THEY WERE DRIVEN BY SEPARATE OBSESSIONS TOWARD UNTHINKABLE GOALS. . . .

PAUL KENYON—A former American Special Agent, he'd come to Yemen for a new chance at life . . . until vengeance gave him a reason to kill.

JOHARA—A dark-eyed Arabian child-woman, her fierce, unyielding passions drew her to the one man it was death to love.

CLAUDIA MALLORY—A beautiful U.S. reporter, her ambitions made her a pawn in a fatal game of passion, intrigue, and international conquest.

PIECE-OF-MY-HEART—A cold-blooded CIA killer, he'd had only one rival in Vietnam. Now he'd been sent to Yemen to terminate a mad prophet. His own twisted scenario included Kenyon's corpse in the bargain.

THE MADHI—The scourge of Allah on earth—a madman with the world's deadliest weapon in his hands, he was a god with the power to conquer a kingdom . . . or destroy the world!

VECTORS

VECTORS

Terry Krueger

A DELL BOOK

Published by
Dell Publishing Co., Inc.
1 Dag Hammarskjold Plaza
New York, New York 10017

Dell ® TM 681510, Dell Publishing Co., Inc.

ISBN: 0-440-19298-6

Printed in the United States of America

First printing—December 1984

PROLOGUE

The Central Highlands, Vietnam/Laos—1968

Paul Kenyon lay facedown in the sandy earth with his feet in a puddle and his chest on the slope of a grave. Mosquitoes danced around his head. He wiped cemetery grunge from his nose and peered over the mound, down through the fog and rain, down to the Montagnard village where he'd lived for months. Despite the monsoon there should have been tribesmen chattering in hootches, some babysans laughing as they were fed. Instead only rain splashing into puddles, trickling from a totem's fanged snout, bouncing off the thick jungle foliage. Someone had ambushed the ville while Paul was in Khe Sanh getting supplies. His tribesmen were dead—that was a given—but what about the girl?

He had a hundred yards to go to the hootches, the only question was how. The grave mounds, the rough-hewn tigers and snakes provided all the cover he needed—for now. Too bad he couldn't take them with him when he had to cross the clearing.

Paul rolled onto his back, closed his eyes, eased back the bolt on his AK-47, and nodded his head for luck. Not that he needed luck. He was *myth.* The CIA called him the free-lance search and destroy operative for the Bang Fai Valley; the Viet Cong some gibberish meaning "bush devil"; and the Marines had a special label: Captain Spooky. Stepping on a month-old jungle corpse was spooky, watching a B-40 rocket take off your best friend's head spookier yet, the Captain was the spookiest. He would stay out in the bush so long the Marines would be certain he was dead, then he'd suddenly materialize inside Khe Sanh's defense perimeter with his game bag full of human ears. The grunts kept their distance from him—to be a free-lancer you had to be *dinky dau,* crazy. Captain Spooky was top gun, the most *dinky dau* of all.

He was the best because he missed nothing.

Another quick look into the ville and he crawled from the mound to a wooden monkey, rose to a crab walk, and slid from totem to grass clump to the mound nearest the village. No battle signs anywhere. He'd lived with the Montagnards long enough to know they wouldn't surrender without a battle, yet there wasn't a thread from bullet-ripped cloth, a spent cartridge, or a bone fragment left. Not even a week's rain could wash everything away. The evidence of the fire fight had been systematically collected and removed so Paul wouldn't find them.

Bad sign.

He'd first heard three months before that some free-lancers had tired of hunting VC and started after each other. The ultimate gunfighter game. In less than a week, he had proof. A beginner, a no-name punk, had tried to frag him within a mile of Khe Sanh. Tried to. One less free-lancer. But if this ambush had been planned by someone good, say Piece-of-My-Heart, Paul would have to be extra careful. He didn't want his heart pickled in a mason jar next to those Piece-of-My-Heart already had.

One final check for movement and Paul sprinted across the clearing, past the gardens, and flattened against the hootch where he had lived with the girl. He noticed a good sign, a sign that told him everything: The gardens hadn't been weeded for weeks. A free-lancer would know that Captain Spooky would spot even *that* small a detail. Thank God. It had only been the VC after all.

He knew the VC: They would be spread evenly through the village, and as soon as one made contact with him, the rest would come running. And there was no telling how many "the rest" were. It would have to be a silent job. He leaned his automatic rifle against the thatching and slid his knife from its sheath . . . a thin, double-edged, sharper-than-razor tool. It sliced well, but he'd designed it for sliding between vertebrae. He called it his Spit. He liked the pun.

Paul put his ear to the thatching. Slurping. Probably rice softened in rainwater. Gook gruel. Since there was no fire smell, the VC was eating it cold. Unusual precaution. He was expecting a special visitor.

No sense keeping him waiting.

Paul would save the VC inside the girl's hut for last. For information. Gliding silently from hootch to hootch, Paul worked his way to the north end of the ville, then back down. He found three visitors. Evidently bored visitors. They must have been waiting quite a while to grow so careless that they'd sit with their backs to the entrance. A number-ten mistake. Paul didn't stop for trophies—he'd be back after the interrogation.

He crept back to the girl's hootch. Still slurping inside. Paul moved around the wall until he pinpointed the VC's location: three feet to the right of the entrance, his back to the thatching. Paul moved to the doorway, crouched into a springing stance, waited until he heard a deep gulp, then glided through the door. The VC's rifle was outside the hootch and the Spit tight to his throat before he could complete the swallow. He didn't spit the gruel out but let it dribble from his mouth, across his chin, and onto Paul's hand. He kept his eyes straight ahead and smiled. His face twitched. "*Chieu hoi,*" he said. Luke the Gook wanted to surrender.

Chieu hoi like hell. Paul kept the Spit to the VC's throat and checked his uniform for other weapons. Only one: a survival knife. Green Beret issue. To have a souvenir like that, he must have been a number-one killer. No wonder the ville was so well groomed.

Paul threw the knife outside, then made the man stand. His head came up to Paul's shoulder. Paul grabbed the top of the VC's shaven head and looked into his face. The man made instant identification—his eyes blinked and his knees wobbled. Paul's shoulder-length hair was matted and greasy, fresh blood sprinkled a month's worth of camouflage paint, and he wore the large viper-shaped earrings the tribal shaman had given him. A bush devil if there ever was one.

"*Chieu hoi,*" Luke said. He was whimpering now. "*Chieu*

hoi." But the bush war didn't acknowledge white flags. That was the rule. The VC played by it, too.

Paul tied the man's hands behind him with a braided vine rope, wedged a bamboo stalk from his back to his wrists to keep his arms fully extended, then threw the rope over the hootch's center pole. Paul didn't go in for torture. While death was inevitable in the bush, prolonging pain wasn't. This was different. This involved the girl.

Paul walked to the carved chest where he kept ammunition and fatigues. He pulled out a piece of the girl's clothing. "*Co?*" Paul asked. Where was the girl?

"*Khong biet,*" the man said. He didn't know? Not likely. Paul tugged the rope until the VC was on his tiptoes. "*Chieu hoi!*" he screamed.

"*O dau?*" Paul asked. Where? His voice was as cold as dead flesh. "*O dau?*" He jerked the rope until the man dangled, his arms straight behind him, his entire weight resting on his shoulder joints. Paul looked up into the VC's face, but in the gray hootch light, all he could see was a grimace. He gave a push, started the man swinging back and forth, then slowly brought up the Spit.

The suggestion was enough.

The man started to babble. Two squads VC slip into ville at night . . . search for bush devil . . . *bac bac* Montagnards . . . kill most, capture rest, search hootches . . . find Yankee clothes but no bush devil . . . prepare ambush and wait three weeks . . . no Yankee can stay in bush three weeks and live . . . main group of VC *didi* ville two days before. . . .

The man promised to show Paul the girl, as long as Paul would kill him quickly.

A deal.

Paul untied the rope and slowly lowered him. They walked from the hootch, across the clearing, and down a twisting jungle path. Birds whistled and called. Monkeys screeched deliriously. Paul knew what he would find. In the VC's business, propaganda, it paid to advertise. This advertisement wouldn't be pretty, but it would be a lesson, a lesson of what happened when he grew weak. He called the girl with whom he lived Little Monkey. She was the reason he stayed in the ville four months—exactly fourteen weeks longer than regulations suggested. The stay-two-weeks-and-move rule was the only regulation free-lancers had. It made sense. Hurt the VC too often in the same quadrant and they came after you. Hard. He'd always kept on the move. Before. But the girl had made him feel human, or something close to it, and that's why he stayed.

The corpse smell was bad even in the cold and rain. Rats by the hundreds scurried as they entered the clearing. Paul found several piles. Arms. Legs. He didn't stop to make identification. He knew them all. He paid Luke back in full, then went back to the ville to collect trophies.

There had been fifty-eight Montagnards in the ville—now there were none. Six months and the hootches would crumble back into the jungle, and the Montagnard smells—the urine and feces and fires and jungle herbs—all would be gone.

All because he had lacked the strength to move on.

It was time to repay the debt. He lived long enough to know that the North Vietnamese let locals do local work. Locals were familiar with terrain and would make their base camp on a hummock near the swamp. Paul knew this and more: The swamp was isolated, noisy, *safe* terrain, and the VC would think there was no chance of ambush. They had numbers. They controlled the quadrant. They would hunt all day, return at dusk, then go out the next dawn. The high water guaranteed they would leave no guards while they were away.

Paul took only his Spit. He left the ville in the afternoon, waded through the flood plain to the swamp, found the camp, and stood in the waist-deep water by the hummock. It was about time he had a bath. All the water in the bomb craters was full of amoebas, flukes, hookworms . . . at least the flood water had movement.

And leeches.

But there were no options. He cut a hollow reed for breathing, then settled into the brown water and became leech bait for six hours. Not even Piece-of-My-Heart would dare do that. One leech fastened to his lip. Another to his eyebrow. He didn't count the ones on his body.

When the full moon crested, he slipped from the water into the camp. One at a time, hands over their mouths, he drove the hardest steel ever forged into the killing spots in the VC's necks. Scarcely any reflex action when done properly. As silent as the night. When he finished with the main group, he waded the length of a football field and gave the two lookouts permanent grins. Hunting was like any other sport. Only there were no cheerleaders, no crowds, no noise at all. Final score: Captain Spooky—10, VC—0.

Then he took souvenirs.

After he finished with the VC, he got around to the thumb-thick leeches. He scraped them off one at a time, like the VC, with his Spit. Hunting had been good, but the price too high. Much too high. And all his fault. Enough nonsense. Guilt was a back-home word; it made sense in the suburbs, on TV, in church. It was an abstract word, and abstractions meant nothing in the bush.

Abstraction or not, guilt was eating a hole in his stomach. Who knew? Maybe the Marines were right. Maybe he was *dinky dau.* Four years earlier, he would have walked out into the mountains, sat under a ponderosa pine, and cried the guilt out. But that was four years ago when he was seventeen. Now he was a thousand. If the ability to laugh and cry was what made humans different from other animals, he'd have to turn in his membership card. He hadn't laughed or cried since he hit the bush.

He held the game bag in his hand and judged the evil weight. A month's hunting—the CIA paid five hundred dollars per ear—that was what, twenty grand? Close to it. He made more per month than General Westmoreland. He might just be the highest paid public servant of all time.

Only in America, he thought.

He scraped the leech from his lip, held it over the game bag, sliced it in half, and let the blood of that final kiss mix with the souvenirs. Then he pulled the string on the bag closed, tied it tight and, with all his might, threw the bag out into the swamp. He sat down on the hummock among the bodies, and instead of crying, he howled like a gut-shot animal.

I.

Al Rattaf, Yemen—April 8, 1981

The "Fiery Serpent" had entered the boy in a sip of stagnant water, eaten through his intestinal wall, matured amid the stomach, colon, and lower liver, then migrated through his trunk and leg, discharging embryos all the way, until it appeared in a tumor at his ankle. *Dracunculus medinensis,* the *Merck Manual* called it. Guinea worm. Somehow the local nickname, "Fiery Serpent," best described the itching and inflammation that accompanied the worm's travels. Paul traced the ulcer back up the boy's leg. If he were a doctor, he'd probably scrape some of the filth from the ulcers, touch a drop of water to it, and watch the embryos the worm had lain become a pulsating mass. That was a waste of time. As a medic, he'd treated more guinea worm in the past four years than a real M.D. would read about in a lifetime. Not that he enjoyed treating it, particularly in a seven-year-old boy. The worm wasn't very wide, but it was long—maybe a yard in this case—and the thought of a malnourished child supporting a parasite as long as he was tall . . .

There was no reason to tell the boy that the treatment wouldn't hurt; another Hippocratic waste of time. This wasn't the suburbs, and the kid hadn't grown up with water beds and Captain Crunch; he was an Arab, and pain was with him every day. If the worm weren't driving him crazy with the burning and itching, he would never have come down from the mountains. When Paul lanced the tumor with a razor, the boy's face remained impassive. Paul poured some alcohol on a cotton swab and cleaned the tumor. At the bottom, perhaps two millimeters wide, moving in the pus and blood, was the worm's head. Most unpretty. Judging from the way it writhed, it didn't enjoy the alcohol bath any more than the boy did.

Which treatment to use?

The ancient method (Plutarch first recorded it two thousand years ago) involved a ten-day extraction, the worm being tortuously wound around a matchstick. Painful, yes. Crude, extremely. Graphic, without a doubt. All things an Arab could understand. It was something the boy would always remember, and you could bet that he would be less apt to drink unboiled water again. In a way he'd been lucky. Guinea worm was one of the nicer things hiding in Yemeni water. There was the bilharziasis fluke, which entered through the skin and destroyed the central nervous system. Or shigellosis. Or cholera and typhoid and all the messiness they imply. The boy must be impressed so he would pass his knowledge on to the rest of the villagers.

"Look," Paul said in Arabic, pointing to the worm's head. He touched more alcohol to it, and the worm's head twitched. He scraped some embryos from an ulcer on the boy's thigh, put them on a slide, added water, brought the microscope from the medicine table, focused, and gave the boy a look.

The boy shrieked and started to tremble.

"Not only has it fed on your juices for months," Paul said, "but it's started to raise a family. Crying won't help. Or praying to Allah. Or passing out. Boiling your drinking water will."

The boy sobbed till he shook. Paul lifted him to his lap and held the boy close till the deep shudders ebbed to sniffles. Even Bedouins understood touching; most primitive people did. In fact, other than the Montagnards, the Bedouins were closer to what Paul considered *reality,* the constant interplay of health/disease, feast/famine, life/death, than any people he'd ever met.

When he first came to Yemen, he thought Al Rattaf, a fishing village on a thirty-mile-wide strip of desert called the Tihama, was the last place he'd stay. Too flat, he thought. Too Moslem. But during his first week a hammerhead shark had swum in past the reef, following the scent of fish entrails, and ate a child instead. Paul hunted the shark, killed it, and saw the diseases that preyed on the fishermen and realized he was needed——for life instead of death. There was no doctor within a hundred miles, so he bought some medical supplies—nowhere near enough, of course—but he had skills to make money in a region without law. He sold his services to a mountain bandit, and within a year he had a generator to refrigerate antibiotics and a traditional mud hut; the clinic was a reality. He hung the grinning shark's skull above the door, and the villagers called him Al Rish, the fin of the shark, because he was swift, sudden, and graceful. He liked being the closest thing to myth the village had.

It meant safety.

The boy still shuddered in Paul's arms. If the worm snapped during extraction, it would discharge its embryos into the bloodstream and cause terrible inflammation. The boy weighed sixty pounds, no more. A long infection would kill him. And ten days of winding could seem like forever.

The boy's arms reached halfway around Paul's chest. Paul had one of those strange paternal rushes that were becoming quite frequent. A sign of weakness but a pleasant one. He would mix Western efficiency with Arabic reality, give thiabendazole orally and gradually extract the weakened worm. Two, maybe three days of winding and the worm would be out—dead or squirming, it would scare the boy. That was as important as the cure.

"When we get it out," Paul said, "I'll put it in a bottle and you can take it back to your village." A battle ribbon. It pays to advertise. When Paul ran his hand through the child's matted hair and dunked it in alcohol, lice floated to the surface. Though he'd never treated a case of typhus, stories of the epidemic that had ravaged Yemen in the mid-forties still circulated. No need to take unnecessary chances. This lad needed a general overhaul.

"Ali Abdul," Paul shouted to his assistant in the next room, "make room for another."

"There are no more beds!" Ali shouted. "No room on the floor!"

"And prepare a bath. One percent gamma benzene hexachloride."

"No room for another licey child!" Ali charged into the room.

Even when he was angry, he moved delicately. He had a smooth, feminine face, and the grace of his gestures parodied his temper. "There is no more money!" Ali said.

The only verses of the Koran Paul knew by heart involved charity and temperance, catch phrases he used debating Ali. Paul said, "*Your* Koran says: 'And let not the possessors of abundance swear against giving to the poor.' Ali winced. Touché. "I'd hate to see your soul in hell over a little greed. Since there is no money in the fund, you and I, Ali, we will share the cost."

"Only the doctor has money," Ali said.

"Stop that doctor nonsense."

"One-fourth," Ali said. "I will pay no more than one-fourth."

"You're the Muslim. You should pay it all."

"Three-eighths," Ali said. "More I will not pay!" He stamped his foot, set his jaw, wrinkled his eyebrows, and glared.

"Half?" Paul asked.

"Half," Ali answered without hesitation.

"For twenty rials a week the muezzin will find room in the hut behind the mosque. He finds nothing wrong with profiting on the Prophet," Paul said. "Give the boy two twenty-five-milligram thiabendazole tablets before you take him." Ali turned and tried to scurry back into the waiting room. "Not so fast!" Paul shouted. "The boy's clothes must be destroyed, and he must be bathed."

Ali grimaced and backed away from the boy's tattered loincloth. Ali had picked up enough Western ways during his eight-year stay at the English school in Yemen's capital, Sana', to grow squeamish around licey children. The only squeamish Arab Paul had ever met. Suddenly Ali's grimace turned into a smile. "There is a leper waiting," Ali said.

"How bad?"

"The ears and nose are gone. The hands and feet look like rats have been feeding. The skull shows through here," Ali said, pointing to his cheek, "and here," pointing to his jaw.

Leprosy was the one disease Paul hadn't grown accustomed to. Maybe it was the idea that it was mega-unclean. Maybe the symptoms reminded him of decay and dismemberment. Maybe just because the disease made him feel helpless. There was nothing he could do in the advanced cases but fill out the papers for the leprosarium in Tai'zz, send a message by radio, and keep the patient isolated until a boat arrived for a journey down the seacoast. Either that or tell him to join the rebels in the mountains: their leader, the Madhi, was rumored to cure leprosy with a touch. Paul felt like handing the lepers bells, patting them on the head (with a *very* long pole), and sending them on their way. Ali didn't seem to mind dealing with them. Maybe they could work out a deal . . . not that Paul liked camel-trading with Ali. "If you fill out the papers," Paul said, "I'll take the boy to the muezzin."

"And bathe the licey boy?"

Paul's hesitation was far too short. "The bath, too."

"And pay for it all? Everything?"

Paul ran up the white flag. "The clothes. Bath. Money. The whole works," he said. There was an old Saudi adage the gist of which was, "Never trade camels with a Yemeni." Six years of dealing with Ali had shown Paul the depths of that wisdom. Who knew if the same genes that made Ali uneasy touching lice-ridden clothes made him at ease dealing with lepers? Who knew anything for sure about Arabs?

Paul drew water for the bath from the communal well, dumped the boy in a metal tub, added the water and medicine, was drenched by the boy's squirming, then brought him fresh clothes. The straw and mud walls of the two-room hut were a foot thick and kept the temperature down inside, so Paul made the boy go outside to dry. Then Paul checked the waiting room to be sure Ali hadn't swindled him. The leper looked as though he'd escaped from one of those fifties Biblical epics: His left leg was a stump, and the hand that held his stick/crutch had only one finger. Paul had no interest in seeing the man's face; he hadn't done badly in his bartering with Ali after all. Paul walked out the back door, took the boy by the hand, and led him to the mosque. The muezzin complained that he had no room. For twenty-five rials he found room.

Thin dust from the sand, thinner and drier than any dust Paul had breathed, hung in the air. It would be hours before the night breeze would blow down from the peaks of Jebel Amhir and sweep the dust out to sea. Only the dust bothered him. He loved the way the sea smells blended with camel dung and the aromas from the *suq,* odors as rich and varied as the merchandise that emitted them. He loved everything about Al Rattaf: the antiquity, the tradition, the simplicity.

There was only one person who might make him leave, and as he walked out of the mosque, past the peddler selling goat meat and yogurt, he saw her leave her father's house, the headman's house, the only stone house in the village: the *'aqil's* daughter. A blue woolen cape covered her white robe, the huge almond eyes were accented by kohl, saffron was rubbed into her eyebrows, and carmine rouged the small slice of cheek he could see between her veil and hood. She was trouble. She was a Muslim—a girl, not a woman—and the daughter of the most dangerous Arab in Al Rattaf.

He walked to the far side of the *suq* to try to avoid her, but she swerved and brushed into him. Did he hear a giggle? There was no doubt about one thing: It was time to be alone. It was a short walk from the marketplace to the beach. He stopped for a drink at the well, the only safe drinking water for thirty miles, then walked past the mud and *dhura-*stalk huts where the fishermen lived in poverty and filth, weaved through the conical huts of the merchants, and onto the beach. He removed his sandals and let the wet sand press up between his toes.

It was either buy a wife or move on. He had the money, and there wasn't anything wrong with marrying an eighteen-year-old. Or sixteen. So what if she turned out to be less than sixteen? Bedouin women matured at their own rate. So what if he'd never talked to her or seen more than her eyes above a veil; the look in those eyes and the giggle that seeped through all those layers of clothing told him enough.

A sand devil swirled up in the Tihąma, roared past him, and scattered over the Red Sea like rain. Tihama. Teen brides. Next he'd have a harem. Not only did he look like a Bedouin, he was starting to think like one. Well, if T. E. Lawrence could go Arab, why not Paul Kenyon?

The sea's smell was a woman's smell, salty and rich. He missed that more than anything. If the *'aqil's* daughter were with him that moment, thin and firm, her skin the color of camel's milk as she rode his hips, her laugh and touch, the feel of her easing him in wouldn't be as sweet as the smell he'd take with him on his hands and mouth.

But she was trouble.

Paul had heard stories, like most stories told in Arabic, plotless and overly poetic but with a clear moral: the brothers hold the suitor down; a *jambiyya* flashes in the sunlight; the *'aqil* wears a tanned scrotum around his neck as a hashish pouch. It had happened to a village lad once before, and Paul didn't want to be forced into killing any of the villagers . . . not even the *'aqil.* If Paul had anywhere left to go, he would move on.

An old fisherman, Ahmed, perhaps, stopped cleaning a yard-long barracuda, uncoiled the entrails from his arm, pulled a branch of qat from the hull of his fishing *dhow,* and held it out to Paul. Paul waded out to him, thanked him with a pat on the back, and counted three rotten teeth in an otherwise vacant mouth when the man smiled. The fisherman cut a thin strip from the fish's stomach, sliced it in half, put one piece in his mouth, and offered the other to Paul. Fried locusts, great. Boiled goat's head, superb. Raw barracuda, no thanks. There could be a tapeworm embryo in that oily flesh just waiting to become a thirty-foot-long uninvited guest at every meal Paul ate. He shook his head, wagged his finger, and gave the fisherman a mild warning. He'd be lucky to change the seven-year-old's habits, much less the seventy-year-old's. A thousand-year-old way of life didn't die that easily.

Paul walked back onto the beach, stripped the top, tender leaves from the qat, put them in his mouth, and started to chew. Just what he needed, a cheek full of sweet dreams. The clouds were so thin and high, they scarcely seemed like clouds. He looked out onto the Red Sea, past the reef waves breaking a mile from shore, past the *dhow* sails scattered along the horizon, and the alkaloid taste of qat faded into the feeling of power that preceded the drug's dreams. He selected a large dune with its curve toward the sun and sat down—you knew it was time to sit down when the sails turned into gulls and flew away squawking.

Paul heard the arrhythmic gait of a camel, and the high vanished. He slipped the thin knife from his thigh pocket, crab-walked to the top of the dune, heard a familiar voice singing, smiled, and slid back down. The hoofbeats grew louder. Paul shielded his eyes just as the camel burst over the dune in an explosion of sand. Its rider was Nuri ibn Sha'lan, Jebeli chieftain, bandit extraordinaire, and the owner of the largest assortment of human noses in north Yemen. Paul once took ears for money, but Nuri's rationale, that those he killed wouldn't be able to sneak up on him in the afterlife, seemed more practical.

"You've grown careless," Nuri shouted over the squealing camel. "Your nose could be the pride of my collection!" He stroked the camel's neck, and she quieted.

"I'll never grow *that* careless," Paul said. "You move in the Tihama like your camel moves at sea." He looked at the pouch hanging from Nuri's sash. "The bag seems to have filled since our last meeting."

"A soldier went to Paradise with no way to smell the ever-blooming date palm!" Nuri laughed. "And a Saudi went to hell with no way to smell the pitch!"

"Be more careful," Paul said, "or some Bedouin will use the money on your head to buy a wife."

"The day a Bedu catches me anywhere," Nuri said, "mountains or Tihama, I'll slice off my nose and hand it to him." He tapped the camel's neck with his quirt. She knelt, and Nuri climbed off her back with a groan. He limped when he walked. "I have carried so many camels that my robe fills with blood whenever I ride—even Shuqra!" He scratched the camel's nose lovingly. "And she is as gentle a ride as my third wife." Nuri walked to Paul, wiped the sweat from Paul's forehead, and spat. "I heard you had the sweats last week. You are crazy. A week from the fever and you sit in the sun." He picked up the branch of qat and spat. "This makes you think much and do little."

"So does love," Paul said.

Nuri jumped, groaned when he landed, then began to circle Paul in a slow, pulsating dance involving pelvic thrusts of innumerable variations. He sang a tribal song of quails and hunters, of how the thrill of the hunt is more pleasurable than the plucking of the bird.

"Right now," Paul said, "I wouldn't mind trying some plucking just to see if I can remember how it's done." At that, Nuri picked up the tempo of his dance, began a plaintive croon, and embellished his thrusts with curving arcs of his arms. One of his swirls knocked sand into Paul's face. "Sit down!" Paul said. "Your heathen ways make me nervous."

Nuri sat next to Paul, sighing as he shifted his buttocks into the hot sand. "Who is this quail?" he asked.

"The *'aqil's* daughter."

Nuri leaned back on his hands and whistled. "She is fresh and new and smells of cloves. It will cost much to see her without feathers."

"I have much," Paul said.

"Thirty thousand rials?"

"Nobody has that much!" Paul said. "I'm no Saudi."

"*That* is your problem. You are an infidel. You cannot marry a believer. It would pollute the village. The muezzin would rather have her dead than married to an infidel." Nuri took a stick of mastic gum from his sash, nipped a bit, then handed the stick to Paul. "Such a marriage cannot be."

The qat taste coated Paul's mouth, but the mastic tasted like pine; it tickled his nose and made him shake his head. "That's why I'm sitting here with a head full of qat," Paul said. Nuri's face was dark and furrowed from the wind, sand, and sun. His mustache and woolly beard held the residue of a month's meals. He was tall and as broad in the shoulders as his camel's rump—no small feat since he fed Shuqra better than his wives. He was the only Yemeni Paul had met who fulfilled Paul's fantasies of sheikhs, white mares, and camel-hair tents.

"The *'aqil* may be a headman," Nuri continued, "but he has the mind of a goatherd. For thirty thousand rials he would marry her to a leper. Bah. No woman is worth that." Nuri gestured toward the mountains, which rose abruptly from the sand thirty miles to the east. "Come ride with me again and we'll steal you all the Bedu women you want!"

Paul had no intention of telling Nuri that he was tired of women who didn't know his name, that he was sick unto death of his annual three weeks of faceless fuckery in Cairo, because that would merely prompt Nuri into a song about geldings and roosters who weren't roosters anymore. And he wasn't going to say that the village needed him, because Nuri would counter that the village had survived two thousand years without him and would probably be right. Instead Paul said nothing.

"You don't argue! You don't shout! You don't even answer!" Nuri said. "From *you* that is an answer!" Nuri took the *jambiyya* from its sheath in his waistband and stuck it in the sand between Paul's feet. "There. Hack your manhood off. It will save me looking for a eunuch for my harem."

"If that were the answer, I'd simply visit the *'aqil,* ask for her, and drop my pants."

"That boy was crazy and stupid. Without friends or relatives. You are only crazy. Give me embroidered slippers. A goat for slaughter. A pound of frankincense. I will be your brother, visit the *'aqil,* propose the marriage."

"And the thirty thousand rials?" Paul asked.

"You are my brother. For a brother such a sum is nothing."

"But I'm an infidel."

"And crazy," Nuri said. "The *'aqil* is a coward. He loves his nose more than his daughter. He fears me, but you, you . . . his water turns the sand to mud when he looks at you."

"Bah," Paul said.

"Do you think these villagers let you use your needles and books on them because you are kind? Do you think the *'aqil*'s daughter giggles and brushes against you because you give them pills? They are Bedus. They are warriors. They know how you found the money to start your doctoring. They know you move without noise. That you never sleep. That you can become like a rock for days." Nuri paused and, for the first time that day, held Paul's eyes. "They know you kill like no other man."

Paul rubbed his eyes with the back of his hand and exhaled in a whistle. "But no more," he said. "No more." He lay back with his hands cradling his head and let the sun warm his muscles. "A question, Nuri," Paul said. "Why did you ride eighty kilometers with hemorrhoids on a camel that isn't broken to offer me thirty thousand rials you didn't know I needed?"

"The government sends a convoy of arms over Kotal Hadur. I have plans for it."

"I didn't know you'd joined the Madhi."

"Joined the Madhi?" Nuri spat. "Another monkey whose tail reaches to Allah—he says. I go where there's money. The Madhi needs weapons. His money never ends."

"Why doesn't he take the convoy himself?"

"He has no followers here. He says it is a land without Allah. The two of us, Paul, we don't need gods, just our guns and knives."

"Sorry," Paul said.

"But you're a hunter of men!"

"An ex-hunter."

Nuri struggled to his feet and began a fast song, a song of how a mare feels between the thighs at full gallop, how the sand tastes when covered by another's blood, how the scimitar rings when it severs a head from its shoulders. Then he paused and added a verse about how women fall at the feet of warriors . . . even *'aqils'* daughters. Paul was certain that verse was ad-libbed. The pitch was different and the words scarcely made sense. But there was no sense trying to stop Nuri's song—its conclusion would lead to his next line of argument. He was a man to whom the aesthetics of a conversation were more important than what was being said: in other words, an Arab. Anyway, two or three more dances and his hemorrhoids would start acting up. Then he'd have to sit down.

Suddenly Nuri stopped in mid-stride and faced Paul. "You are my brother," he said. "I will hear no more talk of rials and convoys! I will go to the *'aqil* this day and barter the marriage contract. Do not try to stop me, or I will take your nose!"

"And the wedding bells will ring tomorrow?" Paul laughed.

"Tomorrow? This is not a heathen land!" Nuri shouted. "A wedding tomorrow? A wedding must be celebrated by everyone. The entire community is remarried with each marriage. It may take days of bartering, then after the *'aqil* consents, the women have a party at his house, the men one at yours. The 'Night of Entrance' follows. Six days. Maybe seven. After a week of hunting, the quail is plucked."

"And when will we pluck the government of its weapons?"

"I will hear no more talk of convoys!"

"Ten days?" Paul asked.

"Three weeks," Nuri said. "Plenty of time for you to learn about your quail."

When Paul nodded his head and started to smile, Nuri started a wild battle dance. Paul covered his eyes and laughed. "You, Nuri, are a bandit."

Nuri laughed, took Paul by the shoulders, and hugged him. The smell of decaying noses was unbelievable. "You, Paul, are a brother."

"You are a trader of camels," Paul said.

"And you, my brother, are the Angel of Death."

II.

Tai'zz, Yemen—April 14, 1981

The Wall, as Claudia Mallory came to call it, wasn't actually a wall but a gutter in which the sewage and rotten vegetables, the rat carcasses and stillbirths of Tai'zz were left to accumulate until the spring rains washed them first into the Wadi Rasyān, then the Red Sea a hundred kilometers to the west. Each Friday for the past month she had dressed as a man, walked with her photographer, Rick Hodges, through the city's *suqs* to the central marketplace, and waited with the five hundred or so regulars, some merchants, but mostly Bedouins and beggars, who attended every execution. Every Friday, the firing squad marched fifteen or twenty Madhists, many in their early teens, up to The Wall, forced them to kneel, and placed M-16 muzzles within a foot of their foreheads. Then, at a prearranged signal so there would be no flinching, the soldiers blew the rebels' brains into the gutter. Later, they'd hang the bodies from the arch of the Bab al Kabir while birds and dogs fought for the leftovers.

It was damn effective media, Claudia had to admit, the perfect show for the Neilsen ratings: complete indifference to life; the gore of shattered craniums; and the most elementary of morals, *obey* or the government will put your head on a pole. Evidently the rebels had little concern for ratings. The Madhi's *jihad,* his holy war, was spreading throughout Yemen.

It was one hundred and three at two in the afternoon, the least comfortable time in the always uncomfortable Yemeni day. The only air conditioning in Claudia's hotel room was a fan-creased newspaper. Perspiration streamed down her thighs and collected in the hollow behind her knees. She pushed away from the typewriter, stood, walked to the window, and studied the ancient buildings, the dirt-caked streets of Tai'zz. Beggars by the mosques. Camels tethered in front of coffee shops. Muezzins calling faithful Muslims to prayer from the towering, phallic minarets. Though the architecture was dreamlike, the assignment wasn't. If it weren't for her reputation for taking stories that no one else wanted, she wouldn't go to the executions again. The marketplace would stink of excrement and clotted meat; last week's bloodstains would still streak the earth, and, quite frankly, she'd seen enough teenagers murdered for one assignment. But, as she always told Rick, an assignment was an assignment . . . she saved her well-turned phrases for the page.

Besides, this firing squad was something special. Claudia sat down on the bed, opened her briefcase, and removed a piece of onion-skin parchment covered by Arabic script. There had been thousands of similar sheets posted throughout Tai'zz. It had taken an hour to translate—time well spent. She read:

A Warning to Nonbelievers

In the name of Allah, the most compassionate and merciful, I, Mohammed al Madhi al Muntazar, your Madhi, have delivered my message. Why will you not listen? Those who doubt my words sin against Allah. They shall forfeit all hope in this world and the world to come. Join my Companions, people of Yemen, before Allah's Wrath finds you!

Remember the Four Pillars of Faith:

The West is the Great Satan
Advancement is Regression
Technology is Corruption
Wealth is Death.

Sinners, you will be told of a miracle this afternoon in the central marketplace in Tai'zz. The tools of Satan have captured some of my Companions. These Companions, my chosen, have chosen the path of martyrdom. They die only in body—their souls ascend into paradise. Remember that to Allah, the body is dung. Only the soul is immortal.

An Imam from the north has been chosen to deliver my words. Nonbelievers, remember that to ignore my word is to bring death to your soul. Watch for Allah's miracles; they are His Word. My Companions, being first in this world, will be first in the world to come.

There is no God but Allah. He is great.

Amen.

Mohammed al Madhi al Muntazar

It was time to go.

Claudia put the parchment back into the briefcase and hid it under her bed, took a hand mirror from her suitcase, and made a final check of her disguise: a long white robe of native cloth (the shopkeeper called it an *'aba*); a curved *jambiyya* in her waistband; an absurd Western suit coat from the 1940s; and the loose ends of her checkered headcloth pulled high to cover her dimples and freckles, those damn freckles, which made her look seventeen instead of twenty-seven. She wore a slip to try to ease the scratching of the rough *'aba,* but it was so hot that the silk stuck to her flesh and worked its way up to her bottom. She lifted the *'aba* and pulled down the slip—something she couldn't do after she left the room.

All she had left to do was to convince Rick; Rick, who was normally drawn to any hint of violence; Rick, who, now that she thought of it, had suggested that they take the assignment in the first place, to attend this final execution.

She removed the chair she'd wedged under the doorknob, checked the back of her disguise with a hand mirror, and opened the door to the hallway, a door so old and neglected it grunted instead of squeaked. She knocked on the door next to hers very softly. Sometimes Rick was her best friend; other times he gave her the willies. She was never sure how to act around him, which was the main reason she found him even mildly interesting.

"Good-bye, Claude," a voice said.

"Open up."

"Enjoy the show," Rick said. "Don't forget to wear your galoshes. Be a shame to get brains all over your sandals."

Claudia twisted the doorknob and pushed. Hashish smoke hung like a veil in the humid room. Rick sat on the edge of the metal frame, plywood support, and Army surplus mattress that Yemeni hoteliers called a bed. His legs were wrapped around the base of a three-tube hookah, and he played with a yo-yo, as he always did when bored. He wore cut-offs and a black Stetson. He smiled and exhaled a cloud of smoke. "Howdy," he said.

"Wrong costume," Claudia said.

"Care to join me for some bunk time?" he asked, patting the mattress.

"Cowboys do nothing for me," Claudia said.

"How about a painter?" Rick asked, pulling a beret from a large box of hats he kept by the bed. "Or a duke?" He put on a homburg. "Or Truman?" He put on a capote, a souvenir from a trip to a gay bar in Paris.

"Try your turban," she said.

"That, my dear," Rick said, snapping out a top hat and affecting an Etonian accent, "would encourage the beastly tendencies already endemic to this beastly little country. Who was it that said 'Foreigners are a filthy nation'? Kipling?"

"Forster."

"A toke for Mr. Forster?"

"No, thanks," Claudia said. "The Wall awaits." She removed her headcloth and shook the long auburn hair down over her shoulders. She had to lift it to keep it from sticking to the sweat on her neck.

"I don't mind the heat," Rick said, scratching his receding hairline. "That hole-in-the-floor shitter is a piece of cake. Cockroaches as big as St. Bernards? That's the romance. But I will not attend another massacre of children."

"Since when? You're always in the front row licking your lips. Besides, we have a job to do."

"Fuck the job," Rick said. He pulled a hair from his beard and chewed on it. "The footwork's done. Interviews taped. Your story's half-written, or *should* be. I have enough glossy eight by tens of stiff corpses and shattered skulls for a special edition of the *National Enquirer.*"

"They've captured an Imam," Claudia said. "There are posters everywhere that say there'll be a prophecy. All hell might break loose."

"All the more reason you should join me on the rack." Rick patted the mattress again.

"I don't compromise my standards."

"And it's no compromise to walk around dressed like Yasir Arab-fat with a goddamn hookah up his keester?"

A strand of hair caught in the corner of Claudia's mouth. First she tried to free it with her tongue, then hooked the curl with her little finger and, with a shake of the head, flipped it over her shoulder. "That's the job," she said.

"*Fuck the job!*" Rick took a deep toke, held it too long, and coughed it out with a laugh. "You're too tall for a Yemeni," he said. "Besides, you'll never fool anyone with all those freckles. Come here and I'll lick some off."

"The Wall, Rick!" Claudia said. There was a six-pack of Pepsi on his dresser. She snapped one out, popped the top, and let the warm fizz run over her hand. She triple-checked the label to be sure it was bottled in the States (her doctor had read her a foot-long list of parasites that were found in Yemeni water) before she licked the cola from her hand. "I'll wait in the hall while you become an Arab," she said.

"No sale, Claude."

She decided to bluff: "Get moving or I'll have your ass."

He called it: "It's yours," he said, and started to undress. She ran into the hallway as his cut-offs flopped against the door.

She wouldn't have any problem finding the marketplace; Lord knew that she'd been there often enough, but, though she didn't want to admit it, she didn't like being in the streets of Tai'zz alone. Maybe it had something to do with being the only woman in the city who wasn't branded with the veil—not that male drag was much better. Maybe it was the fear of knowing what might happen if she were caught. Anyway, she stopped at her room for the Nikon with autowind, strapped it to the frame hidden in the sleeve of her *'aba,* put the headcloth back on and, as she walked from the lobby into the street, started her imitation of a Yemeni's loping gait. She entered the spice *suq,* the only place in the city where the smell of the cloves, frankincense, and coffee was strong enough to battle the sewage and dead animals in the streets—she could breathe through her nose for a change. She walked in the center of the streets so the toilet drains from the upper floors wouldn't empty onto her head. The *suq* was narrow, and the buildings, suede-colored rectangles covered with white latticework, rose three stories, sometimes more, and made the *suq* seem even narrower than it was. You could buy anything in the *suqs,* anything from a wife for your bed to a hunting falcon for your arm, a kettle to fry your food to some qat to fry your mind.

It was like living in the Middle Ages. There were thousands of stories in a twentieth-century country locked in a twelfth-century social system, and she had the best: covering a rebellion led by a reincarnation of a ninth-century Islamic holy man, Mohammed al Madhi al Muntazar, the Madhi. Madhis weren't new. One seemed to appear in the Middle East every fifty years or so—"Chinese" Gordon lost his head to the 1800s' Sudanese version at Khartoum, and in 1979 a self-proclaimed Madhi and 350 followers died in an attempt to seize the Sacred Mosque at Mecca. None of the Madhis had fulfilled the prophecy: to unite all Islam and lead it to world domination; as the Madhi himself put it, "turn the world of war into the world of Islam." Tribal rumors had the current Yemeni Madhi managing every miracle from cleansing lepers to raising the dead, and the people of Yemen were beginning to believe. The Madhi was only a miracle or two and some media exposure away from causing the government some serious trouble.

Claudia tried to blend into the mass of turbans, fezzes, camels, and goats which flowed into the marketplace. She kept her blue eyes focused on her feet. You could find blue eyes on a Circassian tribesman, maybe a Ruwalla, but never on a Yemeni. Besides, maintaining the stride took concentration. She normally wore galoshes to keep the urine and dung off, but today she wanted the realistic clicking of sandals. She glanced up for just an instant and saw a dog urinating on the street. Nothing unusual in that except that ten feet away a man, maybe the dog's owner, urinated a ribbon of twisting script on a building. His name. He took the same pride autographing the building that Picasso took signing a painting. It crystallized her feelings about Yemen: People differed from animals only through intent. She *had* to get the picture: a man and dog pee in tandem while hundreds rush by on the way to a sanctioned massacre.

She walked to twenty feet of the man, her prefocused range, and lifted her arm. The baggy sleeve dropped down. The man looked up. Shit. She tried to tighten the sleeve of her *'aba* around the Nikon and recapture her stride, but her concentration scattered, and she walked like the preppy she had been, all hips and derriere. Rick Hodges, you SOB, she thought, if I get killed over this, I *will* have your ass! The man followed her, the dog followed the man. She stopped and turned. The man stopped. The dog stopped. Claudia broke into a trot. She bumped into a short Bedouin, sidestepped a pile of camel dung, turned at an alley, and flattened up against a wall. She closed her eyes and practiced breath control and, after a few móments, opened them. No man, no dog. . . .

"The man is a lady," the man said in pidgin English.

How did he get behind her!? Claudia assumed a fighting stance and prepared to do whatever was necessary to keep him an arm's length away. He was clean-shaven and covered with dust. He had eyes the color of ripe olives, greasy curls pasted to his forehead, and a psychopath's smile.

"I have not this day," the man said, "bought a single stem of qat."

So he only wanted to camel-trade, the one thing Yemenis seemed to like more than public murder. Fine. The expense account would cover it. "How much?" Claudia said.

"Forty rials buys food for my sisters." He smiled. Green qat residue outlined his teeth.

"Five for your sisters and thirty-five to feed your habit."

"A woman is not allowed in the square on such a day. A woman at the Imam's execution?"

"Twenty," Claudia said.

"Perhaps the authorities . . ."

"Thirty," Claudia said. Much too fast. The Ripper smile crawled back onto his face.

"Forty or my cousin, the soldier, arrests a man who is a woman who is an infidel."

Claudia's performance had been pathetic, but the cost of pathos was cheap this time: forty rials. She found her wallet in the endless layers of *'aba,* counted out the bills, and handed them to him. She had no intention of turning her back until they left, but the man continued to stare at her. "Forty's all you get," she said.

"I will serve you for a day," he said.

It wasn't that he looked trustworthy, but Claudia had needed a translator since she arrived. Arabic was a web with a thousand tortuous threads, and she wanted to understand *all* of the prophecy. "Pancho," she said, "you're hired."

"My name is Abdullah Mohammed."

"No doubt," Claudia said. "Lead on."

There *was* something special about this execution. Normally boys would sing and dance while an old man kept time on an oil drum. Normally the gamblers took wagers on which bodies would convulse the longest, as peddlers hawked oranges and warm Pepsis. Normally there would be a grandstand stuffed with government officials and a military band. Not today. Even the street vendors had been replaced by more soldiers than Claudia had ever seen at an execution. And an unusual crowd it was: bankers, money changers, and something new, a scattering of official-looking Saudis.

"Why Saudis?" Claudia asked.

"The Saudis own everything," Pancho said. He wrinkled his nose and spat. "They do what they want."

"Where are the Bedouins and beggars?"

"Gone."

Claudia rolled her eyes. "*Why* are they gone?"

"The beggars and Bedouins believe the Madhi's words. The government is afraid of those who believe. This Imam knows the Madhi."

Birds gathered on the minaret high above the square. They'd incorporated the Friday executions into their feeding schedule, and since the soldiers were late, the birds were restless. Like the birds, the crowd grew uneasy, shifted, and whispered long before the prisoners were marched into the cordoned-off area in front of The Wall. Most of the rebels were young, thin-chested, and dark from the sun—typical Yemeni youths. The Imam was a different story entirely. Taller, fairer, no doubt a Ruwalla from Saudi Arabia, he had black hair that fell past his shoulders and was matted with grease and sand. With a nose that was more rectangular than wedge-shaped, skin that could have been eaten away by acid rain, and the most insanely burning eyes she'd ever seen, he reminded Claudia of gargoyles she had seen crouched on cathedrals in Venice.

"This Imam was a leper," Pancho said. "The Madhi touched his flesh and made it clean."

"You believe that nonsense?" Claudia asked.

Pancho spat.

From the looks of the Imam's complexion, it was possible. Great. But there was something special about the Madhi's followers. Of the sixty or seventy she'd seen die here, not one had whimpered or pleaded, not one had shaken at the knees or fallen into a faint.

Things did not go as the government had planned. The Imam laughed at the reading of the death sentence, and when a soldier was ordered to silence him, he stared the soldier down. When he talked, his voice erupted like a spring in the desert. If Bedouins had been present, there might have been trouble, but this was a staid, staid audience. The Imam's voice was almost a song. Pancho didn't translate. Claudia nudged him with an elbow. When he still remained silent, she stepped on his foot.

"Patience," he snapped. He leaned over and whispered. "The Imam says that the soldiers will die of Allah's Wrath, if they shoot."

"What's that?" she asked

"The plague. He asked the soldiers if they don't already feel the swelling here"—Pancho touched under his armpits—"and here"—he touched his groin.

"That all?" Claudia asked.

"He says that the Madhi will call down the plague on a village of *munafiq.* That this will prove the Madhi is the chosen Guide of Allah."

"What's a *munafiq?*" Claudia asked.

"Believers who have turned their backs on the Prophet."

Claudia had seen enough crowds to sense the point when they would turn into mobs. This one was close to that transformation. An officer signaled for the executions to begin. The Imam laughed maniacally. Pancho's dog howled, and the birds on the minaret scattered in a flutter of black wings. Suddenly, all the prisoners were laughing and the crowd cheering and she couldn't hear the officer's commands. He drew his pistol and approached the Imam. They stood there, nose-to-nose, trying to glare each other down, as the dogs howled and the birds settled back on their perches. This was the essence of Yemen for Claudia—machismo on the rampage—a world where men would rather have a sister dead than dishonored and would starve a daughter to feed a mare. Claudia hoped they'd stand there till they both passed out.

That was not to be. When the officer fired his pistol under the Imam's chin, the bullet exited in a red spray and lifted the Imam six inches off the ground. The spray was still in the air when his body fell into The Wall. The dance began.

The firing squad approached the Madhists, there was the heavy thump of muzzle blasts, and the bodies were thrown head over heels. Then Pancho walked toward the firing squad, stood within ten feet of them, holding out his hand as if to greet them. The crowd swept forward, and Claudia lost sight of him.

She would have left, but the scene demanded photographs. Why use Rick's when she could get the copyright? She took a shot of two crows sitting on a jagged cranium and one of a dog already feasting on a Madhist's still-jerking leg. She planned her last shot—the stiffening bodies hanging in a breeze, concentrating on the Imam's scarred face, a frozen death mask. But his body wasn't hanging with the others.

Before UPI assigned her Rick, she'd taken her own photos. Her Nikon shot rolls from the last helicopter leaving the embassy during the fall of Saigon, in the gore of Idi Amin's torture chambers, as soldiers shot children during the Soweto riots. Which is why, when two soldiers leveled their rifles at her, locked her in handcuffs, and smashed her Nikon on The Wall, she wasn't sure if it was really happening or was one of the many stories she'd once covered but had, in the rush, forgotten.

III.

Al Rattaf, Yemen—April 15, 1981

Nuri walked three steps ahead and refused to talk, and Paul didn't know why. Maybe it was part of another ritual—there had been ritual after ritual, nonstop, for the past week. Nuri stopped abruptly when they reached the shade of the *'aqil*'s four-story house, and Paul almost ran into him. "The bartering was long and hard," Nuri said. "The *'aqil* said he would rather die than marry his daughter to an infidel. It was the choice I finally had to offer him."

"Th—"

"Quiet!" Nuri interrupted. "Only if you are quiet will you keep from making heathen mistakes."

Paul shrugged and looked up at the house. It "turned its back," faced away from the *suq* as was the custom with wealthier families throughout Yemen. The three windows that opened onto the Red Sea were alabaster, because Yemeni tradition said the rays of the setting sun were harmful. It was another of those seemingly useless traditions with beneficial side effects: the temperature on the west side of the house was always cool, and the filtered light was perfect for reading or, Paul imagined, admiring the skin tone of a lover's back. Nuri started up the first stair, then stopped and turned around. "You have bought presents for the villagers?"

"I sent Ali to Tai'zz three days ago and told him to buy two bales of qat. Wadi Dahr qat. He returned with them this morning."

"That is a good thing," Nuri said. "Without presents to give the villagers, when they bring you your wife, you will have many visitors throughout the Night of Entrance."

Nuri pushed open the latticework door on the ground floor and led Paul inside. Cattle stalls? Some oxen munched *dhura* stalks; two riding camels and a small herd of milk camels clustered in the middle of the floor; and Paul's sacrificial goat, suddenly groomed and with ribbons in its beard, was tied to a pillar in the corner. Nuri approached one of the riding camels, a dun-colored, lightly built animal, and lovingly scratched its hump.

"What a beauty!" he said. "An *omaniya* from the hills by Maskat. I offered the *'aqil* my third wife for this beast, but he would have none of it. Now I must come back to steal her."

"When will I see her?" Paul asked.

"The beast or my third wife?" Nuri laughed. "Soon you will see the girl's shape."

"What's her name?"

Nuri reached over and covered Paul's mouth. His hand tasted of mastic and sweat. "Will your heathen ways not stop even in the house of her father? It is her name to give, not mine. I can only give you my name. Nuri. There. That must satisfy you until tonight."

They walked through a storeroom and up a massive flight of stone stairs. The living quarters on the second floor were as elegant as any Paul had seen in Yemen. The windows were stained-glass crescents, Oriental rugs covered the walls, the beams were of carved *'ilb* wood, and brass ornaments, antique weapons, and pottery hung from the pillars. Shrieks and pounding drums pulled them up another stairway. They entered a pavilion crowded with guests, not men *or* women, but both. Paul saw the *'aqil,* a tall, obese man in a white *'aba,* checkered turban, and black headband, across the room. When he noticed Paul, the *'aqil* turned his back. Men stayed at the fringes of the room throwing dice and smoking hashish—women ruled the ritual of marriage. A row of black-veiled women hypnotically pounded goat-skin drums, while others danced, writhed, uttered high-pitched trills around a kneeling figure covered by a green shawl. Ritualized birth screams. Death screams. They were giving birth to a woman, mourning the death of a girl. And who knew better than Bedouin women that life can't be created without death?

Faster and faster the women whirled, shrieked, wailed till Paul thought the walls would collapse. The frenzy began to enter him despite his attempts to distance it: He had the urge to strike at his own breast, claw his own face.

Nuri pushed him to within three feet of the kneeling figure. "The *'aqil*'s daughter," Nuri said.

The women moved like gyres and tightened their circle around the couple. Round and round through the clouds of hashish smoke they whirled till the shrieks of pain became shrieks of horror. The room began to spin, and Nuri helped Paul kneel.

The noise stopped when an elderly woman walked through the crowd, uncovered the top of the girl's head, and pulled out black hair which fell past the girl's waist.

"The *haria,*" Nuri said. "A relative chosen by the girl. She has only been married once. That will bring you luck. She must stay at the clinic until you decide if you want to keep the girl."

The *haria* stroked the girl's hair, then stopped, gave her a reassuring pat through the shawl, took a silver comb from her shawl, and made a part. When she finished, she took a stick of carmine and traced a red line. Paul had seen enough primates in heat to recognize the symbolism: labial folds. When he started to edge toward the girl, Nuri took his arm and held him in place. The *haria* helped the girl to her feet and led her through the crowd. The girl giggled as she passed.

"What is this?" Paul whispered. "More of your Arab torture?"

"I could say it was a lesson in patience, but that would not be true," Nuri said. "Everything has a reason. The longer a fig ripens, the sweeter its flesh becomes."

"If it sweetens too long, it rots."

"She must be bathed, perfumed, given new clothes. You must be patient. First you will come to her, then she to you."

The girl vanished through a door at the far end of the pavilion as the dancing, the tongue-trills and shrieks resumed. Again the drums stopped, and the men gathered for an all-day poetry competition, long, lyrical verses about peeling pomegranates or the smell of the sea. When it was Paul's turn, he told of a lover's breath as hot as the *khamsin* wind and white limbs that would curl around a lover's waist like grape vines. They were staccato verses with little attention to rhyme or meter, verses which, like Paul, made little sense, because they were hopelessly lost in passion.

Somehow the *Mus-ha,* "The Wiping," didn't seem the proper name for the most subtly erotic ceremony of the day. "The Stroking" would have been better. "The Caressing" better yet. The gentle sensuality of the ceremony was a break in an otherwise harsh existence. Though it was another in a long line of Arab paradoxes, by this time Paul was ready for anything.

After hours of singing, dancing, and poetry, Nuri led Paul down a long hallway lighted by oil lamps. Gypsum mosaics flickered as the breeze from Paul's movement stirred the flame. Nuri stopped him at a wooden gate, opened it, and they walked up another flight of stone stairs. The lone window in the women's quarters was a stained-glass palm tree which was open to let in the moonlight. The girl, again covered by a shawl, sat on a pillow in the center of the room. The *'aqil,* the *haria,* and a scribe surrounded her. The muezzin, normally the man to finalize wedding contracts, was absent.

"She is naked beneath the shawl," Nuri said, "and the material is thin as breath. It is not yet time for *that* kind of intimacy; for now another kind is more important. Touch only her face and head. Say little. Learn through your fingers."

Paul kneeled on a cushion beside the girl. The shawl was so delicate, it rose and fell with each of her breaths. He couldn't tell its color; everything was black and white in the moonlight. When he reached out and touched the material, a ripple flowed through it like water.

"My name is Paul."

"And I am Johara," said a voice as fragile as moonlight.

"I have watched you often," he said.

"All eyes watch you."

He touched the shawl where he thought her cheek would be, and when he drew his hand away, she followed it as a baby would follow its mother's breast. And with his fingertips, stroking more gently than he thought killer's hands could stroke, he learned that she would sigh when he touched the soft spot behind her ear, that she was ticklish in the hollow beneath her chin, and that her nostrils flared as her breath quickened. He learned that she would nibble his fingers when he brushed them across her lips, and that her cheeks were so smooth he could scarcely tell them from the silk. He learned as much from her in those silent moments as he had learned about other women in years.

"You are the most civilized people I've ever met," Paul said.

"Your eyes have finally opened!" Nuri laughed. "The scribe is here. The contract can be signed if you wish."

Paul nodded.

The *'aqil* sat on a cushion by Paul, pulled up a foot-high table, and unrolled a parchment. Paul could see only the deep ridges above his eyes and his hooked nose. The scribe signed, then Paul and the *'aqil,* but the *'aqil* refused when Paul offered the traditional clasping of arms. Paul held his gaze until the arm reached out.

"Now we must wait at your hut," Nuri said. "Soon she will come."

Paul stood, bowed to the *'aqil* and scribe, and walked from the room.

"I cannot imagine what keeps your heathen tongue from wagging about this final delay," Nuri said as he led Paul down the stairs.

"And I cannot imagine how I have lived this long without her."

"Give her this," Nuri said as he handed Paul a single, tarnished rial. "A token. Take it back only when she leaves you or you send her away."

Paul paced around the bedroom—just that morning it had

been the examining room. Why hadn't he bought a bed? At least a cot. Anything would have been better than the rug by his trunk. He'd slept on the ground for fifteen years, but she'd never had jungle training. She'd think he was a heathen! He sat on the edge of his teakwood trunk, then stood, paced, and restacked the bales of qat. Wadi Dahr qat . . . there would be few *dhows* putting out to sea and few meals of *dhura* gruel being made in the next few days.

Paul took Nuri's arm as he walked to the door. "I will come to your camp in a week, my brother," Paul said.

"Your quail is a glory," Nuri said, "but don't sip from her cup too often. She will take your strength. The soldiers will only be Bedus, but their rifles reach for miles."

They clasped arms, and Paul watched him walk into the darkness. "Be gentle, my Shuqra, my love," he whispered to the camel. There was a deep groan as the camel's awkward gait thumped down the *suq* and into the Tihama.

Though the temperature was in the eighties, the breeze from Jebel Amhir replaced the humidity of the day with dry mountain air, and the singing and drumming from the *'aqil*'s sounded as though they were just down the street. Paul lighted an oil lamp and walked back to his trunk, a chest as large as a casket, the only thing he'd taken from the Montagnard village. Covered with carvings of monkeys, bamboo vipers, and human skulls, it now held his weapons and doctoring gadgets—his old life and new.

The drums and shouting seemed louder. When Paul looked out the window, he saw a twisting procession of oil lamps and clapping hands. At the head of the line was the *haria* leading Johara on a donkey. Paul had visions of a shivaree but remembered Ali's bales of qat. These Yemenis were a practical group, quality qat in exchange for a peaceful wedding night; he could close the clinic till Sunday.

The *haria* helped the girl down from the donkey and waited till Paul distributed the qat. The crowd scattered in the darkness. Johara and the old woman followed Paul into the hut and waited in the outer room as he walked into the bedroom. He sat on the trunk and waited.

And the lights in the next room went out.

And Johara appeared at his door.

And she didn't wear a shawl but a white *qamis,* which draped to the ground, and a transparent veil over her head. Her face was long, almost oval, and the single dimple in her chin accented her full lips. Her nose was small and her cheeks traditionally high, but her eyes were still her dominant feature, wide and almond-shaped, dark as the Black Stone at Mecca.

"The old one will listen," Johara said, "but she will not hear. That is why I chose her. We may do what we will do."

He made room for her on the trunk and motioned for her to sit down. There was no sign of nerves in her graceful stride, and he wondered why *he* had to regulate his breathing to keep his hands from shaking. She brushed against him as she sat down. He removed her headband and lifted her veil. Her hair was worn high in plaits with flowers and gold coins intertwined throughout the braids. It was cool inside, but she was covered by a film of perspiration. He touched a finger to the hollow beneath her chin and brought it to his lips. Fresh and sweet. A blend of everything he loved most about Yemen. "You taste of cloves and the sea," he said. His passion stirred, but again he regulated his breath. Move slowly. Gently. Who knows how old she is? Be both father and lover.

She ran a finger down the bridge of his nose and tasted it. "You taste of the chase and the kill," she said.

He reached over and touched her hip, then realized that he might be more father than lover after all. Her eyes broke from his and watched him pull his hand back shyly.

Her lips curled into a pout. "I am sixteen," she said. "Twice my father would marry me. Once at twelve to a cousin. Again at fourteen to the son of an *amil.* To him I almost said yes. I told my father I would take poison and he would get nothing for me." She rested on her knuckles and leaned toward Paul. "I grew afraid you would never ask."

"Am I so easily understood?"

"You are Al Rish," Johara said. "And you are my husband."

Paul cupped his hand behind her neck and rubbed the soft spot behind her ear. "Last week I had the fever and could dream only of battles. Do you know the coral islet that looks like a mushroom at low tide? When my dream calmed, I saw you there." He sighed and wondered why he had told her that.

"And I'd wait for you in the *suq,*" Johara said. "Once I slipped from the women's quarters and followed you. I watched you bathe in the surf." She opened the front of his shirt and touched the purple scar by his sternum. "I wondered what you had done to earn this," she said. She eased her hand down the front of his pants, past his stomach. "And I wondered what I must do to earn this."

He kissed her neck and tried to lock her taste into his memory. He removed her sash, opened the *qamis,* and let it slide from her shoulders. He didn't touch her with his hands, just his lips, as he moved down the slope of her neck to her breasts. Her nipples, smelling of spice and the color and shape of candy kisses, were hard even before his beard touched them. He let his tongue rest and play there for just an instant to see if she would tense from the teasing, a tension which would later need relief in spasms, then continued down the flat of her stomach until the hair around his lips mingled with the hair between her legs. She pressed tight against him, tasting of cloves and tidal pools, joined her hands behind his head, and held him as she shuddered and smiled. He let his hands linger on the curve where the small of her back became her bottom. Then he rose and blew out all the lamps but the one above the rug so the night would hold all but their corner.

"Tomorrow we will go to your mushroom rock," she said, "and watch our reflections join in the water." A glimmer from the flame caught in her half-open eyes. "Tomorrow. Tonight there are hours until dawn, and I am not tired at all."

And soon they were together on the rug, and his metaphors of hot wind and grapevines became understatements, and he was soft with her and her thighs opened for him, spread wide for him, and her ankles were hesitant when they were at his calves but grew more and more urgent as they moved up from his thighs to his waist to lock at the small of his back, and she pulled him in and she held him and pulled him, and his mind filled with the sea and the sky, and then she was curled against his side, asleep.

He tossed on the rug, turned and coughed, and realized he couldn't sleep while there was someone by him. He had trained himself not to trust anyone that much. It was the end product of all his training—she might awaken and he'd be too vulnerable, too unaware. He sat up with his back against the chest, snuffed out the final lamp, and watched her in the moonlight. He stayed that way till she stirred and looked up at him.

"Will you not sleep with me, my husband?"

"I'm sorry, Johara. I've forgotten how."

He expected her to act hurt, to waste words when they would have no meaning or effect. But she was a Bedu and knew that words were just sounds. Her hand reached out and found him, brought him to life, and guided him. Afterward, his head in her lap, she stroked his hair till he fell asleep.

IV.

Tai'zz, Yemen—April 15, 1981

The dungeon stank of excrement and mildew, and the light was so poor that even Claudia's red sandals looked gray. She'd spent the night sitting cross-legged on the bunk, away from the rats, squashing roaches and listening to condensation drip from cell bars. While her cell was hardly first-class, it was a pleasure dome compared to those she'd seen on the way up to interrogation. She had seen men hanging by their feet, men chained to walls. One was tied to the floor with water pooled up to his ears, his face torn where the rats had been at him. The guard took pleasure in showing her the horrors.

But the tour didn't have its intended effect. She was frightened, but fear was light-years from panic. Fear cleared the mind. Scared, Claudia was rational. But pain made her panic. And when she panicked, she was useless.

Besides, there was a method to her treatment. The detours in her trip up from the dungeon and the relative luxury of her cell showed staging. She wasn't dealing with goatherds. So the problem became just how far she could push her interrogator before he quit playing with her mind and started hurting her body. If she could be certain that Rick had contacted the American consulate, she would demand her rights, but if he was locked somewhere in this chamber of horrors, she'd have to do what she was told.

The door at the top of the stairs was thick and rusted. She was handed over to a huge soldier with the smallest eyes and forehead she'd ever seen. His nose was hooked and it twitched each time he breathed, and his bushy nose hair looked like a rodent's whiskers. She nicknamed him Mickey Rat. He led Claudia into a moldy room with five doors—no doubt a central clearing-house for the disposition of prisoners—and removed her manacles. Claudia preferred her cell, the raw meat smell and blood-stains on this floor were hardly reassuring, but the fear in the air here was worse. She kept telling herself that she had two things going for her that other prisoners hadn't. She was an American. More important, she was media.

He stared at her from behind his desk. His nose twitched. She turned her back to him, but that didn't stop him from staring. She could feel his eyes. His chair squeaked as he pushed it away from his desk. Footsteps. They hesitated for just an instant, then came toward her. He grabbed her breasts.

Claudia jumped but not much. Just for an instant, she tried to ignore him, but the groping fingers hurt. She couldn't scream or flail—that would only excite him. It was probably what the routine was designed to provoke. She tried to think of some Arabic but couldn't come up with anything. She screamed, "Get your paws off me!" hoping that this animal knew that much English.

No response.

"Off!" she snarled.

His fingers probed harder. They found her nipples.

That left only two options: grab his genitals and yank till he passed out or killed her; or bite his hand. If she went after his testicles, he'd certainly hurt her. The bite would convey her message and still leave him a variety of responses. She chose the fleshy part of his palm that fortune-tellers call the Mount of Luna and bit so hard and held on so long that when he finally pulled away, skin remained between her teeth. She sat back and waited for his punch.

It never came.

He stood about ten feet from her, grinding his teeth and fingering a huge *jambiyya.* He was following orders, the expression in his eyes indicated he was trying to decide whether to slit her throat—then face The Wall—or sit down and behave himself.

He sat down.

His actions told Claudia: one, she *was* something special; and two, the man who gave Mickey Rat his orders wasn't pleasant. He didn't look like the type to pass up violence unless he was afraid, and he didn't look as though he scared often or easily.

Claudia sat back and sighed. The bloodstains on the floor remained, but most of the fear dissipated. After about fifteen minutes, a red light flashed on the wall behind his desk. He grunted and motioned for her to follow.

On the way up from the dungeon, Claudia had visualized the interrogation room: cramped white walls, a single chair, a naked light bulb. She was wrong only in color. The room had once been white but had long since faded to yellow, then brown. Her interrogator stood outside the bright halo of the light bulb. He had liver-colored splotches on his face, greasy hair, and his crisp uniform couldn't hide his fat. He was a human slug, and his voice complemented his appearance. There was nothing human in it, nothing at all. "Sit," he said.

Claudia sat.

"How familiar with pain are you, Miss Mallory?" he asked.

Maybe he was mean but not terribly bright. His accent gave away his Western education; he had to be familiar with international diplomacy, the Geneva Convention, the rights of American citizens. Since he knew her name, he'd either found her press credentials or Rick had made it to the consulate.

"You were caught impersonating a man," the interrogator said. "You took photographs where photographs are not allowed." He took her by the chin and moved her eyes toward the bright light bulb so she couldn't see his face. "Either could be considered espionage."

"You should post your regulations," Claudia said through clenched teeth. She tried to regulate her breath to maintain control. "It would clear up a lot of misunderstandings."

He touched her behind the ear. His voice softened and his accent grew more affected. He moved out of the light bulb's glare. The markings on his epaulets indicated he was a lieutenant. He was one of the ugliest men she had ever seen. "Minor transgressions can be overlooked," he said, letting go of her chin.

Claudia lowered her voice. "And which of my transgressions aren't minor?"

"Your association with an assassin for the rebels."

"Never met him."

"He has a dog."

"Pancho?" Claudia chuckled but not loudly enough to be disrespectful.

"I know of no 'Pancho,' " the lieutenant said. He grabbed her chin again and made her look into the light bulb. "You were seen with Abdullah Mohammed. I want him."

"We have a mutual interest in art," Claudia said. "We met accidentally."

"Nonsense. He knew who you were and when you would leave your motel. Without publicity the rebellion will never expand beyond the Highlands. *You* are publicity. Many have known of you since your arrival. We are not all 'goatherds.'

"There are things you will do for us," the lieutenant said. "Perhaps you will tell me who arranged for your meetings with the rebels. Twice you were able to lose the men I assigned to you." He leaned over her. His face was within six inches of hers. His breath stank of rotten teeth and rotting meat.

If he had pushed her or slapped her or called her whore, she might have eventually told him what he wanted to know. Maybe. Instead he put his hand on her knee. She tensed and began to shake. She tried to control the anger in her voice. "Even reporters have ethics," she said.

The hand moved up to her thigh. "Ethics can be fatal."

The first rule of "Cat and Mouse": Once you decide to extend your claws, you'd better become a lion as fast as possible. She caught the lieutenant's eyes and held them, then brushed his hand away. "Enough," she said.

His eyebrows pursed, then he pushed the intercom button on the wall. "Corporal Sadid," he said, "take Miss Mallory to one of our collective cells."

Claudia set her jaw and held his glare. It was a bluff time. The game had moved beyond anything else. She kept her voice as even and calm as she could. "I'm media, not some freak in town to buy hash and qat."

He looked up at her in disbelief. "You really don't understand, do you?"

Claudia had been in enough tight spots to know that when you're bluffing on borrowed money, there's no backing out. She looked straight into his eyes. "Uncle Sam has a way of evening things out. Throw me in with those freaks, imagine your assets frozen."

Mickey Rat walked into the room, still rubbing his hand. The lieutenant said, "Corporal Sadid is a simple man, a man without knowledge of international diplomacy. He is, however, an expert on finding out what I want to know."

"You put the hurt on me, and the media will make enough noise to hold up, if not stop, your military aid." She waited for the lieutenant's comeback—the rules of camel trading demanded a comeback. Nothing. Silence would cost her momentum. She continued, "Your Marxist neighbors to the south would love that. They're experts at taking over your border towns—until American hardware starts pouring in. If you think I'm worth stopping that, I'm flattered. If not, I want out."

That was it. Her last bluff. She couldn't escalate things any further without drifting into absurdity. Only one thing left to do. She waited.

Something glorious happened. Something truly unexpected: The lieutenant changed tactics. He abruptly motioned for Mickey Rat to leave the room, and his face of ice melted into a sugary smile. A pause. "We are both persons of culture," he said. "Perhaps we can come to an agreement that will benefit both of us."

Claudia was too surprised and relieved to analyze his strategy. Since she wasn't sure how to respond to him, she didn't.

"I must have knowledge that would be useful in your story," he said. "Perhaps you may have information that will benefit me."

"I don't reveal sources, period," Claudia said.

"Then censored information if you wish."

"A trade?"

"A trade like any other." His eyes told her nothing. When he noticed her staring, he turned away. "Perhaps it may be even better than a trade for you. I will give you information so you can write your story with, how should I say it, equality for *both* sides?"

First of all, Claudia was a reporter. This animal was now a news source, something she could deal with.

"How often have you met with the rebels?" he asked.

The question seemed harmless enough. "Three times," she said.

"Always in the Highlands?"

"Censored," Claudia said. "My turn. The Madhi has a fortress in the mountains, Bustān al Kaf Maryam. The Bedouins say it materialized from thin air." Time for a prod to his ego. "They say you can't find it."

"The insect has a gift for scattering lies," the lieutenant said calmly. "Yemen has few roads. All are watched. If we don't know where the fortress is, it doesn't exist. If we did . . . there are airplanes."

"But the Bedus believe."

"The insect knows that what is, is not as important as what appears to be."

"He's an image-maker." Claudia smiled. "Think he was educated in the States like you?"

"Perhaps *you* should be a detective," the lieutenant said. He smiled, but it was a mask. "His past is a ghost. Have you met anyone who has seen him?"

"No. I heard he rose from a cave in Samara after a thousand-year nap. That he eats nothing but sand and rock. That he talks directly with Allah. That he intends to wipe the Middle East clean of all traces of Westernization . . . which would include you."

"As a nonbeliever," the lieutenant said, "perhaps you should know that he has declared *jihad,* holy war. It is the *jihad*ist's duty to put all nonbelievers to the sword. Some would rather kill Christians than go on the pilgrimage."

Claudia shook her head. "I heard his primary *hadith* is that his followers 'exert themselves through heart, tongue, hands, and sword.' He puts the sword last on the list. You put it first."

"I've met him only in war."

The lieutenant smiled, then turned his back on her and walked out of the room. Moments later, he returned with a small, leather-bound Koran. He handed it to her. Five one-thousand-dollar bills were pressed in its pages. "This could be a most profitable story for you if you treat my government favorably. Forget what you have seen today. Leave Yemen immediately."

The lieutenant was nervous. Rick. It had to be Rick. Rick had reached the consulate, the foreign service was raising hell, and that's why the lieutenant hadn't had time to soften her up properly. "The name Rick Hodges wouldn't mean anything to you, would it?" Claudia asked. She handed the book and money back.

"It would," the lieutenant said. "He's been in the building since this morning." He pointed to the door at the far end of the room. "He has even less sense than you. If that's possible." He walked her to the door, opened it partway, then held it. Mickey Rat had reentered the room. The lieutenant pointed toward the money.

"No, thanks," Claudia said, shaking her head.

"Then you are in danger as soon as you leave this building," he said. He took her chin in his hand for a final time. "Should word of this insect's tricks spread, should his army grow, he could top Khomeini and form a world of Islam from southern Russia to the Cape of Good Hope. And oil would stop. And trade. Who's to say what your people and the Russians would do if the oil stops? Nuclear war? Perhaps."

The line could have come directly from a CIA operations book, which would explain the money and perhaps the change in tactics. "If you please?" she said, nodding toward the door.

"I would be careful which shadows you pass," he said.

The door opened into a huge room with brick walls. The only decoration was the picture of the country's president, a man who looked like Omar Sharif in a khaki uniform.

"Hey mahn, you miss me?" a voice shouted. Rick sat on a podium playing with his yo-yo. He did a "Walk the Dog" and a "Cat's Cradle" as Claudia walked across the room to him. She gave him a mock round of applause. He wore the traditional *'aba* but had replaced the turban with his black Stetson, a paisley scarf, and sunglasses.

As the adrenaline rush faded, Claudia could feel both of her hands shake. She pulled Rick to his feet, almost crying "Jesus, Rick, you make fun of these goons, and they'll gouge your liver out!" She snatched his sunglasses and scarf and put them in her suit coat.

"Where's my reward?" he asked.

Claudia leaned over and kissed him on the forehead.

"A start," he said. "How'd they treat you?"

"Mostly strong-arm. A little sugar. A couple days to soften me up and it would have worked." She wrapped her arms around his neck, drew tight against him, and kissed him deeply. "Thanks," she said. She left her arm around his waist as she drew away. She laughed weakly. "You wouldn't believe the people they keep in their dungeons. It's like the bar scene from *Star Wars.*"

Claudia leaned against him and put her head on his shoulder. She'd had enough for one day. "It's been a day and a half since I slept or tasted food," she said. "Let's get out of here."

She kept his arm as they walked back through the *suqs.* Once they were back in his hotel room, Rick went to a restaurant of sorts and came back with hamburgers and roasted *dhura.* He lifted the top of the bun and drew back in horror. "You'll have to pretend the hamburgers are beef," he said. "If your imagination isn't that strong, I'll disinfect them with Jack Daniel's."

"I'd pass out," Claudia said. "I have to pack first."

"Pack?" Rick asked. "The notes, first draft, and film are safe and sound in the consul's desk."

"It's time to leave. How soon can you get tickets?"

"Hold on, Claude. You were the one who insisted on staying. I know for damn sure you couldn't have followed up the Imam lead from a cell."

Claudia flopped back on the mattress. "Things have changed.

It was made clear that unless I play along with the security police, I end up at The Wall. The guy who interrogated me has a playmate even you wouldn't want to meet." She ran a hand through her hair and made a face. "Jesus, it's been a month since I've had a hot bath! I want to be in Sana' by this evening, on a plane by midnight, and halfway to Cairo by dawn."

"Sorry. No can do. Things have changed."

"Rick," she said, "*I want out!*"

Rick held up his hand as if to ward her off. "Take a deep breath, count to ten, and listen," he said. "After I dropped the goods off at the consulate, I spent the rest of the evening following up on the execution. This place is alive with rumors."

"No rumors exist that will make me stay another day in this barbaric hole."

"No? Try this one on. That Imam? Wasn't with the others, was he? Rumors have it that a team of American specialists have been called in to examine the body. That Imam's a most unusual specimen, indeed. Seems that not only was his leprosy in remission, but he was growing back fingers and toes."

"Nonsense."

"So I thought, so I bought a leak at the consulate. Seems there *is* a team of American bacteriologists and dermatologists that landed in Sana' last night, and now they're staying at the Beit adh Dhuyūf as the personal guests of the Yemeni government."

"Which is all lovely," Claudia said, "but you failed to have registered on one small point. I said my ass is on the line."

"That's not all," Rick said, ignoring her. "You were at the execution. Remember the substance of the Imam's prophecies?"

"In short, he said the Madhi would call down a plague on assorted persons for assorted reasons."

"He did."

"Who did what?"

"I told you there were rumors! I've never seen anything like it, not even in those days before the fall of Saigon. Everyone who took part in the firing squad, all sixteen of them including the officer, are dead."

"Knives, garrotes, or guns?"

"Of the plague, Claude, *the plague!*"

Claudia did a double take. It couldn't be. This had to be another of Rick's schemes. She forced a yawn. "At least we've had our boosters," she said.

"Listen to me, Claude. P-L-A-G-U-E. Got it? The leak said there have been only sixteen cases of the plague reported, *only* sixteen. All sixteen members of the firing squad got it; all of them died within six hours of the first symptoms. That kind of virulence makes the Black Death seem like a runny nose.

"The government has forbidden all incoming flights and ships. You can leave, but you can't come," Rick said. "If the second half of the Imam's prophecy comes true, if some village gets wiped out by the plague, then we're sitting on the biggest story since the Resurrection—and *it's all ours!*"

Claudia dropped her head into her hands and rubbed her eyes. This wasn't real—that was the only thing she was sure of. Her circuits were overloading; her systems were shot; she needed a rest. That plane ride could wait until morning, after all.

V.

**Bustān al Kaf Maryam, the Yemeni Highlands—
April 15, 1981**

Even as a child, when the breath of Allah first lifted him beyond the torment of his epilepsy, Talāl ibn Saud, prince of the House of Saud, knew his destiny: to become the sword of righteousness on the Saudi flag. He would slice all things from his world that did not obey the Law. He would follow the Path, become the beloved of Allah, sip from the cup of truth. He was told the path to becoming an *auliya,* a saint, would be one of anguish; it was the only road the wealth of the Royal Family couldn't pave with gold. He would listen to no words but the words of Abdullah-i Ansari, a voice of God:

> O God, whosoever comes to know you
> And raises the banner of your love
> Will cast off all that is other than you.
> What use has he of his soul who has known you?
> What use has he of offspring and family?

Talāl was a foolish child, and a foolish child can become a fanatic youth.

First he petitioned his father, then King Saud himself, for the right to turn his back on privilege. He wasn't satisfied with salvation in the Hereafter, he wanted it immediately. At twelve, he was sent to Mecca to study law with the *ulama.* When even the answers of those learned men proved shallow, when all words became echoes and lies, he chose to go to the heart of the faith, to find the Real behind the ninety-nine names of the divinity. He chose to follow the mystic's path.

He left the Arabian peninsula, crossed the Gulf of Oman, traveled on foot through Pakistan, and settled in Punjab. There he abandoned the *'aba* for the Sufi robe, the turban for the *tasbih*, the throne for the prayer carpet. He tried to cleanse the dust of the world from the mirror of his heart by meditation and self-mortification. He would slice all things that weren't Allah from his body, even if it meant his death. He entered a prayer cell at sixteen, a five- by eight-foot stone room that was always cold, always damp, and waited for the love of Allah to fill him.

And he waited.

He waited until he discovered the bitter truth behind the sayings of Farid Sani. Each day Talāl would rise and repeat the prayer over and over:

> Let me not sit at another's door, O Lord, I pray;
> And if I am to be kept thus, then take my life away.

Even that simple request remained unanswered.

Talāl spent twelve years traveling the Path to God. He stopped at each of the first six way stations, drank only fetid water, ate only crusts, concentrated all his being on Allah but never found satisfaction. He squandered his youth and his right to succession in a stinking cell, waiting to hear God's music, and heard only silence.

Somewhere in his readings, perhaps in the works of San Juan de la Cruz, Talāl had read that failed mystics became the greatest heretics. There was more truth in those words than in any others he had read. He decided there were other ways to the truth.

He abandoned a worn-out path for a new road—and great wealth makes any earthly road a highway. He returned to Riyadh and the Royal Palace, then traded his robes for a student's blazer. The road led West, first to England where he studied a new poetry: formulas, theories, calculations. Cambridge led to Harvard, Harvard to Cal Tech, physics to chemistry to molecular biology. A new set of saints appeared: Einstein, Mendel, Watson, and Crick. What miracles this new road held!

Instead of trembling in prayer, he studied. Instead of fighting off snakes while men with wild beards shouted insane prayers, he sat in comfortable lounges, conversing with men in lab coats. They didn't speak in riddles and songs but in a language that mapped life. He learned to be an architect whose buildings last instead of a singer whose echo fades. Life was a swirling stairway with numbered steps, and one needed knowledge, not luck or prayer, to control it. When he had learned enough, when he had found and bought the best people, he returned again to Saudi Arabia.

He needed money to construct his new road, secret money. Millions weren't missed in a land whose wealth grew by billions each day. In the West it would have been called embezzlement; he considered to call it *zakat,* charity. After all, the money financed a holy war. The time was right, Islam splintered and weak. He had learned his theology well and knew the prophecy of the Madhi—the proper timing, the proper miracles, and all Islam would flock to him.

He chose Yemen, the most primitive Arab country, the most fertile Islamic soil, for his garden. The materials for the fortress that would be his base were flown in from Ethiopia by helicopter to an unchartered peak near Jebel Ash Shu'ub. Within five years, the shell of the fortress, camouflaged from the air by a ridge, hidden by peaks on three sides, was finished. All workmen and pilots were paid well for their silence, then silenced permanently before they could betray. Then the lab. For enough money, black-market supplies were available—from France, Russia, the U.S. herself—in boxes marked medicine, wheat, or rice. Soon centrifuges, spectrophotometers, Laminar hoods, incubators, radioactively labeled nucleotides, restriction enzymes—the list seemed to go on forever—were collected and assembled. Then came the hardest task: assembling the research group—the men who would manufacture his miracles. But offer a scientist ten, fifteen times what his university pays him, and even that task becomes simple.

The holy war was easiest of all. Some guns, some promises, enough money to the proper chieftains, proper men to spread proper rumors, and the *jihad* was reality. Talāl knew the words of the Prophet so well he could twist the Law until even the poisons were coated with sugar paste. It was simple to run a rebellion by proxy. Not once in three thousand years had he set foot in Yemen, yet his legend continued to grow. He performed enough miracles by proxy to be sure his name stayed on the lips of all true believers.

He made only one error in two decades: placing trust in the wrong man. A lackey, an insect, Muhammed ibn Abdullah al Qahtani used Talāl's preparations and strategy and stormed the Sacred Mosque at Mecca. But that was to have been the final act of the *jihad*, not the first. Could he have really believed the House of Saud would deliver the throne to three hundred fifty maniacs? Fortunately, of all that group, only al Qahtani knew the rest of Talāl's plans. A proper distribution of rials to the proper members of the Saudi National Guard assured another false Madhi died before the prophecy was fulfilled. Only sixty-three fanatics survived the siege. Talāl attended their beheadings as a lesson on the cost of impatience.

When it was finally time, he drove south from Riyadh by limousine, crossed the Yemeni border at Nejran, and rode two hundred kilometers south on camels to the village of Huth. There he abandoned even camel trails for the eighty kilometer crisscross through the Highlands to his fortress, Bustān al Kaf Maryam, the Garden of the Resurrection Flower. Everything was ready. It was time to begin.

Talāl sat down on a wall of native rock and looked west over a courtyard filled with his followers to the bare peaks of the Highlands, the jagged ranges that rose from the valleys like the spine of an enormous reptile. Even from a distance of a hundred kilometers he could see the humidity that hung above the Red Sea and the Tihama. It was the perfect place to kill a village. Poor. Isolated. He had no followers there. He was close enough to Al Rattaf that he could collect specimens and information before anyone else arrived.

The preparations were finished at Al Rattaf, the groundwork laid in Tai'zz: the Imam gave the prophecy before he died; retribution had been taken against the firing squad; connections with the Western press established. There would be no more need to start rumors; the miracles would be their own medium for exaggeration. And when the word of the miracles reached other Islamic countries, he could leave these cold peaks, raise the sword of righteousness and bring it down on the necks of those who doubted. It would be his great gift to the world: certainty, direction. He would give to others what he had not been able to find for himself.

He walked from the wall back into his prayer cell. Even here the odors of ethanol, acetone, and the beef-broth smell of phenol leaked down from a lab outside the containment room. All that was needed was for the word of the miracles to be disseminated. The messenger from Tai'zz had arranged even that: The entire world would hear of Allah's wrath. The American would be led to the proper places at the proper times. She was a gift from Allah.

The hallway to Talāl's study was dark all day. When he passed a follower, the man dropped to his knees in the position of salaam and remained there until the Madhi's footsteps faded. Talāl sat down at his desk, toying with the dry stem that always went with him on his travels, the *kaf maryam,* the resurrection plant. In dry seasons the leaves fell, the branches folded inward, the roots loosened, and the plant would be carried in the wind like a wicker ball until it reached a wet spot. Then it would take hold in the moisture, return to life, and burst into bloom.

Talāl was the resurrection plant, and this fortress was his garden. Saudi Arabia had been a desert, so he pulled up his roots, curled into a ball, and blew first to Punjab, then to the West, and finally settled in the barren Highlands of Yemen. Here he had taken root and, within hours, would send forth seeds that would bring the entire Middle East to blossom.

VI.

Al Rattaf, Yemen—April 16, 1981

Johara was the perfect lover, a lover without taboos, habits, or expectations. She cared about *now,* not before or after. Why, she asked Paul, did he reminisce about yesterday and worry about tomorrow when he had today? It was a tough question, a question to which he first pleaded ignorance, then stupidity. She'd have to be patient, he answered, and in a year, maybe two, she could unteach him all that he'd learned growing up in the West.

In the new light he could see traces where perspiration had dried on her neck. He wanted to lick the salt from behind her ear, wake her, and join with her at sunrise just because he'd never done it before. Slow down, he thought, *slow down!* You are Al Rish. The shark must be strong. If he learned the quiet of her sleep, someday it would kill him.

But he couldn't help himself. He sat back and watched her breath play with the folds in the sheet. Then, like a child, when the light grew brighter and he knew that life in the *suq* would begin, he stroked her thigh until she turned to him. She didn't say a word, just smiled and opened her arms and legs.

"Have you been awake long?" she asked when they finished.

"Too long. You're too strong to watch sleep."

"You talk in riddles. No one is stronger than Al Rish."

If only she knew. He stood, walked to the Montagnard chest, removed the branch of Wadi Dawr qat he had taken from the bales, and held it out to her.

She frowned. "Why chew qat when there are so many other things to do?"

"Why not?"

"I chewed only because I was in purdah. Every day with the same rugs and games and faces. Now that everything is new, I will never chew again."

"I thought it would make our love better," Paul admitted. And again, without wanting to, he played the child. He made a silly, disappointed face, and Johara, like a mother distracting a spoiled child, chewed his qat, washed away the strong taste with coffee, and made love to him again. It was too painful to fall in love for the first time at thirty-five. It stripped him bare. He wished he could cover his naked feelings with his hands.

The sounds of the wakening village poured in through the window: songs of fishermen mending their nets; the pounding of hammers in the salt quarry; the cries of a shark vendor who started his rounds at the far edge of the village. "The law says I must not leave this room for a week," Johara said. "If we are to see this mushroom rock, we must leave now, before others see me." When she rose, took a robe from her bag and began to cover her body, Paul almost cried out. Again she seemed to read his mind. "If the *haria* wakes, she will try to stop me. If the village learns, I will be disgraced." She began to put on her veil.

"Don't wear that for me," Paul said.

"I wear it *only* for you. I wouldn't go naked before other men!"

Again he was the heathen. She'd have to be patient with him. He took her hand and they tiptoed past the *haria,* out the front entrance, and into the suq. Either no one saw them as they left the village, or no one acknowledged their breach of tradition with a nod or cry of welcome.

As the tide moved out, the beach sparkled with a film of water. They took off their sandals and let the waves wash their feet. It was so early, the humidity hadn't yet gathered into a haze; the air was clear and the Highlands looked close enough to step over. A ridge of seaweed and shells had been dropped by the receding tide. Paul stopped to examine an occasional shell, but he always poked the weeds first as a precaution: a sea snake might be hiding in the tangle, or a man-of-war might have been caught in a swell and washed ashore. A mile from the village, they passed a clump of mangrove, a sand dune gathering scrub brush, and a pile of rotting pearl-oyster shells. Soon the islet appeared to their left, an enormous pink mushroom in a meadow of blue water. They put on their sandals so the coral wouldn't cut their feet.

It was a hundred-yard wade through the tidal pools. The water was clear, and they watched eels and rays dart away as they approached. The islet was at least twelve feet high, so Paul let Johara climb first and helped her with his hand when she couldn't find a spot to lodge her foot. Once they were atop, they could see miles past the reef to the west and deep into the mountain valleys to the east.

Johara dropped to her knees and began to crawl around, to search through the sand and brush. She looked up at Paul. "Once I found the nest of a sea bird here." She knotted her eyebrows, cocked her head a bit to her left, and continued the search.

"Was that long ago?"

"Ten years, maybe eleven. All years are the same in purdah."

"But you didn't wear a veil then."

She laughed at his nonsense. "Children don't wear veils!" Then she shrieked in surprise as she found an egg.

"At this moment," Paul said, "you are a child with her toes in the sand, yelling like the discoverer of a new world because you found an egg. I can't share the expressions on your face."

"Then I will take the veil off!" she said. Paul imagined her setting her jaw, and how her lips curled and her nose turned down when she made up her mind. She turned away from the village, hunched over, removed the hood of her robe, and swept the veil back off her face. Then she sat back on her hands and smiled at him. She crawled to the rim of the islet. "Our reflections!" she shouted, and motioned for him to join her. When he was near, she turned and nipped the end of his nose. "I am the one to take the nose of Al Rish!" she shrieked.

"Given with pleasure," Paul said. He patted the sand in front of him. "Here," he said, "your flowers have wilted." She scurried in front of him and giggled, then squirmed in the sand. Suddenly she was a sixteen-year-old girl on the beach with her boyfriend, in love with the unaccustomed naughtiness and mystery. Paul slid the robe down to her shoulders, massaged her neck till she purred, then slowly unwound the plaits in her hair. She stared into the sea.

"Have you brought a weapon?" she finally asked.

"Just a knife," Paul said. "I always have my knife."

"You should carry more."

"We'll cross the flats before the tide rises. It's too shallow for sharks now."

"You are the shark. Sharks should fear only hunters."

He finished unknotting the last braid on her left side before he turned her head toward him. "I was a hunter before I became a shark. There was only one person in Yemen strong enough to take my nose." He laughed.

She didn't. She turned away, and he continued to unwind her hair. Paul looked up and followed her gaze into the sea; reef waves began to break a mile offshore. "My father and the muezzin hate you, hate how you came from the outside and grew strong." She looked into his eyes. "If they hurt you, I will kill them!" Then she looked back into the sand. "The muezzin said our marriage breaks the Prophet's Law."

"So does chewing qat. *No one* refused my gift."

"My father has guns."

"But I have you," Paul said, untying the final plait in her hair. "Comb," he said, holding out his hand.

Her eyes opened in amazement. "I tried to sneak it in my robe."

"Al Rish hears, smells, sees everything. Don't worry about me."

He took it from her and combed her hair till it was rich and full and glistened in the sun like a wet rock. The wind off the sea increased, and she transformed into a woman with wild hair and full lips. "You must stand and look at the village," Paul said.

She cried out. "Someone may see and think I am your whore!"

"They will know that you are my wife and that you are stronger than other women."

Her hair settled at the small of her back. "Then I will stand," she whispered, as though the village might be listening. "I will stand *now*!" Her tone indicated that her mind was made up, a tone he could have distinguished in a gale at a hundred yards. As she stood, the wind blew from her left to her right, whipped her robe like a flag and swirled the hair in front of her face. She stood until the wind began to calm, then flopped into the sand before her hair settled and uncovered her face. "I can't go back to the village without my veil," she said.

She would kill him with her vulnerability!

"Don't wear it when we're alone," he said. "It hides what you feel and think, and I don't know how to act."

It was low tide, so they walked in the wet sand between the water and the mangroves. Gulls circled overhead, squawked at Paul and Johara, staked out territory, and fought for abandoned minnows and mollusks. A gull swooped within six inches of Johara's head and, when she picked up a rock, held it in her hand and, in elaborate Arabic curses, dared the gull to come back within throwing range, Paul realized again how well he'd married. They walked past the pile of oyster shells. Soon they would be visible to the fishermen on the jetty. Paul took her hand and led her into the last stand of mangroves before Al Rattaf.

"We can return to the hut with no one seeing us," Paul said.

"The streets are narrow and crowded," Johara said.

"But the people are noisy and blind." Then he showed her how it is movement that makes things visible, and that controlled movement is camouflage. He showed her that in the Tihama where the sand is almost white and the sun is close, eyes can't adjust to shadows. The desert hunter is brother to shadows, the dark side of buildings, the lee slope of sand dunes. They decided to buy her cloth like he wore, mottled cloth the color of sand, which became one with the desert without movement, and make her slacks and a blouse. They crawled from the mangroves to the dunes, to the buildings at the fringe of the village, to the streets. Only a dog saw them and growled, an animal that knew them well but was frightened to see humans move with the grace and cunning of animals. Johara laughed as she climbed through the back window of the clinic, giggled, and mimicked the faces of the camel-stupid men who had walked right past them.

"It's a century since they were warriors," Paul said.

"I will go out every night and steal until we are as rich as my father." Johara laughed until she was out of breath.

Paul heard an argument in the waiting room. The *haria* was trying to quiet a man. It sounded like Is'mail, the spice merchant, his voice distorted by fear.

"Patients," Paul said, not realizing his pun until after he had said it. He raised Johara's veil and kissed her as a wife instead of a lover for the first time. "I will deal with him quickly." Paul opened the door and walked into the waiting room.

"He knows not to disturb you today!" the *haria* shrieked, pointing to the spice merchant.

"The boy is alive with fever," Is'mail said.

"Then I'd better see what's wrong," Paul said. The boy's lips were cracked and the inside of his mouth dry and covered with a white film. That the boy's breath was terrible wasn't unusual; what worried Paul was that it was terrible in an unusual way. When Paul touched the boy's forehead, he was careful not to show surprise. The kid was hot. One hundred and four at least. "How long has he been like this?"

"A half-hour. Maybe an hour. He was playing and started to wobble. When he fell down, he couldn't get up. He didn't know me."

Paul wondered where Ali was—he must have had a hell of a qat hangover not to be in by eight. Just this once, considering the occasion, Paul would forgive him. Paul found Ali's rectal thermometer on the desk. The child was delirious; he'd bite an oral thermometer in half. "Johara," Paul said, "bring me the gallon of cold water and a tray of ice from the refrigerator. Then take whatever buckets we have, fill them with water, and refrigerate them."

"She must not go outside!" the *haria* said.

"Then *you* will go to the well," Paul said. "*Now*!"

The old woman picked up a bucket and scurried out the door as Johara went into the examination room. "Dip the rags in cold water," Paul shouted, "enough to cover his body. Then fill a towel with ice for his head." The number-one priority was to stabilize that fever. The boy already had chills.

Paul took the boy's pulse. It was shallow and erratic. "Did he complain of a sore throat?" Paul asked. "A stomachache or backache?"

"He complained of nothing."

Good. It wasn't typhoid. No pink macules on his face, so it probably wasn't typhus, either. "Diarrhea?" Paul asked.

"Nothing," the man said, "he just fell down!"

Scratch shigellosis and, thank God, cholera. The boy's forehead was dripping with sweat. "Please hurry with those towels," Paul said.

Johara hurried back into the room, her arms full of wet rags. "Help me with his clothes," Paul said.

"She is a woman!" Is'mail yelled.

"I don't have time to talk," Paul said. "You have three choices. One: sit down, shut up and stay out of the way. Two: go back to your shop until I've brought his fever down. Three: take him home and watch him die."

The man sat down behind Ali's desk.

When Paul slipped the *'aba* from the boy's shoulders, he saw the swelling, the bulging lymph nodes in the boy's neck. The sight was beyond response. A single nursery rhyme kept repeating in his mind:

> Ring around the rosey
> Pocket full of posey
> Ashes, ashes, all fall down.

Paul reviewed the symptoms of every disease he'd ever encountered and prayed that one of them would match the almond-sized boils. Anthrax, no. Relapsing fever, no. Malaria, no. Yaws, no. Maybe it was meningitis—God, let it be meningitis! When he pulled the *'aba* down to the boy's waist, he found the ring around the rosey in the armpits; when the robe was completely removed, there was massive swelling in the groin. Paul instinctively took a step backward. "Go sit down, Johara," Paul said softly. "Get away from the boy."

The *haria* returned with a bucket of water. "Stay in the hut," Paul told the old woman. He motioned for Is'mail to come to the table. "Put these rags all over his body," Paul said, "and put the one with ice on his forehead. I have to make a call." Paul walked through the examination room door, closed it behind him, and walked to the radio. He wasn't above asking for help when he needed it.

He flipped the on/off switch, turned the hand crank on the generator, and waited for the light to flash on. Nothing. He cranked harder. Still nothing. He cranked until his arm hurt, but the power light refused to turn on. It had never failed to work before.

There was no more time to waste. The weekly boat from Tai'zz was due in two days, but that was too long. The spice merchant had a motorcycle. It was only a half-day's drive to the hospital in Sana' by motorcycle, then another two hours' flight back by helicopter. Not great but the best he could do. He took a sheet of paper from his trunk and wrote a quick note in English so only the doctors in Sana' could read it:

Al Rattaf, April 16

Dear Dr. al Shohaty:

I'm treating a boy who appears to have the bubonic plague. I have limited antibiotics. I can treat him, maybe a few others, but I have no idea how many cases will develop. Please send help.

Paul Kenyon

Paul walked back into the waiting room. "Is your motorcycle running?" Paul asked Is'mail.

The man nodded.

"Is there anyone other than your employees and members of your family who knows how to operate it?"

"Jamaal, son of the shark vendor, sometimes gets supplies for me in Sana'."

"Perfect," Paul said. "Give him this note and tell him to get to Sana' as fast as he can. You return to your house, close up the shop, and stay there. Talk to no one but Jamaal. No one in your family, none of your clerks are to leave your house until I say it's all right. *Now hurry!*"

The man took the note and ran from the house. My God, Paul thought, I stepped right into the fourteenth century. The plague wasn't just a disease, it was a disease elevated to symbol . . . the corpses and rot in the religious paintings, the Black Death of the fictions. It was a disease that was part of the cultural heritage, a disease with its own vocabulary: the buboes distanced through language to the childish "ring around the rosey"; the massive deaths to "all falling down"; and the "ashes to ashes" of dust-to-dust fame. He hoped his treatment was better than a "pocket full of posey." Perhaps reducing the plague to a child's game was the only way the psyche could deal with such horror. What to do? What to do? If he didn't bring the temperature down, it wouldn't make any difference. He put the bucket of water in the refrigerator and came back for the child.

"What is wrong?" Johara asked.

He'd have to quarantine everyone who'd been in contact with the boy, but Johara was different. Paul rubbed the backs of his hands over his eyes. "Would your father take you back into his house for a few days?"

"What is wrong?"

"Just until I come to get you. Two days? Maybe three?"

"What is wrong, Paul?" It was the first time she had called him by his first name.

He whispered to Johara so the *haria* wouldn't hear. "Plague. If he starts to cough, that means it's pneumonic and that it can be transmitted through his spittle. I looked inside his mouth."

"Then someone will have to take care of you."

"I have at least a day before the symptoms appear in me. By

that time, someone who knows what to do will be here." Paul turned his back on her. "The boy, the *haria,* and I will remain here. You will return to your father. I don't have time to argue."

He visualized her jaw setting. Her eyes pursed. "I am *not* the spice merchant! And *I* don't have time to argue!" Johara's tone indicated that she'd had enough of his nonsense. "I will pull my veil high so the plague can't get in."

Paul couldn't help smiling.

The boy began to shake. When Paul picked him up and carried him into the examination room, he felt the deep, bubbling sound in the boy's lungs: rale. It was the pneumonic plague, and it was beginning to consolidate. "You may stay with me, Johara," Paul said, "but over there." He pointed to the trunk. Paul covered the boy with fresh towels and inserted the thermometer into the boy's anus.

Then he took the *Merck Manual* from his trunk. He was amazed how fast he adjusted to reading English. Only ten percent of plague victims had boils in multiple locations; the boy had them every place possible. Pneumonic plague took half as long to kill and half as long for symptoms to develop as bubonic plague: two days. Fortunately, by that time the cavalry would have arrived. Something was wrong: Boils weren't supposed to appear in pneumonic plague.

It made sense that the spice merchant's family would be first to be exposed. They handled merchandise from all over the Middle East. A rat with infected fleas could hide in any spice shipment, and the sailors on those ships frequented the filthiest quarters in the world.

Paul checked for a lesion from the flea bite but couldn't find one. He didn't have the equipment to do a white blood count, but a bacteria culture might be useful to the doctors. He used a needle (the way things were developing, he'd do more needle work in this one day than during the past year) to withdraw pus from the buboes; there was no need to chance spreading the disease by lancing. He injected the sample into some agar gel and covered the petri dish.

The boy began to writhe.

The *Merck Manual* had good news. Contrary to legend and religious belief, the plague was just another bacteria. He had antibiotics—he wasn't in the fourteenth century, after all. "Prompt treatment reduces mortality to below five percent," the book said. Those were his kind of odds. The plague would be a piece of cake.

"Prompt treatment" included: 0.5 grams of streptomycin intramuscularly or 500 milligrams of tetracycline intravenously every three hours. He had both. Plenty of both. At those dosages he could treat twenty persons for a day. He wasn't much good at finding veins, so he took one hypodermic needle, one vial of streptomycin, drew the antibiotic into the needle, gave it a squirt for effect, put the needle in the boy's bottom, and gave the boy's immune system an intramuscular helping hand. Paul withdrew the thermometer: 105.8. The boy's fever was approaching the upper limits of the disease.

"More towels," he said. He only had two trays of ice left. The water the *haria* brought wouldn't cool for hours, so the streptomycin had better take hold soon or the boy might suffer permanent brain damage.

Paul changed the compresses and put a fresh ice pack on the boy's forehead. He tried the radio again. Still no go. Current wasn't even reaching the on/off button—the thing must be completely blown. He took out his remaining medical books and sat on the far side of the room from Johara. He wanted to find out everything he could about the disease; he never had liked surprises. How quickly would the antibiotic lower the bacteria count? The level of the toxins produced in his bloodstream would drop accordingly. How quickly would the disease consolidate? Would there be a crisis? It would take fast, thorough reading.

Paul wasn't fast enough.

The boy went into convulsions. They were convulsions beyond shock, beyond epilepsy. The pain must have been incomprehensible, because the boy's face was locked in a bizarre grimace—there would have been screaming, but the muscles in his throat were so contracted that no screams could escape. Could it be a reaction to the drug? As antibiotics went, streptomycin was clean. Minor nerve damage only with prolonged use. Some malaise, maybe. A headache. The boy reacted as if Paul had injected Drāno into his system.

And Paul quickly learned why people once believed only the hand of God could destroy so thoroughly. The boy's buboes had been the size of almonds when he arrived; now they were like small apples, red, tender. Already they were turning dark. The boy's bladder emptied onto the table, but it was like no urine in the world, purple, almost black from blood. The convulsions grew so strong, Paul had to strap the boy down to keep him from falling onto the floor. Then he injected phenobarbital and, when that didn't work, phenytoin to ease the convulsions. No sale. The convulsions seemed to feed on his drugs. When spittle the color and consistency of grenadine drooled from the corner of the boy's mouth, and the dark blotches that indicated subcutaneous hemorrhaging appeared on his skin, Paul knew the boy would die. Paul applied more compresses and stroked the boy's forehead just to have something to do with his hands. Within fifteen minutes, the buboes had burst, the stench in the room doubled, and the boy was dead. His face aged seventy years in an hour, wrinkled, faded; his eye sockets sunk like wells. Paul had seen a thousand corpses, more, but none approached this one in stench and waste.

Paul had to prepare himself; there would undoubtedly be more like the boy. He looked up at Johara. She appeared confused but not panicked. To her, Paul was Al Rish, and Al Rish could solve any problem. Paul walked back to the radio and began to crank the handle hard. *Hard.* The son of a bitch had to work!

It didn't work.

"I sent the father away because I knew the boy would die," Paul lied to Johara.

Her eyes told him she knew he was lying, that it was important she lie also, that she act as though she believed him so he could continue to think and function. She played the role well.

The cause of the boy's death had to be kept secret until the medical team from Sana' arrived. The people's fear of the plague could be as deadly as the plague itself. Thousands were stoned to death, thousands more burned alive during the Black Death when the survivors of the plague lashed out at something they couldn't understand through something they could kill. Always the attacks came against outsiders, Jews or Moslems. Paul had no reason to believe the village's reaction toward him would be any different. He hid the boy's body under a tarp, then took a mop and tried to clean up the filth the boy's body had made.

Before he had finished scrubbing the table, two, then three more voices began talking to the *haria.* He walked into the waiting room and closed the door behind him. There were six new victims, all boys between six and ten, all with fever and chills, incipient boils, and dripping sweat. Whatever kind of plague this was, it followed new rules: It was more sudden, virulent, graphic than the normal strains.

He had six sick kids on his hands, and in a village of three hundred, he would probably expect more. But they weren't kids anymore; they were guinea pigs. Statistics. Test cases. He had to learn about this disease and learn about it fast. He would give two of the children nothing and let the disease progress at its normal rate. One would be given tetracycline intravenously, another tetracycline orally. Paul would have to give one boy a shot of streptomycin to see if the first dose was bad. He would give the last boy tartar emetic. Paul had no idea why; it wasn't an antibiotic, but it was the strongest drug he had.

He took the children into the examination room and closed the door. Johara helped with the treatments; sitting around doing nothing would only make her feel frightened and helpless.

Paul went back to the fathers when he finished. Time to play research scientist. Sherlock Holmes with a hypo and stethoscope. The six new cases were all from poor families and couldn't have come in contact with the spice merchant's son. If the plague wasn't spread through contact, how was it spread? And why did it attack only young boys? Perhaps the plague's most reliable quality was its indifference to its host: men, women, infants, octogenarians, dogs, cats, or rats, healthy or sick, it cared not in the least.

"Anyone found an unusual number of dead rats?" Paul asked.

They hadn't.

If the carrier was rats, there would have been contact with livestock through the medium of grain. "Any sick livestock?" Paul asked.

Again nothing.

"Have any of you seen *any* other sickness?"

"My daughter is sick," a fisherman said. "The same fever and lumps."

"Then why the *hell* isn't she here?"

"You are a man. She is in purdah."

It figured.

Twenty minutes of questioning revealed one thing: Everyone who had a daughter between the ages of six and twelve had a sick daughter. The same symptoms. Same timing. But the sons were their pride. Paul was the doctor, and the doctor would help. He sent the men away and went into the examination room.

The two children who'd been given antibiotic injections died within minutes of each other. The child who'd taken tetracycline orally had plum-sized buboes. The untreated boys were in the best shape of the six, and that wasn't good. Paul needed something he could see. Something he could use a tourniquet on. Even lepers suddenly seemed attractive. He felt helpless, outmatched. Then he realized something even worse had happened: Patients had stopped coming. "How much does the muezzin hate me?" he asked Johara.

"How much water is in the sea?"

"Would any villagers take their sick to him?"

"Most. Those who know only the village."

Bacteria didn't exist to the muezzin, and if they did, they would be in the permanent employ of Allah. Paul, the unbeliever, would be cast as the magnet drawing every evil in the world to Al Rattaf. . . .

He should have gone for the gun barrel sticking through the window. His reflexes, all his experience told him so, but there was an override on all his circuits, and her name was Johara. He reached her and covered her with his body just as he heard two explosions: a small pop followed immediately by a roar. He'd never been shot by anything like the projectile that slashed through his deltoid and lodged in the floor. His arm didn't explode and he didn't go into shock. The bullet was much slower; he could feel it rip tissue. But there was still pain.

Pain was a problem. Paul either had to conquer it or enter into an alliance with it until he was through killing. Each time he'd been shot, the first impulse had been to give up—that guaranteed a sudden end to the throbbing—but self-survival was his prime directive. Pain proved to be his ally. It reduced him to a state of pure, if hampered, sensation. There would be no intellect, no empathy to interfere with a job. Never corner a wounded human, he always said. It should only take one arm to deal with these goatherds.

The goatherd coming through the window hadn't bothered to reload; a rookie. A seventy-year-old rookie. It was Ahmed, the fisherman who gave Paul qat not a week before. Paul wasn't in the mood for handicaps. He snapped Ahmed's spinal cord with a kick to the throat before the old man could draw his *jambiyya.* He finished the old man with his knife, then picked up the musket. It was a flintlock covered with gold etching. Its barrel was long and the stock thin and cut-off: a camel-riding musket. "This belongs in a museum," Paul said.

"It's my father's," Johara said. "He has others."

"Any automatic weapons?"

"A few. In case bandits from the mountains attack."

Paul bent over and examined Ahmed. This was a fisherman, not a hunter of sharks. Paul smelled his breath to see if he'd been drugged or given alcohol. *Nada.* Then Paul found something more interesting on his neck: plague boils.

"No wonder the old man was so brave," Paul said. "The muezzin probably promised him reservations beneath the ever-blooming date palm in return for my head." Paul closed the old man's eyes. "I hope he gets his spot, anyway."

Johara touched one of the buboes. "We may have the plague, too."

"There will be others outside," Paul said, ignoring her. "Think hard. How many guns does your father have?"

"Ten at most."

First Paul gave himself a tetanus shot, then crawled to his trunk. He squeezed the wound to raise the level of pain. *Harder.* Harder until he almost cried out. Pain as an ally. Pain as a friend. The men outside were no longer friends. Feel only the pain. "Stay put," he told Johara. He handed her the Mannlicher and took the machine pistol for himself. "Ever shoot?"

She shook her head.

"Keep the open end pointed at the window. You see a body there, pull this," he said, pointing to the trigger.

"The *haria* was a good woman," Johara said softly.

And Paul understood why he hadn't heard the old woman scream at the gunshots. "I won't let her suffer," Paul said.

He kissed Johara, stuffed several extra clips in his belt, and crawled over the dead and dying children. He dragged one of the cadavers with him and threw it into the waiting room to see if it would draw fire. Silence.

Plague or not, the muezzin hadn't convinced anyone else to enter the clinic. Paul looked up at the shark's head. The myth of Al Rish still had its effect. It pays to advertise.

The *haria* was slumped over the desk; Ali's books and paper were scattered on the floor. Her face was knotted in agony and her fists were clenched. Paul killed her quickly, a single jab above the plague boils to the medulla oblongata. Pithing. White-bellied frogs. The only term that remained with him from high school biology.

Question: How to get out?

Though it was quiet, Paul knew that rifles would cover the door and windows. If he had a canister of smoke screen, he would have no problem. But this wasn't Nam. No luxuries here. He'd make his own camouflage, create his own distraction. He dressed the *haria*'s body in some of his extra clothes, sat her in Ali's roller chair, and propped her against the door. He crawled over to the window. Then he shot the *haria*'s body to knock it through the door and onto the street.

It wasn't silent anymore.

As the *haria*'s body jerked with bullets from the rooftops, Paul slipped through the side window. Surprise! He was across the street and with his brothers, the shadows, before a shot was fired at him. The first five men Paul found were armed only with scimitars and *jambiyyas.* Some were sick with the plague, others just careless. Not that it made much difference. None of them saw Paul. Five without a shot. Without a sound. As silent as the shark.

Paul planned to take them all without a shot, to attack from the shadows with his knife. He was invisible. But he saw a man with a musket creeping toward Johara's window. It was a hard shot, a moving target at sixty yards, and he didn't have his left arm to use as a rest. It made no difference. It was Johara the man was attacking. His chest blew into the back of his *'aba* as he bounced off the clinic's wall.

Paul wasn't invisible anymore.

He heard three automatic weapons, an AK-47 and two M-16s, as they destroyed the ledge where he had been. Had been. He was back in the shadows. He would stay there till the job was finished. He didn't care if it took all day. He was better at night. He knew how to wait.

The villagers didn't.

One at a time they broke from cover, tried to escape the shadows and the terror, and one at a time Paul shot them down. He intentionally drew fire each time, so he could learn where the automatic weapons were; one atop the spice merchant's roof; one in the minaret above the mosque; one on the roof of the *'aqil*'s house. Paul had no trouble guessing who held the last two guns, but he couldn't imagine Is'mail shooting anything, much less a human.

Paul still had two clips. He was as well armed as the villagers. There was a time he would have dropped the pistol and finished the job with his knife. Aesthetics. But those days were over. It was no longer a game with a scorecard but the defense of territory. Johara had changed all the rules.

Is'mail wasn't atop his roof. He sat where he always sat at that time of the day—at his counter. He was dead of the plague, his head scattered a pile of incense and cloves. At least the spices eased the stench of the suppurating buboes. It was a house of the dead. A nightmare house. The wife and two daughters were dead in the women's quarters, and the son was sprawled in a hallway where he had died trying to crawl from his dead father to his dying mother. Perhaps his death was most pathetic, the most moving sight Paul had seen all day. He clutched a toy cat as though it were an amulet.

Toughen up! Paul pinched the wound again. There were at least three more killings to do. A dog, the house's sole survivor, whimpered in a corner. Paul would have liked to have joined him. Whimpered in unison. Howled. But there was no time.

There *were* footsteps on the roof. An adult could only walk on the support beams; the rest was thatching and wouldn't support the weight of a child, much less a man. Paul waited until the sound was directly above him, then fired two five-shot bursts. He needed only one. A man fell through the thatching and onto a table. The muezzin's assistant. A young man who was studying the Prophet's Law. He was rumored to be the muezzin's lover. Well, no one was perfect, not even religious leaders. Paul didn't have to wait long for the muezzin's visit. The old man burst through the door of the spice shop, cursing and crying, his M-16 firing wildly. Paul fired a single shot into the muezzin's forehead. A black turban rolled into the street. Neither of the last two corpses had plague boils. Maybe there was something to this Hand-of-Allah nonsense after all.

Twelve down and one to go.

But Paul didn't have to kill the *'aqil.* Maybe it was the turban in the street, maybe just the knowledge that he was the only one left. Paul heard a single muffled shot, a sound he'd occasionally heard in Nam when a muzzle was inserted into someone's mouth and the trigger pulled. Suicide might be painless, but it was certainly no way to gain entrance to the Garden of Paradise.

There was no one left to fight. Judging from the corpses in the huts and on the streets, there might not be anyone left, period. Only Johara! Let Johara be alive! Paul shouted her name as he ran toward the clinic. He looked in through a window.

She was.

Johara insisted that Paul clean his wound and apply sulfa powder before they searched through the village for survivors. Though the cries of infants and young children tumbled down the street, she wanted to be sure the doctors from Sana' arrived before Paul and she left the clinic. There was no telling how many murderers might be waiting in the street.

Paul knew the doctors wouldn't be coming.

He envisioned the young cyclist growing dizzy somewhere on the high mountain trail and thinking it was merely the height. He would stop to rest and wouldn't have the strength to rise. Maybe the disease hit him suddenly and he swerved off a cliff to his death. Paul hoped for the suddenness of the latter.

At five in the afternoon, when they heard the shuffling of a child's sandals in the alley by the clinic, Paul and Johara knew they couldn't wait any longer. They moved the corpses from the clinic to a hut across the alley—at least the bodies could decompose there without the interference of dogs and buzzards and living human eyes. Paul and Johara checked house by house for survivors, and house by house they found the same scene: men and boys sitting in the main room, their buboes burst, their faces already tinged gray with death. Women died in the women's quarters, sprawled over pillows, unable to escape purdah even in death. In the poorer huts where there was a single room, families died together. Buzzards circled overhead. Dogs went crazy. Some growled, tried to protect their dead masters, while others just ate. There were no dead animals in the village.

All human survivors were seven or younger. Good thing they were so young. The years would turn the experience into a dream, a fiction that would seem less real the farther they moved from it. Twenty-six survivors in all, eighteen girls and eight boys. All survivors over six were female.

So Paul and Johara became the parents of a large, hungry family. Goat or camel milk would have been the best food for most of the children, and there was plenty of livestock squealing for overdue milkings, but that would take too much time. With ten boxes of formula, some water from the well, and a little stirring, they had a nutritious meal *en masse.* When they finished with the feeding and cleaning up, Johara asked Paul to go to her house. She didn't ask to come along. He put the pistol in his sling and walked out of the clinic.

He covered his face with his handkerchief to ease the stench as he walked through the fly-buzzing streets. The walk gave him time to think. He didn't want to think. The whole thing made no sense. He didn't mind whys, but this series of whys had no logical progression. Why were Johara and he the only survivors? Why should animals and young children be spared? Why was this strain of the plague so thorough? The only accounts of ninety percent plus mortality during the Black Death were in the nunneries and monasteries, where cloistering increased contact and precluded escape. There was no cloistering in Al Rattaf. The answer was simple: the disease couldn't be. The stench of this nightmare, the twisted corpses that lined the street were beyond logic and therefore just a dream.

Paul walked into the *'aqil*'s house. The animals in the downstairs manger were hungry and restless and moved toward him as though they expected to be fed. The plague had spared the *'aqil*'s house.

The *'aqil* hadn't.

Johara's mother and younger sisters were in the women's quarters, dead, single bullet holes in their temples. Not a plague boil in the bunch. The *'aqil*'s head was scattered across the house's stone roof. Paul had to chase buzzards away before he could drag the man's body downstairs to his family. Paul closed all windows and doors and walked back to the clinic. The *'aqil*'s entire family seemed immune. Maybe the same gene that saved them would also save Johara. Where would Paul find his immunity? He must write down as many observations as possible, so that when the authorities finally arrived, they would have a foundation to begin their experiments.

He wrote until the sun was well set, till the last children were asleep and scattered on the floor throughout the clinic and the only sounds outside were the buzzards and dogs. He wrote until he saw Johara wobble, then stumble and catch herself. He approached her slowly, calmly, sat her in his chair and felt under her arms.

Plague.

Johara said nothing, just looked at him with a strange, peaceful smile. Paul knew the smile wouldn't last long. Johara was too healthy, too strong. Within hours, he'd be begging her to die, sitting back and watching helplessly as she shriveled and screamed and cursed him for his helplessness.

He took her hand and spoke gently, rocking back and forth on the balls of his feet. "In America," he said, "when a man takes a bride, he doesn't give presents to her father but to her."

"What does he give?" Johara asked.

"Certainly not an old rial like Nuri's!" Paul tried to laugh. "A ring. Would you wear my ring?"

She smiled.

Paul walked to the trunk and removed the ring the CIA had first given him when he walked into the jungle alone, a bulky ring decorated with an eagle clutching a burst of arrows in its talons. He slipped it onto the third finger of her left hand. "They have a ceremony where meaningless words are spoken," Paul said. "Kiss me instead."

As she bent to kiss him, he twisted the arrows on the ring in a full circle and pushed down—it sent a needle, barely a scratch, into her finger. She scarcely winced. He took her hand, led her to the rug in the corner, and let her lie, curled like a child with her head in his lap.

The shellfish toxin worked swiftly, painlessly. She was asleep within a minute, and her death throes weren't death throes at all, just a gentle shiver which started at her heart and moved ever so quietly out through her fingers and into the night. It was like the ripple that had passed through her veil when he first touched her.

Paul left her on the rug, emptied his Montagnard chest,

dressed her in the wedding *qamis* and veil, combed out her hair, then laid her in the chest. She was still young and beautiful.

Though he could use only one arm, he tied his Army shovel to his back and dragged the coffin through the *suq* and into the Tihama, deep into the sands beyond the flapping wings and snarling dogs. He might not have much time, so he worked quickly. He hurt, but he needed the pain to keep him awake and moving. Physical pain could reduce deeper hurts.

The moon over the Tihama was high and robbed the already colorless desert of whatever color remained. He dug a grave with one arm into the side of a dune. The lee side. He would have liked to have gone straight down, but the arm wouldn't allow it. Instead he used the shovel like a hoe and scraped a three-foot-deep grave, a grave whose sand wouldn't blow away. He dug wildly and his wound reopened; blood fanned down onto his shorts. He was so weak and hurt so badly that he couldn't tell if it was the fever from the wound or the plague that was devouring him. Either way, he needed to complete this final act, an act of love, to counter the rest of his life. All his other actions had been chance, mindless encounters without logic or meaning: he would complete the burial so the sand and teak could protect her body. It would be more than he had been able to do.

Then he would sit down by her grave and wait for death.

He was tough, gnarled; the scavengers would find sweeter meat in the village. He pushed the coffin into the grave, wound a single *shauk au ajus* blossom into Johara's hair, and kissed her on the forehead. Then he took Nuri's tarnished rial from the strap around her neck, closed the coffin, and one spadeful of sand at a time, he sent her away.

VII.

Tai'zz, Yemen—April 20, 1981

"I can't hear you!" Claudia shouted as she tapped the telephone's mouthpiece with her finger.

The phone's answer was a series of bleeps and clicks.

She glanced around the American consul's library: the leather-bound books; the thick pile carpet; the yellowing rubber plant in the corner. She banged the receiver down on the desk, then tried again. "I need some strings pulled! Cash for bribes! A helicopter!" Her voice trailed off as the static grew louder.

The line went dead.

"Connections always this bad?" she asked.

The vice-consul shook his head.

"Speak up!" Claudia said.

"It's never happened before. It started right after we got the news about the plague village." He looked directly into Claudia's face, an indication he wanted some eye contact. His voice took on the tone of foreign service expertise. "The government says it's the rebels." A pause. "The rebels would undoubtedly blame the government."

"Who would you blame?"

"I lack sufficient data to take sides."

Great. An android. "You must get daily reports out," Claudia said. "How?"

"Telegraph."

"Where *is* this telegraph?"

"At the headquarters of security police."

"Remember," Claudia said, her voice as cold as ice, "I've already been there." She closed her eyes and tapped her fingers on the desk, then took a spiral notebook from her pocket and wrote a letter detailing her needs. "If the line clears, send this," Claudia told the vice-consul. "Should it begin to slip your mind, remember that the home office shows its appreciation in dollars, cents, and influence."

She walked from the library to the balcony, approached the stairway, and took the stairs two at a time until she reached the lobby. She nodded to one of the Marines in the anteroom, and he opened the heavy metal door. When she stepped out of the air conditioning onto the portico, she hit a wall of hot air, staggered, and her momentum carried her into a Bedouin. They went down together. She was up first, apologized, and offered him a hand up.

He pressed a note into it.

She continued the masquerade, apologized again, then sat beneath the huge cypress in the courtyard. It must have been fifteen degrees cooler in the shade, but the nonstop spy games kept her blood pressure and temperature up. She glanced at the note:

> Ten tonight. The Mosque of the Learned Imam in Janadiya. Twenty kilometers N.E. *ALONE.*
>
> Abdullah Mohammed

The affair was developing a reality she found altogether unpleasant. What had made the trip to the dungeon tolerable was its suddenness. She had not had time to think, only react, so it seemed like a dream. She looked at her watch. Five. Five hours till ten. Too long to think about who might be waiting and what they might do. The next move was hers; not Rick's, nor the rebels', nor the security police's. She stood, walked through the consulate's iron gate, crossed the bazaar to the café where Rick sat drinking a Pepsi, and sat down next to him. The fact he was starting to look good meant trouble. Granted, she'd been too long without a man, but he would be insufferable in an intimate relationship. He'd try to make her his property, and it would be time to find a new photographer.

As she looked around the bazaar, Claudia noticed the men

who had been tailing her since she left the dungeon. They wore Bedouin robes and sat beneath a small palm tree. "They been here long?" Claudia asked.

"Since you went in," Rick said.

"Any more?"

"Two behind the consulate. More at every street corner coming into the bazaar. You've become quite the celebrity."

"I'm starting to receive fan letters," Claudia said. She bent over as if to whisper something to Rick, then pressed the note into his hand.

He read it while pretending to adjust his belt. When he looked up, he was frowning. "Why is it every time you get that moon-in-June look in your eyes, something comes up that keeps me from going the distance with you?"

Claudia shrugged.

"At first I thought you were just a tease, but dammit, it's been almost three years. Try me, Claude, you'll like me."

"I like you," she said, "which is why I can't try you." A pause. "Think the note's for real?"

"Who delivered it?"

"Not Pancho." She looked up at the men beneath the palm tree. "What if it's a setup?"

"What options do we have?" Rick asked. "My leak says it's two hundred and fifty miles to the village. With all the roadblocks, a car would be useless even if we could shake the security police."

"How about cross-country?"

"We'd die of thirst."

"But what if the plague didn't get the village? A two-hundred-and-fifty-mile rumor is pretty faint."

"There'll be no help from the home bureau," Rick said. "And if we don't move pretty soon, this story will be so cold we'll never revive it."

Claudia sat back in the rickety cane chair, rocked, and rubbed her hands over her eyes. She pointed to the note. "Does alone mean *alone*?"

"Everybody wants a piece of poor Claude," Rick says. "I think she needs a sidekick."

Claudia touched his hand—affectionately—and said, "It's time we do some business with the competent members of the consulate."

They stood and walked across the bazaar, back through the iron gate, and waited for the Marine to open the door. They had shaken the security police twice before by exchanging clothing with the consulate's servants, but this time the price of new identities went up. Maybe the servants had heard about her brush with the police; they insisted on three times the payment to carry out the ruse. Three times the payment for three times the risk.

The hooded *'aba* Rick handed through the bathroom door could have walked in on its own. At least it was white—she could see most of the stains. When she came back into the library, Rick was dressed in white, too. The butler who wore Rick's clothes sat by the front window, just far enough into the shadows that only the clothes, not the face, could be identified.

At six o'clock, the consulate's ten domestics, a boisterous, oversexed group, barged through the rear entrance on their way home. They shoved and shouted, argued over the bloodlines of wives and racing camels. Claudia watched two members of the security police from beneath her hood. One counted heads. The other shook his head as if to say such nonsense would come to an end if the Saudis ran things.

Claudia and Rick stayed with the group for ten blocks, then strayed into a coffee market. They exited through a rear door, entered a spice shop, exited under a side awning, then headed back. The only way to reach the Bab Sheikh Musa, the gate in the northwestern wall of Tai'zz, was to pass by the consulate.

Six o'clock was the closest thing Tai'zz had to a rush hour. Farmers left the bazaars with their unsold crops. Merchants and moneylenders closed shop. All the cars and motorcycles in the city jammed into the three main streets, honked, swerved, and stirred up huge clouds of dust that made breathing painful. Since the vehicles bunched toward the center of the streets, Claudia walked next to buildings.

Beneath the drains.

The buildings grew smaller, became one story, and Claudia and Rick walked through the Bab Sheikh Musa and back four hundred years. Black goat-hair tents clustered around the city walls, and she could barely hear Rick whistle above the squealing camels. The valley flowed northeast . . . fields of green onions and *dhura* were outlined by red and brown ridges. They walked past a wall that had been crumbling since before the start of the Renaissance.

Rick wasn't in a talking mood. He took out his yo-yo and played silently with it. Farmland extended halfway up the sides of the ridges in an elaborate series of terraces. The soil was old, overused. The walls that lined the path didn't rise as much as the path sunk: the result of three thousand years of trampling feet and hooves. She spread her arms in a wide circle and turned. "This is beautiful!"

"Forget about the landscape," Rick snapped. "Worry about staying alive."

"No wonder this place breeds holy men!" Claudia said.

Rick grabbed her shoulders and spun her around. "Dammit, Claude, you've been in a blue funk for almost a week! These people want to put the big hurt on you! Their bullets are for real!"

"I know," Claudia said softly. "I know." She relaxed until he let her arms go. The indentations from his fingers hurt. She stood, arms akimbo, with her head cocked to the right. "What if?" she asked.

"What if what?"

"What if the Madhi is what he says he is?"

"Shit!" Rick said. He buried his face in his hands and shook his head.

"I'm not saying he is, but what if? It would explain the cured lepers and the selective plague."

"Then we look for his bag of tricks. We've uncovered charlatans before."

"No charlatans with nature in their back pocket." Claudia leaned against a frankincense tree. Its fragrant limbs intertwined like whips. There were no people in sight, so she swept back the hood of her *'aba* so the evening breeze from the Highlands could cool her scalp. "I don't claim to understand how he does it," Claudia said. "That's why I'm so interested."

Rick reached out and massaged the back of her neck. 'Sorry," he said. "If you don't start putting some distance between what is and what you *hope* is, I'm gonna lose you." When he pulled his hand away, he brushed a finger along the rim of her ear.

"If you're not careful," Claudia said, "you could turn a lovely professional relationship into something else."

"I've been working on it."

"Would it be worth the story of the century?"

Rick pondered for a while. "What do you think?"

"Not yet," Claudia said. "Not quite yet."

The minaret above the Mosque of the Learned Imam hadn't looked like much when she first saw it, just a black needle in the moonlight. As Claudia and Rick left the road and followed a path that wound through miles of scrub brush, the minaret's gallery with its ancient latticework and hexagonal walls became increasingly more impressive. But it was the strangest place for a secret rendezvous that Claudia had ever seen.

Maybe that was part of the plan. Pick the spot in Yemen most vulnerable to ambush and hope the security police would ignore it. The flatlands were scarred by enough crevasses and rises to hold the entire Yemeni army, and the wild brush grew all the way to the mud wall that surrounded the shrine: the mosque, minaret, courtyard, everything. It was ten when they arrived at the shrine, but no one waited for them.

Then ten thirty.

At eleven it was still just Claudia and Rick. It was cold but too dangerous to start a fire. Claudia wasn't crazy about the white *'abas* they wore—they stood out in the moonlight like toadstools. There was nothing they could do but sit by the wall, snuggle, and listen to their stomachs growl.

Rick moved well in the darkness, more gracefully than she ever imagined. He didn't sit on his butt like a Boy Scout roasting marshmallows but squatted instead—like the Vietnamese. "I didn't know you had Oriental blood in your veins," Claudia said.

Rick raised his head and sniffed like a wolf. "The night brings back Nam," he said. "I learned you can move fast in any direction from a squat. When you're sitting, all you can do is crawl backward with your buns in the air. All I had was my camera, Claude. I either learned the tricks or took my trip back to the States in a body bag."

"You don't talk much about the war," she said.

"Neither do you, and you spent most of your time in Saigon. The sort of shit you saw in the dungeon I saw in the bush every day. And it wasn't just the slopes who did it. I bivouacked with grunts who made Jack the Ripper look like Billy Graham."

"And that wasn't enough?"

"I didn't say I didn't like it. Maybe it's the rush. The nights like this. Tonight it all seems this close." He held his hand within an inch of his nose.

"Know what, Hodges?" Claudia said. "For all your cool, you're a hell of a lot crazier than I am."

"Know what else, Claude? My ass is coming out of this alive. Know why? I don't expect a freeway to the Hereafter, so I won't get careless looking for it."

They were five thousand feet above sea level. Their breath formed clouds. Bra, designer panties, and a layer of native cloth wasn't much protection against a frost. Things were too quiet. There wasn't much wildlife left on the plains by Tai'zz; three thousand years of interacting with civilization took its toll on wild animals. Claudia wanted noise. The yowling of a feral dog would have been welcome, the buzz of an off-year locust divine.

Rick's head cocked. "Visitors, Claude. Let's hope your Pancho is one of them."

He was.

There were twelve in all, all dressed in the standard rebel garb, black *'abas* and turbans, all with mud rubbed into their faces to ease the moon glare. Each carried an automatic rifle and had extra clips strapped to his chest. "The note said alone," Pancho said in crisp English.

"I couldn't be sure it was from you." Claudia wrinkled her nose at his change in dialect. "Are you you?"

"I found the West repulsive in many ways," he said, "useful in many others. If I hadn't lived in the West, I couldn't bear to associate with a woman like you."

Claudia bit her lip. "This is Rick."

"He is why we didn't come down earlier. He goes back to Tai'zz."

"*Au contraire,*" Claudia said.

"We have checked into your past. His is unknown. A man with no past cannot see the Madhi."

A loud explosion. Claudia looked up. Flashes of gunfire from the minaret. Claudia flattened as a line of bullets kicked up dust ten feet from her. Two thuds to her left. A rebel flew back over his feet and lay writhing, gut-shot. More gunfire from behind the wall. More from the far side of the courtyard. More from the bluff above them. Pancho lay facedown in the dust next to Claudia. "How?" she shouted.

"We were here at nine. They must have arrived before!"

"Did they write the goddamn note for you?" she asked.

The rebels returned fire. One of their spent cartridges rolled against Claudia's ankle and burned it. When her leg jerked, she kneed Pancho. "Where to?" she shouted.

He pointed to one of the paths that dropped to the plain. Then he moved fast, almost imperceptibly, like a spider descending on something caught in its web. A rebel tried to follow him. There was the sound of a pumpkin shattering on a sidewalk. The man's body continued three steps, but his brainpan stayed by the wall. The lieutenant had her against The Wall, after all.

A rebel close to her tried to stand. Someone fired from the rise above the mosque—it was lovely in a macabre way—blossoms of fire. It sounded like someone hit a mattress with an ax handle—*hard.* The rebel's body flew past her, his legs twitching, his hands opening and closing in spasms.

Time for an exit.

Claudia picked up his M-16, a gun she'd learned how to fire, if not aim, in Nam. She'd never shot anyone, hoped she wouldn't start now, but she wasn't about to let these goatherds defend her. She stripped some clips from the dead man's robe and fired a short burst at the ridge. Her muzzle blast should have drawn fire.

It didn't.

Most of the fire was concentrated on three rebels huddled beneath the wall. It was impossible to count the bullets that thudded into it. The wall began to chip away. A rebel tried to stand. Bullets quickly cut him down. Pancho nudged her with his foot and pointed to the path.

Claudia shook her head. "If we don't cover them, they're through."

"They have a spot in the Garden of Paradise," Pancho said.

A rebel moved, just twitched, and took a bullet in the thigh. The Yemenis weren't supposed to have Starlight scopes.

Rick! Where was Rick?

He squatted behind a clump of brush that grew from a mound. Maybe twenty yards from Claudia. Bullets sparked off rocks and kicked up dirt all around him.

"I didn't know the Yemenis were this well trained!" Claudia shouted.

"They're not," Pancho said. He fired into a window in the minaret, then yanked on her arm.

They made it to the sunken path. Claudia hadn't felt her body move—the adrenaline made it airy as moonlight. Once behind the wall, they could supply covering fire. The remaining rebels made their break. Five made it, though one dragged his leg behind him, bones grating with each step. That only left Rick.

"I'm not leaving without him!" Claudia shouted.

"He is a dead man," Pancho said.

Rick looked at her, shrugged, then broke from cover, kept low in a crouch, zigzagged his way Nam-style toward the path.

And went down.

Not straight down, as in the World War II movies or the Saturday morning Westerns, but more as if he'd been pulled by a rope tied to his waist. He doubled up, legs still churning, and spun in crazed circles like an injured cricket.

Claudia discovered she had lived her entire life under a misconception: Pain wasn't the only thing that made her panic.

She went over the wall for Rick.

There was no thought about her not making it because she'd be damned before she let Mickey Rat and the lieutenant lay their hands on her Rick, and she was halfway to him when she went down; her legs kept pumping, her hands clawed the air, and she hadn't been wounded, just tackled, and the rebels were dragging her back, so she shouted Rick's name to let him know she was sorry, that maybe she loved him and maybe that's why she couldn't let him close, and then she started to flail her arms, kick and scream, do all the things she prided herself on never doing, but more hands grabbed her and dragged her down a brush-lined path to a palm tree where the camels waited.

When she began to swear, Pancho stuffed a rag in her mouth. And it wasn't the gunfire, not the blood dripping from the wall, nor the sight of Rick going down that stayed locked in her mind for the rest of the night but the taste of that rag. The taste summarized all Yemen, all three thousand years of Bedouin culture: blood, semen, sweat. That's all she could think of as they strapped her hands behind her back, blindfolded her, tied her to the back of a camel, and rode off into the darkness.

Blood.

Semen.

Sweat.

VIII.

Al Rattaf, Yemen—April 23, 1981

Maybe he stayed at Johara's grave so he wouldn't be alone. Maybe he stayed because there was no place left to go. No matter, Paul stayed. He stayed until he was too weak to return to the clinic, till he reached the point where the loss of blood was more serious than the wound.

Other than the constant buzzing of flies, millions of flies, more flies than he'd seen in Vietnam, there weren't many sounds in the Tihama. The wind rolling sand against his face. A lizard scurrying past. Sometimes the flapping of buzzards' wings. Buzzards. God, they were vile, ugly, the last thing he wanted around—particularly while he was alive. If one landed by him, he'd brain it; not that buzzards had much brain. They seemed all mouth and gullet. Paul hid beneath some scrub brush and grabbed the shovel. A squawk, a flutter of wings, and they were gone; either his movement scared them, or they were part of his imagination. Hard to tell which, the white-hot sun curled his brain. Bird watching ended on day two when his eyes swelled shut. It became a world of shadows and outlines.

Paul brushed at the flies that coated his bandage. Blowflies. They'd lay eggs under his skin if they could get to the wound. Uggh! When one walked across his nose, he felt each footstep. His brain said swat it, but he had no strength left. It walked where it pleased. He breathed deeply. Even the dust that coated the brush, the rocks, the inside of his nose, couldn't take the edge off the sweet stench from the village. The perfume of death. It had been bad at Hai Vahn Pass, worse in the cold and rain at Hue, but he'd been mobile then. Now that his moving days were done, he finally understood the meaning of a poem he'd read in high school about lilacs and Lincoln's death.

But at night, the cool wind swept down from Jebel Sharah and blew the decay, the nightmares of Nam and Al Rattaf, off into the Red Sea. At night, dew formed on his lips and pooled in his eyes, and though there wasn't enough moisture for healing, there was plenty for memories. Paul discovered his mind had an immune system that healed with images instead of bone, blood, and tissue. Memories. Strange, the other times he'd been wounded, the thoughts were of the future—things would be better when . . . well, when was here, and things had only grown worse.

One memory returned over and over . . . a week after high-school graduation. Twenty miles into the mountains. Thirty miles from people. He found a lake so deep it was black despite its snow-fed water. Three cutthroat trout swayed in the snowmelt like strips of silk. He jumped in the water. He couldn't help it. After thirty seconds, it hurt too much, so he crawled out and lay naked on the shore. A breeze off the snowbanks and the hot sun alternately warmed and cooled him.

A sound.

A harsh, abrupt sound that had nothing to do with the mountains. A voice. "Jesus!" it shouted in English. Footsteps thudded in the sand. A shoe nudged Paul. "This one's not ripe!"

Mountain sounds were infinitely preferable to human sounds.

Paul tried to open his eyes, maybe move an arm or leg for effect, but it was no sale. He just lay there and let the voices discuss his future. After six years of hearing only Arabic, English sounded gruff, lopped off. No sentence was longer than ten words, and the relentless progression from point to point to logical conclusion took all the surprise from conversation. It was a language for scientists and storekeepers, not poets and wanderers.

And these weren't Arabs speaking English. "Far out," "number one," and "honcho," sprinkled their sentences: Nam slang. And it wasn't only the idioms that showed their nationality. Arabs would have grabbed him under the arms and dragged him through the sand; abrupt, practical, like Yemen. These men rolled him onto a stretcher and carried him back to the village. They plopped him onto a cot, stripped him down, and applied cold compresses. Standard procedure. Whoever administered the IV was a pro; Paul scarcely felt a thing. Then came the thermometer, the stethoscope, and an injection that robbed him of images, healing or otherwise.

When Paul woke, the swelling in his eyes had gone down, but cloth, probably gauze compresses, kept the world black. The room buzzed. Electricity. The familiar acoustics told him he was back in the clinic, but there was one hell of a lot more electricity being used than could be provided by his single generator. He had wires fastened to his head and chest—wires that would be attached to machines monitoring his vital signs. Whatever dripped into his arm from the IV was a magic potion. Instant strength. Whoever had arrived in Al Rattaf had brought the twentieth century with them.

Hands took Paul's pulse, checked his temperature, adjusted the catheter, and changed his fluid bags. Without a single word. They took enough blood samples to start a bank. Paul had plenty of questions, but he decided to stay in a coma until he discovered who these folks were and why they were in Yemen.

Footsteps on the mud floor. A cold stethoscope on his chest. A pause. "How about an arm?" a voice said.

Hardly enough information to justify coming out of the coma.

"Your ECG shows you're in there," the voice continued. "Vitals are strong." Another pause for Paul's response. "There's a hell of a lot we don't know about the plague. You should know better than anyone how little time we have."

Paul lifted an arm.

"Left leg," the voice said.

It was stiff, but Paul raised it.

"Tongue."

It was so swollen, Paul wasn't sure it would fit through his mouth, and it felt like a balloon that had been scoured by steel wool. What if it popped when it hit the air? The tongue depressor tasted woody.

"You'll live," the voice said.

Paul still wasn't sure that was the prognosis he wanted to hear.

"Say, 'Mary had a little lamb.' "

His tongue wasn't ready for acrobatics. If it had to be English, he'd better stick to the basics. "Who are you?" he asked.

"A friend."

Exactly the line Paul hoped he wouldn't hear. "Well, friend," Paul said, "maybe you can tell me what happened in Al Rattaf."

"Soon. Right now you need fluids. Today's selection includes Pepsi, Gatorade, Cranapple juice, and Kool-Aid—cherry, I think."

The list answered all Paul's questions about where the visitors were from. The Americanization of Al Rattaf. "How about water?"

"You need the sucrose."

"Pepsi, then." The familiar snap of the cap, the splash, the fizz—it was right out of yesteryear: flashes of basketball games, grade-school dances, and a first drunk (mixed with 151 rum). The carbonation tickled Paul's nose. None of the outside sounds indicated how the village had been changed. No barking dogs. No squawking crows or buzzards. A jeep started. Two voices spoke English—a third, with an Arabic accent, joined in.

"How about trying 'Mary . . .' again. That tongue could use some exercise."

"Find my notes?" Paul asked.

"I assumed they were yours." The man unwound the gauze from around Paul's head, then lifted the compresses from his eyes. Returning to the world of light wasn't like the hocus-pocus in the television melodramas—no darkness easing into light, then soft focus, then clarity, but a sudden explosion of white. Paul blinked, squinted, and squeezed his eyelids tight. Tears poured from his eyes and dropped onto his wrists.

"Good," the voice said. "Give those tear ducts a workout. The more moisture you can gather, the faster the sandpaper feeling will vanish."

When the voice finally became attached to a shape and the shape to a body, the shape was round. And the first color Paul saw was the one color he hoped he'd never see again. Olive drab.

Shape and uniform equaled a lifer. The name stencil said Colonel Owens; the arm patches said doctor. "I could have used you about a week ago," Paul said.

"So we saw. We were busy elsewhere. Now, about your notes. They added more questions to a list that already runs into the next world," Colonel Owens said. He motioned toward the door. "My standard advice would be plenty of rest, but there are people waiting to see you. An armful of Dexedrine would give you a lift, but it's imperative we do nothing to alter your body chemistry."

"A guinea pig?"

"You're the sole survivor out of a village of two hundred ninety. Quite an honor. It makes you living data."

"You didn't find any kids in the clinic?" Paul asked. "Twenty? Maybe twenty-five?"

"You're the *sole* survivor," the doctor said.

Paul rubbed his temples, stared at the rafters and thatched ceiling, then around the room at the new machinery. "Let's get at it," he said.

Though Paul's legs were out of practice, they had an excellent memory. After ten minutes of stumbling around the room, he was ready for the street. Colonel Owens gave him sunglasses to ease the glare, then helped him through the door.

Things had changed in Al Rattaf.

A ghost of the plague stench still hung in the air; maybe that would never leave, but the stock and dogs were gone. And the crows and buzzards. Even bloodstains were scraped from the walls and shoveled from the dirt. Black smoke hung in the air—gasoline, maybe napalm. And a long-forgotten smell: charred flesh. It answered Paul's questions of what they'd done with the bodies.

Al Rattaf had been birthed into the twentieth century in less than a week. The number of steel-hulled ships at the dock made it look like a Navy base, and the number of Caucasians, uniformed and otherwise, brought back entirely unpleasant memories of landing zones, combat bases, and villes-turned-compounds. It reminded him of Da Nang, where the beach terminated at the jungle. *To terminate.* An ugly verb. The last time he'd used it, it had had a specific meaning and he'd been a different man.

Quonset huts.

There were Quonset huts all along the fringe of the village. And a chemical perfume, a disinfectant smell might be closer—not that it had much effect on the plague stench. The doctor led Paul into a Quonset hut with olive drab walls and a black roof. They sat in a room with tin walls, metal swivel chairs, and metal desk covered by wood-grain contact paper. Portable U.S. of A. Another culture modernized, yet trivialized.

It wasn't really surprising that there were more Anglo than Yemeni soldiers. The plague had implications that reached far beyond the Middle East. What if it broke out in New York or L.A. . . . two voices in the hall outside the room. One straight American, the other more English with a heavy Oxford/Yemeni inflection.

Two men walked into the room.

Number one was a lieutenant in the Yemeni Security Police—never a welcome sight. The second man was even more disquieting. He was a man in desert fatigues who moved with a grace beyond grace, the type of fluency a ballet dancer might develop if his life instead of his ego depended on each movement: a hunter of men. He had a full beard. Sunglasses. No identification patches. As intentionally nondescript as he could be. He was a top-level operative, no doubt about it. If he wasn't CIA, then he wasn't far removed from the Company coffers. Paul could understand why the World Health Organization would get involved; maybe the Disease Control Center. But why spooks? The chubby Yemeni sat in a chair by Colonel Owens; the hunter sat on the desk and smiled. "So *you're* Paul Kenyon," he said.

The stress on the contraction was hardly reassuring. "You've done your homework," Paul said.

The man took off his sunglasses, opened a manila envelope, and read a computer printout. "You grew up in Montana."

"I was a kid in Montana," Paul said. "I grew up in Nam."

The man on the desk looked up. The corners of his mouth

twitched as though, at other times, he might have broken into a smile. "Didn't we all." He had large, sparkling eyes that constantly moved and evaluated. The kind of eyes you'd expect to find at a meeting of atomic physicists . . . or at a war crimes trial. They held Paul's stare. There was territory being declared here; the gathering seemed more like an interrogation than a conference. And the hunter was experienced—he knew the opening moves of an interrogation dictated the outcome.

Paul sat back in the chair and smiled. "Your play," he said.

"Mine comes later. Right now you belong to Colonel Owens."

"Now," the colonel said, "the plague?"

"My notes. They contain everything I learned."

"They told us nothing we didn't already know."

"You make the plague sound as common as clap," Paul said.

"Perhaps. Here. We came to Yemen to investigate the plague long before we heard of Al Rattaf."

Paul inhaled, held his breath for an instant, then popped the air through his lips. "Okay," he said, "one last time. One: It's too virulent to believe. It takes three, maybe four hours from first symptoms to death. Two: When you catch it, you're through. Period. Three: Forget antibiotics; they only make things worse. Four: The symptoms are not of this world. Take the description in the *Merck Manual* and multiply by ten. Five: If it spreads beyond Yemen, the world is in for some very heavy shit."

"Which leaves only one question unanswered," the Yemeni said, blinking his watery eyes. He smiled stupidly.

"Which is?" The question was obvious.

"Why are you alive?"

Yes. Definitely a valid question. "No idea," Paul said.

"Nonsense," the Yemeni said.

"I have an honest-to-God fondness for humanity," Paul said. "Whatever I know I've either written or told."

"Then my question becomes what portion of humanity you're fondest of," the Yemeni said, the bristles in his nose twitching as he talked.

The hunter apparently didn't think they had enough time to play a game of twenty questions. "We lack agreement on why you're still with us," he said. "The doctor thinks it was something physiological. Lieutenant Bu-jahl has a more suspicious nature. He thinks you work for the Madhi."

"Then the lieutenant's about as smart as he looks," Paul said.

The lieutenant's smile didn't change—nor the wrinkles on his sloping forehead. "You have, of course, heard of the Madhi's prophecies," he said.

"His world of Islam?" Paul asked.

"More recently, the plague," the Yemeni said. His hairless cheeks rolled with each word.

"Christ. I've heard he cures leprosy. That he chats with Allah. I also know a Jebeli who thinks he's a werewolf. The Madhi and the plague? That's one I missed. All we heard from the outside was from sailors on the supply boat . . . they weren't a talkative group."

"Possible. All possible," the Yemeni said. "Even so, things remain unanswered." He stood, took two strides, looked into Paul's face, and blinked. He was wonderfully ugly . . . if such a thing were possible.

"You find me amusing," he said. He gently touched Paul's wounded shoulder. "This gunshot is amusing. Perhaps you find it amusing that gunshot wounds aren't a plague symptom." He grabbed the wound and squeezed.

The arm exploded. Paul closed his eyes, bit down the scream, and breathed evenly until the pain was under control. Then he stared at the Yemeni. Hard.

"Perhaps you agree it is unusual you sent no message for help. Unusual and amusing. I find great amusement in making people answer unanswered questions."

The toad-man wasn't so entertaining anymore. It would be easier to explain the lack of message than the wounded shoulder. "You'll find a boy on Kotal Shaharah," Paul said. "He has the message. The radio wouldn't work."

"The radios never work when their capacitators are removed."

"The *what* was removed?"

"Of course, you didn't bother to check."

"If anything was gone," Paul said, "you took it."

"Nonsense," Lieutenant Bu-jahl said. "I don't sell antiques."

"Why would I wreck my own radio?" Paul asked.

"A question which returns us to my original hypothesis," the lieutenant said. Under other circumstances, his feigned-air Sherlock Holmes might have been funny. "You were collecting data about the plague and sending it to the Madhi by radio. The villagers discovered you. The wound resulted from their attempts to stop you."

"There's one constant about the plague—now or four thousand years ago: Those who have the plague hate those who don't. People don't like what's different."

"And you're *very* different. You're alive. Perhaps there are other ways you're different?" the lieutenant asked.

"I'm American," Paul said. Not much of an answer, granted, but the best he had.

"Your blood type is *O,*" Colonel Owens interrupted. "You can't find them more common. What did you eat?"

"Fish. *Dhura.* What everyone else ate."

"Drink?"

"There's only water from the communal well."

"We analyzed it," the colonel said. "It's not Perrier, but there're no unusual bacteria counts."

"What did you learn from the autopsies?" Paul asked.

The hunter leaned forward. "Three days of dogs, buzzards, and heat leave enough to scoop into a shovel. No more. What we found was consistent with data from Tai'zz," he said.

"Tai'zz?"

"The other outbreak of the Madhi plague."

The Madhi again. "A few more details about the Madhi might help," Paul said.

"You were the medic for Al Rattaf?" Lieutenant Bu-jahl asked.

"No argument there."

"And who had a better opportunity to infect the village?"

No comment on that one.

"And who but a rebel," the Yemeni continued, "would need to keep heavy armaments in his dwelling?"

Ouch. "There are bandits in the mountains," Paul said. "Heavy armaments keep them in the mountains."

"Perhaps, then, you will explain why we found bullets from your weapons in some of the villagers?"

The drift of the conversation was taking Paul closer and closer to a reef. Time for a change in course. "I was the outsider."

"Of course, you had no problem killing twelve persons," the lieutenant said. "Nonsense. You had help. Your rebel friends came too early, before the plague finished everyone. Shooting broke out. You were wounded. The rebels overlooked you in their retreat."

"The *'aqil?* The muezzin?" Paul asked. "They didn't have the plague."

"Perhaps you killed them before the symptoms developed," the lieutenant said. "Since they are dead, we'll never know."

The hunter grew impatient. "What we *do* know is that you're the only one left," he told Paul. "If you weren't, you'd be the lieutenant's property. He does his job. His nickname isn't 'Hamburger' because of the condition of his face." The hunger stroked his beard, smiled ever so slightly, then rested on his hands. "The doctor has two more days to find out what makes you so special. Then we try some medieval methods."

"Sometimes," Colonel Owens said, "the concerns of science transcend a single person's well-being."

"Easy to say when the well-being isn't your own," Paul said.

The hunter stood. "For the next half-hour, Mr. Kenyon's well-being is my concern. *Alone,*" he said.

The Yemeni and the doctor took the hint. They stood, walked from the room, and closed the door behind them. Gently. Then the hunter walked behind Paul. He placed a hand on Paul's shoulder. He wore a bulky ring decorated with an eagle on the third finger of his left hand. The eagle's talons clutched a burst of thunderbolts. Not a pleasant sight. "Captain Spooky," the hunter said, "you have this way of ending up in the damnedest shit!"

It was as though Paul had been woken by a gunshot from one of those death sleeps in Nam, one of those sped-up, shot-down, five-days-on-the-move-with-five-hours-to-sleep adrenaline bomb bursts that left him more exhausted than when he'd lain down. It was like Hue all over agin: sitting on the rubble of the Citadel, pinned down by snipers, and knowing in your bones that General Giap and twenty or so battalions of gooks were getting ready to drive tanks and punji sticks right up his ass.

"Who are you?" Paul asked.

"You were the stomp-down, slickest fucker there was. Period."

At least he didn't claim to be a friend. The label, the slang, the inflections, the sentence cadences, they brought it back, all of it. The bush. The months alone. The jungle noises. The muscle spasms as the Spit sliced a spinal cord. It was all within touching distance again. Twelve years trying to escape those images, that guilt, and the man's language led Paul back by the nose. "Captain Spooky died on birthday number twenty-two," Paul said. "He crawled out of the bush, wiped the paddy grunge from his face, dug the slime from under his fingernails. He turned in his game bag and headed for the States. They didn't zip him in a body bag. Maybe they couldn't tell him from a dink. Maybe there wasn't enough left of him to be worth their while."

"Fate," the hunter said. "It *had* to come down to you and me." His laugh was unhinged, but not as unhinged as his eyes. He popped his knuckles one at a time, then strummed his fingertips on Paul's wounded shoulder. "You don't look much like Superman, but you must have some spit left to grease twelve villagers."

"I repeat," Paul said. "Who . . . ?"

"Moons ago. Many moons."

"Where?"

"Nam."

"Thanks," Paul said.

"Khe Sanh."

"Which whittles it down to ten thousand or so."

"*Or so.*" The hunter's voice was right at the edge. Paul hadn't heard anyone that close to going over since he heard his own echo during the days after the Tet Offensive. But this guy had none of the secondary symptoms. No pacing. No fingernails chewed to the cuticle. No twitching eyebrows. Salesman, psycho, slope-eater, preacher, this man had incorporated it all into one smooth machine. "Call me Piece-of-My-Heart," he said.

Captain Spooky's other half: the man-grunts would always fill in the blank within their mega-duel fantasies . . . imagine Captain Spooky and Piece-of-My-Heart one-on-one, knife versus garrote, in ten acres of bush. They could have sold ten thousand tickets at a grand per. "You really keep some gook's heart in a mason jar?" Paul asked.

The man smiled. "It pays to advertise. It got me a rep and a name."

"Heavy shit," Paul said.

"But not like yours. The Spook-man is still number one in Company tales. That's the rub. As long as you breathe, you'll stay number one."

"Things were crazy over there," Paul said.

"Some of us liked the crazy."

Things had floated far enough into free-lance days. The chat was maybe an inch from a glove across Paul's face . . . if he fought Piece-of-My-Heart with a wounded shoulder, *his* heart would end up in a mason jar. "You're still with the Company?" Paul asked.

"After free-lancing, what was left?"

"I turned medic."

"Only after three years of mercenary work in Ethiopia. On the wrong side."

"You've researched well."

"The day the Company forgets Captain Spooky, it won't stay the Company for long." Piece-of-My-Heart leaned over until his face was inches from Paul's. "Twelve years is a long wait. Being able to wait is what separates the hunters from the killed in action."

"Color Captain Spooky KIA," Paul said.

Piece-of-My-Heart turned and walked to a wall. When he

strummed his fingers against the tin, the entire hut echoed. "Imagine my surprise when I'm given an assignment and your name turns up as a possible contact. The Spook-man on my computer readout. Then the name of the plague village was your village. But I knew you'd make it. It's the way you are."

"The Company behind this?"

"Uncle Sam waste this action on wilderness? Hardly. The Company knows nothing about this plague, but they want to know everything. I have *carte blanche:* Quonset huts, scientific teams, air strikes if it comes to that. The Middle East is unstable enough without the Madhi."

"It's been Madhi this, Madhi that, all afternoon."

"It's his show. He calls the shots, folks start dying."

If it was the Madhi's show, then . . . there was pleasure in revenge, a quickening of the pulse, a high-five, super sense, Dexadrine rush without the needles or teeth grinding. Revenge brought clarity to the world, trimmed away doubt, provided a sense of purpose that blended decision and action. Paul's voice dropped into a flat whisper. "Perhaps I should visit this Madhi."

"I came after you once," Piece-of-My-Heart said.

"The Montagnards told me."

"I waited for two months at Khe Sanh for you to show. I gave you an hour, then picked up your trail at Langvei, humped hill nine-eight-one, and dropped down into your preserve. Poetry, man, hunting the Man on his own turf. The kind of poetry that makes myth. Lost you but came on the trail of some Vietnamese Rangers—shit, you could have driven a goddamn tank down it. I *knew* they wouldn't last long leaving that kind of advertisement, but I was in a rut. Maybe they knew where you operated. Maybe an hour after I joined them, we humped into a ville. The gooners were waiting. *Bac-bac* time. I mean to tell you the meat popped off those dinks. I was thinking, dog-tag-in-the-mouth-time for yours truly."

"Would my ears have gone into the body count?" Paul asked.

"I reserved a spot for them in my medicine bag." Then Piece-of-My-Heart's eyes were back in the bush. "I found a paddy and cut a breathing reed. Got it in my mouth. Nasty stuff.

Worms. Gook sores. I shit for months. I was lucky. The gooners did a number-ten knife job on the Rangers. I didn't hear anything, but when I crawled out of the paddy, I found what was left. Not much. I could have gotten angry. Piece-of-My-Heart hiding in a paddy? I left your trail and took after the gooners. When I finished with them, your trail was cold. Too slick. You were just too slick."

"Since you're here to measure hard-ons," Paul said, "you'd better keep me from your lieutenant. There's not much myth in greasing a cripple."

"What would the Company do to me if I put pleasure before work? An early retirement," Piece-of-My-Heart said. The eerie smile was back. "I'll try to work something out."

"Tell Bu-jahl that I can kill a dozen villagers solo, and the rest of my story might ring true."

"Negative on that one. He likes challenges, a virtuoso when it comes to a hot crowbar and human flesh." Piece-of-My-Heart pushed a button atop the desk. "Colonel Owens has a number-one efficiency rating. We'll put our hopes with him. If you're special, he'll find out why." Then he paused. "One way or another."

"He sounds as dangerous as either of us."

"Two days from now, you'll know for sure," Piece-of-My-Heart said. "And two days can go by most *ricky-tick* . . . or faster."

IX.

Bustān al Kaf Maryam, the Yemeni Highlands—April 23, 1981

The Madhi held audiences only between the hours of five and seven, when the sun slipped far enough toward the horizon to pour through the open balcony and reflect off the mirrors in his study. The two thousand mirrors. The mirrors which, when activated, created illusion, chaos—some parts of the room would be locked in darkness and other parts lighted so brightly it was impossible to see—and they blended and merged. Only the raised prayer carpet where the Madhi received the faithful was spared the sense of dislocation: a true magic carpet.

Talāl borrowed the idea of psychologically altering a room from the design of Gothic cathedrals. Medieval churchmen knew that the more thoroughly a worshiper was prepared to receive God's miracles, the more complete his devotion would be. So they attached mazes to their entranceways to confuse, condition their flock. How glorious the colored windows, the organ music, and choirs must have seemed after a week of drab, medieval life. Talāl did them one better. He consulted psychologists and architects while designing the study—now the labyrinth of a hallway, the distorting mirrors made Talāl divine . . . between the hours of five and seven.

Long red rays streamed in over the courtyard and lit the study with an aura. A scuffling. Footsteps in the maze. Stumbling, hesitant footsteps. The man must have reached one of the right angles where the maze narrowed, and fallen.

Talāl had never murdered before. At least not with his own hands. There were lessons to learn, lessons in death. The killing would be a first step, not unlike the first steps on the pathway to Allah. Would that this path had fewer details! He touched the arabesque in the upper left corner of the prayer carpet and started the motor that turned the mirrors. The room became a tangle of flashes, darkness, imbalance . . . once Talāl had tried to walk when the room was like this and had taken five minutes to grope back to the carpet.

The footsteps stopped at the end of the maze.

"Enter, child of Allah," Talāl said. A man crawled into the room and stretched into a position of full salaam. That this man, Ali Abdul, the medic's assistant from Al Rattaf, was the one to infect the town was fortunate. A very expendable man. He was a groveling, simpering, useless man who would break under torture or, more likely, brag in conversation . . . and what good would the Madhi's miracles be if the faithful learned they were produced by men instead of Allah's Wrath?

Talāl lowered his voice. "The seeds you planted in Al Rattaf have borne blossoms of death, whose fragrance already draws the faithful to the Highlands like bees to frankincense. Your reward will be a spot by me in the Garden of Paradise."

The man whined like an excited puppy. His smell . . . his commonness . . . Talāl grimaced and wrinkled his nose. His hands trembled, and it took effort to keep his voice from breaking. If he couldn't kill this insect, then . . . "Come and be blessed, my child."

The man began to crawl in the wrong direction; he was in danger of going onto the balcony. "Let my voice lead you," Talāl said. He began to chant one of the prayers from Abdullah-i Ansari's "Intimate Conversations with God":

> Allah,
> You are kind in your strength,
> Radiant in your beauty,
> And know no limits of space. . . .

The man changed direction. Talāl took an airgun used in mass inoculations from his waistband. It would scarcely hurt the man.

Just a slight prick as the dose entered his system. Just a few milligrams of shellfish toxin: enough to kill a dozen men.

Ten feet now. The man followed Talāl's voice like a beacon:

You know not of time
There is none like you. . . .

Two yards away . . . a yard. The man stopped and looked up, his eyes lost in Allah's radiance. Talāl placed the gun against a bare spot in the man's neck:

You are close to the knowledge of man
Yet you are far from what we imagine you to be.

And pulled the trigger. Ali Abdul's mouth opened more in surprise than pain, tried to form words but emitted no sounds. He twisted his head, rose to his feet, took several steps, and fell, then crawled all around the room, broke a mirror, and finally curled up beneath the radio transmitter and just lay there trembling. Talāl turned off the motor and the mirrors stopped. He walked toward the quivering body. It twitched, quieted, jerked three, four times violently, then quivered.

Why wouldn't it die? Talāl kicked it. And trembled. Not a scream, not a sound, not a trace of blood, and still Talāl trembled. He shook for this commoner. This filth. If he couldn't even take this life without fear, how could he kill those who must die in the later prophecies? His brothers and cousins? King Khalid?

He kicked the body. A dull thud. He kicked it harder. And harder. He kicked it until his fear was replaced by rage. When he sat down on the carpet, his hand was still. He nudged the body with his foot. Garbage. Lifeless garbage that would never tell the secrets of the miracle at Al Rattaf.

The ululating call of the muezzin rolled in from the domed minaret at the far side of the courtyard. It was time for *Asr,* the late-afternoon prayer. Prayer was nonsense; twelve lonely years in a stone cell had taught Talāl that, but ceremony was necessary. It was ceremony that cemented faith. Only the five daily appearances for prayer, only five, and his followers willingly became martyrs like the corpse on his floor.

As Talāl walked onto the balcony, he ran his fingers along the hand-chiseled tracery shaped like crescent moons. Already his followers, his companions, were clustered around the fountain in the middle of the courtyard. As soon as they saw him, they fell to their knees. Even from a height of thirty feet, they were impressive: dressed in black robes and turbans; almost four hundred strong; his personal guard. He looked past them, out past the walls and minaret, past the mountain's overhang, north toward Mecca. He lifted his eyes toward the overhang, opened his mouth, and chanted, "Allah-o-Akbar!" His voice echoed past the walls and out into the valley two thousand feet below.

And the Companions echoed his call. He led them through the ten steps of prayer, told them to rise, blessed them, then reentered his study. He didn't stop at the prayer carpet but continued to the back of the room and opened a door that led to the corridor. There were things he had to know about the vector before he left for Riyadh, and only Corbin, the group leader, could give him definitive answers. The light in the corridor was blue, artificial. He opened an iron door, stepped into the airlock, watched the safety door slip down from the ceiling behind him, and waited for the pressure to equalize. Then he opened the door and walked into the lab.

The air reeked of ethanol and pyridine. None of the group, the molecular biologists, the biochemists, the lab personnel, were in. The light above the Culture Containment Area was flashing, which meant it would be at least an hour before they'd be decontaminated, an hour before they could answer his questions. Too long.

He walked past the spinning centrifuges. A yeast smell rose from the fermentors. Petri dishes filled with *E. coli* were scattered all over the lab carrels. At least the toxic cultures were locked in compartments labeled BIOHAZARD.

Jacob's door was open. When Talāl looked in, he saw him thumbing through some manuscript pages. He was an American with a patrician nose and white hair that could have been copied from one of Michelangelo's frescoes of the patriarchs. His eyes didn't sparkle; they burned with a blue flame. And what was best, he was the ideal servant. As long as Talāl treated him as an equal, gave him freedom to run whatever experiments he wished, the promise of oil and gas rights, and guaranteed his safety after the *jihad,* he did whatever was asked of him. He liked dealing with Americans, and this scientist was American to the core. A true mercantilist. Talāl sat next to him.

"The DNA coded for plague toxins functioned perfectly," Jacob said. "Of the hundreds in the village and the twenty children we tested, not one survived."

"How do you explain the medic?" Talāl asked.

"I can't. Yet," Corbin said. "Maybe he didn't drink the water. Maybe he didn't eat the qat. Since he's American, his routine may be different. My guess is that he somehow managed to find one of the control mechanisms—accidentally."

"And you don't like to guess," Talāl said.

Corbin leaned back in his chair and smiled. He reached for a cigarette and, remembering Talāl was in the room, put it back down. "We'll find out as soon as I talk to your man from Al Rattaf."

"Impossible," Talal said. "He died."

"That raises problems," Corbin said.

"He was educated. Somewhat. And a Bedouin. His mouth said too many things to too many people."

Corbin cupped his hand over his mouth and rubbed his chin. "Still, that presents problems. If the vector remains in the medic's system, it can be isolated, discovered. If the Americans run genetic and immunological tests and the vector's still there, they'll discover precisely where the Madhi's ability to prophesy comes from."

"But they won't have that opportunity," Talāl said. "The faithful will liberate him from his own people. He will visit us along with the female reporter."

Corbin strummed his hand against the top of the desk until some paper clips began to jiggle. "If there is any chance that he'll be recaptured, either the plague must be triggered or his body must be destroyed. There must be no tests!"

"Either the medic will be here in a week," Talāl said, "or he will not *be.*" He stood and began to pace around the desk. He took some lab reports from the top of the file cabinet, then looked at some computer printouts detailing the virulence of the vector. He abruptly turned back to Corbin and leaned over the desk. "Are you certain it's safe for me to be near someone who has been infected?"

Corbin put his hand on Talāl's shoulder and steered him into a chair. Corbin paused until Talāl calmed, then said, "Since there are no bacteria involved, there is no chance for infection. Even if the vector could enter the air, and it can't, it would die instantly." Corbin nodded his head. "You are completely safe."

"It will be awkward to make them all ingest the triggering mechanism," Talāl said.

"No need. We produced a second option," Corbin said. He walked to the file cabinet, opened a drawer, and removed a small black gadget that looked like a pocket calculator. He handed it to Talāl. "This emits enough microwave energy to raise a portion of a person's body temperature four degrees . . . just enough to trigger the plague toxins. It's been tested. This is how your man in Tai'zz was able to get to the firing squad. There are only two limitations. One: you must be within ten feet of the victim. Two: it must be pointed at them." Then Corbin smiled. "Of course, with your connections, you should be able to get within ten feet of anyone in the world."

Talāl bounced the microwave device in his hand. "This will simplify things with King Khalid and Sheikh Yamani." Talāl's smile grew larger. "Their deaths will open a void only the Madhi can fill." He ran his hand through the tangle of his beard. "How long from the time the toxins are triggered until the first symptoms appear?"

"Two hours for fever and chills. Then delirium. Another thirty minutes for tachycardia, dyspnea, and tachynea. There will be severe lymph node enlargement, buboes, within three hours."

"How long until a man can no longer ride a camel?"

"That depends on the size of the man. No one could last longer than two and a half hours," Corbin said.

"And death?"

"Six hours—unless antibiotics are administered. They trigger a superpromoter . . . then half as much." Corbin looked directly into Talāl's eyes. "I watched the children myself. It isn't pretty."

"That's the point, isn't it, Jacob? Allah's Wrath is never pretty. And the faithful *must see* what happens to those who oppose the Madhi. I have had the Companions post the prophecies of the King's Camel Race throughout Saudi Arabia. People will come to the race to *see.* What the faithful see with their eyes, they will tell with their lips. The word must spread so that when King Khalid dies at the Sacred Mosque, no soldiers will oppose the Companions who sweep in from the desert. Once we control the Sacred mosque, we control Islam. And if Hussein doesn't believe, or Khomeini, or Khadafy, any of them, first a Companion will visit them, then the Wrath of Allah. And the faithful will believe. Allah-o-Akbar!" Talāl laughed, placed his hand on Corbin's shoulder, and asked, "Are you sure you can be me until I return?"

"If being you only involves leading prayer fives times a day, then certainly," Corbin said.

"As long as you hold audience only in the study, only at the proper time, the mirrors will make you divine and disguise those Anglo blue eyes." Talāl began to stroke his beard. "Convince the reporter. Infect several Companions if necessary. The news she takes with her will be history."

"Then you will become the stabilizing force in the Middle East," Corbin said, "the man of the century."

"And you," Talāl said, "will have all that your work requires . . . who can say what miracles you may yet discover." He took Corbin by the shoulders, hugged him, then turned and walked through the lab and back into the corridor.

The next two weeks wouldn't be easy. Talāl would have to temper his will, thrust it into hell fire so that when it emerged it would glide through any obstacle like a hot knife through yogurt. There was little to learn from killing a faceless beggar . . . but his brother, Ja'far, had a face. And his cousins. His will would harden as he sat beside their bodies and watched the plague reduce them to filth, harden so that when it came time, Talāl could kneel at King Khalid's feet, look up into his eyes, smile, and trigger his death. The *ulamas* once told Talāl that there were great lessons to be learned from watching great suffering, and that killing was the most intimate of acts. If that were true, then he would finally give his relatives the intimacy they deserved, and in return they would teach him the greatest lesson of all.

X.

The Foothills of the Yemeni Highlands—April 25, 1981

Claudia stood just inside the shadow line of the cavern, took *off* her sandals to ease the rawness between her toes, and leaned against a stalagmite. What she would have given to sit down, but sitting was no longer possible. Five nights of trying to synchronize the cadence of her derriere with a camel's irregular gait had given her an inch-wide strip of blisters . . . and it wasn't as though she'd never ridden. But a camel's stride was as incomprehensible to a Western tail as Arab culture was to a Western mind.

A camel squealed toward the back of the cave and tried to wriggle free of its leg bindings. One of the rebels brought it a handful of *dhura* stalks and it quieted. Down in the Tihama the wind rose, then dropped thin cones of sand. It was beautiful. Once all this craziness—the plague, the killing, the personal loss—had graduated into memory, she planned to return to Yemen and see all the terrain she missed traveling at night. Two hundred miles of mountains and sand, and every inch of it in darkness. Not that she blamed Pancho for traveling at night with government planes buzzing the Tihama from dawn to dusk.

But that was the only thing she couldn't blame him for.

She'd seen more government patrols, more helicopters and Land Rovers than she thought existed in Yemen, and it was all because of the village. She lifted the binoculars to her eyes.

The Red Sea was blue and brilliant with a lace-fringe of waves breaking a mile from shore. Who named it red? It was as lucid blue as the sky it joined at the horizon. The fishing village looked like no Yemeni village she'd ever seen, more like a jumble of Fort

Bragg and the *Arabian Nights:* Quonset huts erected outside the mud and *dhura* stalk dwellings; a flotilla of modern ships dwarfed the *dhows* in the harbor; men dressed in khaki, both Anglo and Yemeni, patrolled the streets. Perhaps they were investigating the plague outbreak.

Perhaps.

And it could be that the evil-looking sand pile in the Tihama was a mass grave.

Could be.

And the black scar on the beach might have been where they burned the putrified bodies. Or where a gas tank exploded. Or a thousand other things. That was the problem with the entire assignment. There were too many maybes, could bes, ors, and what ifs for her liking. She needed proof. A bacteria culture would be a start, but seeing the disease in progress would be optimal. Maybe a corpse or two. She shuddered. Rick might be a corpse.

Guilt started up.

Again.

'Nuff of that, she thought. Mourn him when you can do it right. Get your fanny in a hotel room in Cairo, put on one of his hats, the capote, maybe, have a yo-yo in one hand, a double martini in the other, several boxes of Kleenex within reach, then break loose with the tears.

Already she'd saved up enough cries for a year.

God, she hated emotional outbursts, but she'd never seen a friend gunned down before. Others, sure, but not a friend. Faceless folks weren't the same, statistics that enlivened her writing, black characters on a white background. If she hadn't learned to distance herself from her stories, she would have gone crazy years before. But Rick was no statistic. Statistics didn't make up stupid puns or soften at the eyes when she flirted with them.

Claudia missed him, she honest-to-God did, but he was gone, gone, gone.

A tear streaked her cheek. So what if she'd grown to rely on him? What was wrong with that? Hadn't he relied on her too . . . ?

. . . and look where it got him.

Enough.

Self-flagellation wouldn't help Rick, and a distracted mind would lead her into danger . . . without him to lead her out again. She thought of their first assignment together, a feature on atrocities committed in Cambodia. She and Rick were strolling down a path in the Dangrek range when their Thai contact suddenly disappeared. A setup. They were about to enter a jungle clearing when Rick put a hand over her mouth and rolled her into the underbrush. At the time, she didn't know him from the Yorkshire Ripper. Rape flashes followed, thoughts of her body oozing into the jungle rot. Within ten seconds, no more, a squad of Khmer Rouge walked into the clearing with their standard assortment or trophies: heads, arms, genitals, all without bodies. Once they were gone, Rick led her back to the Thai border. They hitched a ride back to Nakhon Ratchasima in an ox cart. How had he known? she asked. She hadn't heard a thing. So he started an anecdote about his days as a photojournalist in Vietnam, then smiled and changed tactics. Reincarnation, he said. He'd been a tiger in a previous incarnation, therefore his jungle knowledge and sharp senses. During his other lives he'd acquired tastes for the *I Ching,* Tantric yoga, and tall women with auburn hair. For two weeks, he maneuvered every discussion into debates on the *Kama Sutra* and how his tiger instincts made him invulnerable.

The camels squealed and struggled as the meeting of rebels disbanded. Pancho walked through the water skins and *haulinis* in the sand and said, "It is agreed by all. You stay."

It wasn't time for a counteroffensive just yet. Psych-op instead, a matching of minds. Pancho was a better camel trader than most, so Claudia had to invent new tactics each time they argued. Her silence seemed to confuse him.

He wrinkled her face. She was destroying the rhythm of the game by not making a counteroffer. "Once we have rescued the survivor, there will be a chase. We do not need wounded women," Pancho said. "You must see the Madhi. It is commanded. Less than a week."

"Unless I see the inside of that village, you can tell the Madhi

. . . no deal." Pancho winced. Claudia's sole enjoyment since the kidnapping was tormenting him. She did it for Rick. For the indignity of being tied to a camel. For fifteen hundred years of women in veils and *purdah.* And he couldn't do a thing in retaliation—he wouldn't have been baby-sitting her all through Yemen if the rebels didn't need her as much as she needed them. "What good are words, prophecies, if I don't have visual proof of the plague?"

"The survivor should be proof enough."

"What if he's another of your props?" Claudia pointed toward the village. "What I see down there is the Americanization of Yemen. I saw the same thing in Sana'. The mound, the burn, the soldiers could be the result of the plague or about a million other things." She held his glare, something which, judging from his growing discomfort, women never did. "I need to see about these victims, not just hear about them."

"The discussion is finished," Pancho said. "Such a mission is too dangerous for a woman. You stay."

"I don't see it, I don't report it," Claudia said.

He took a step toward her, expanded his chest, and clenched his fists. King Kong time. But Claudia didn't buy it.

"I'm not writing for goatherds," she said. "How can I convince my readers of this Dark Age mumbo jumbo if I don't believe it myself?"

"You stay!"

"It's your rebellion," Claudia said indifferently. She turned from him, lifted the binoculars to her eyes, then looked back at the Tihama.

Pancho returned to the back of the cave and called the other rebels around him. They took turns drinking putrid water from a goatskin.

There must have been two hundred soldiers in the village and an equal number of civilians. If there was a survivor, he'd be the most valuable piece of information on earth, and springing him wouldn't be easy. The story was developing into one of those situations where her curiosity was apt to get her killed. But this assignment had moved beyond career expectations and self-preservation to that seldom-used part of her psyche: honor. Even the sound of the word grated on her and made her squirm. Each time she'd decided to be honorable before, it wasn't long before she realized how dangerous it was. She *owed* Rick this story. This and much more. It had become their story. Their by-line.

The village was protected by guard dogs on all sides but the west . . . there the Red Sea did more than an adequate job. The only route with natural cover was straight down the foothills to the Tihama, then to follow the dunes. But the last dune was a hundred yards from the village. A hundred yards too far.

The chattering in the back of the cavern stopped. Pancho picked up a handful of sand and threw it against the back of a camel, which, in turn, tried to nip his leg. A different rebel approached Claudia. "You come," he said in perhaps the worst English she had ever heard.

The Red Sea was a huge black hole in the night. The only lights in the sky were from the moon and a scattering of stars. The village mimicked the sky. It, too, was dark except for the windows in the Quonset huts and a single light in a dwelling at mid-village.

How it stunk, even from two miles away! The smell of burning petrol; an antiseptic odor, as though it had rained disinfectant; and a sweet, malignant, scary stench that counterpoised the others.

The plague?

Maybe. But she had no worries; she couldn't catch it; she had her plague boosters. But what good were boosters against a disease that had moved beyond science into religion. At least Pancho had an in with the Madhi. She stayed close to him in hopes of divine protection.

They tethered the camels to some scrub brush a mile from the village, then crept from dune to dune, always on the shadowed side of the crests. The moon was neither full nor high, but it shined too brightly. There could be no soldiers anywhere.

Claudia raised her head above the dune, and the wind sprayed sand in her face.

It surprised her that she could move so quietly until she realized she couldn't have been noisy if she wanted to; the sand swallowed every movement and sound. She had a black *'aba* over the white one Rick had given her, her feet were strapped to her sandals to prevent clicking, and mud was rubbed into her face. She looked just like a rebel . . . which had both advantages and disadvantages. As long as she stayed in the deepest shadows, she was invisible, but if she were seen, she'd be just another rebel. Another dead rebel. There'd be no chance to flash her press card or ring the consulate in Tai'zz.

And there were soldiers out there waiting.

She was sure of it. Sure, the village looked quiet and natural. Sure, the guards in the street looked nonchalant and the music from the Quonset huts was comfortably loud, but that was the point. It seemed too perfect

It had to be a setup.

Her heart beat so loudly, Claudia was sure it would give them away. "A trap!" she whispered, pulling on Pancho's sleeve.

He tried to quiet her.

"Even the dogs are quiet!" she whispered.

Pancho placed his hand over her mouth. Claudia wasn't sure if she saw his cocky smile or merely sensed it. "Where there are Yemenis," he whispered, "there are believers."

What was that supposed to mean?

Five other rebels went first, then Pancho grabbed her hand, gave it a jerk, and led her across the open sand. It flew up into her mouth as she crouched low.

The guards dogs were dead. Stretched on their sides, mouths open, tongues coated with sand they had eaten. Poison. Which explained the line about believers. Another hundred feet and they flattened against the first building.

The windows in the Quonset huts had red-and-white-checkered curtains: no longer any doubt that Americans were inside. The slang confirmed it. Claudia peeked through a window: crew cuts, a chess game, a cluster of men around a Monopoly board. What Americans were doing in Yemen presented a stream of questions she didn't have time to answer.

One question she couldn't avoid: If the shooting started, whose side was she on? No way she'd gun down Americans, but if they saw her in her rebel outfit . . .

. . . a door opened.

A marine and a man in civvies walked from the hut and stared right at her. She stopped breathing. The dark clothing must have worked because they glanced up and down the street, then entered a windowless Quonset. She didn't shake, but when she ran her tongue around her mouth to collect saliva, it was as dry as if she'd been gnawing sand all day.

Time for some objectivity. She needed plague signs. There was no chance for corpses after all this time, but she expected to see *some* animals. Rats were everywhere in Yemen—everywhere except this village. What it lacked in rats it made up for in flies. Millions of flies. They streamed into her face as she walked.

All the rebels moved well but none as well as Pancho. They stayed on the shadowed side of the street until they were within a hundred feet of the mud hut with lights. Then three of the rebels crouched low, ran across the street, and bellied toward the hut.

Footsteps.

Two Yemeni soldiers stood guard in front of the hut; a third marched up and down the street, pausing to look in dark alleys. The marching guard turned into the alley by the hut, unbuttoned his military trousers, and urinated a stream against a building.

Before the soldier could shake off the last drops, a rebel stood behind him. A *jambiyya* flashed. Claudia had never seen a man's throat cut before. There was no scream, hardly a noise at all, just the scraping of blade against bone, then a deep liquid gurgling. The rebel dragged the man farther into the shadows, his pants around his ankles, his hands clawing at his throat as thought that would help.

After half a minute, the soldier emerged from the darkness—taller, more graceful. An oxlike rebel crawled up some stacked crates to the roof of the hut and crept along the supports. He crouched above the door, jumped when the marching soldier reached the guards, then slit one guard's throat. When the second guard turned, the rebel in uniform jerked back his head and sliced him to the spinal column. The guards' legs convulsed as they were dragged into the alley.

When the rebels returned from the shadows, they wore Yemeni uniforms. One entered the hut and, after a minute or so, emerged with a tall bearded man. The rebel pointed toward Pancho, and the tall man glided across the street toward them. Claudia *used* to think Pancho was graceful. No more. The new man moved like moonbeams or the wind in one long, continuous flow instead of individual movements. She couldn't see much of him: a nose crooked enough to show he could take care of himself; deep-set eyes that flickered in the moonlight; an angular face that could have been hewn from native rock. "Abdullah Mohammed?" he asked Claudia.

She pointed to Pancho.

"You well enough to ride?" Pancho asked the man.

"I better be," the man said.

The rebels dressed as soldiers stayed behind as the rest of them crept along the street back to the Tihama. Claudia tugged on Pancho's *'aba,* then nodded toward the rebels in front of the hut. "Why?" she whispered.

He looked at her as if to say only a woman, an infidel, or worse, *both,* could ask so stupid a question. "The guards will change in six hours . . . as long as they have someone to change with."

Three more martyrs putting down their lives as a down payment on a small plot in the Garden of Paradise. There was an old adage that the most dangerous creature on earth was a man who wasn't afraid to die. Claudia believed it now.

"If things go well," Pancho whispered, "we'll be in a cave in the Highlands before they discover he's gone."

Which should have been Claudia's clue. Nothing had gone well since she arrived in Yemen—why should it suddenly change? Just as Pancho finished talking, a huge Yemeni stepped out from around a corner. His eyes were as large as moon glow and he held a huge *jambiyya* high above his head. It was broad, curved, beautiful in the way it caught the moonlight like a white flame, hypnotic as it began a wide arc toward her throat. Then she realized the man holding it had escaped from her nightmares back into reality.

Mickey Rat.

XI.

Al Rattaf, Yemen—April 25, 1981

If Paul was to play an active role in his own future—in determining how and how long he would remain alive—then this was the night for action. Tomorrow promised the Yemeni lieutenant and hot crowbars; tonight, just the three Yemeni guards outside the clinic and the one in the examination room. Those were odds down considerably from the squad of CIA sharpshooters who had guarded the clinic since Paul became strong enough to walk. The problem was what lay beyond these guards. An escape to Nuri's? The Yemeni army? Or Piece-of-My-Heart waiting in the darkness?

The Yemenis would almost be too easy, and Piece-of-My-Heart knew that. Since he had no more concern for international diplomacy than Paul—which was none at all—if the Yemenis wouldn't let him complete the vendetta, then he'd find some way to work around them.

Like abetting Paul's escape to set up a one-on-one . . . it would be the kind of bravado that myths were made of.

There was scarcely any noise outside: two men talking in Arabic by the front door; the shuffling of the third guard's feet as he walked up and down the dusty street; and the generator and the freezer's electric motors, which made no more noise than a June bug buzzing against a screen door.

The inner guard sat under a bright Coleman lantern, reading an Arabic edition of Marvel comics. He'd pose no problem. Neither would one of the door guards. It would be the other two who'd be difficult . . . all four must be taken without noise. A single shout or gunshot would wake the camp and finish the escape attempt—not to mention finishing Paul.

His shoulder was still on fire, which wasn't right. Maybe he was flexing it too soon, testing it to learn which stresses it would and wouldn't take. Maybe Colonel Owens had left something raw or untied when he did the surgery. It made no difference. It would be strong enough for the guards if Paul could lure one of them inside. . . . Paul heard a soft splashing against the alley wall of the clinic, the unmistakable sound of a bladder emptying. That could be just the distraction he needed. He listened more closely. A sound . . .

. . . bone scraping against steel?

Once you'd heard a throat being slashed, there was no mistaking it. Something—someone—had just had his throat slashed and was being dragged behind the clinic. Paul looked toward the Coleman lantern. The guard continued to swing across the skyline with Spider-Man. He never looked up from the page.

Relax. Clear the mind of all thoughts but the hunt, the adrenaline buildup, the aching muscle, the heightened senses. Paul's breath slowed and evened. He felt for something he could use as a garrote.

A scratch on the wall. It was too high up for a cat and much too loud. A cat would have to weigh two hundred pounds to make that much noise: close to Piece-of-My-Heart's weight.

The guard's head looked up from the comic. His eyes followed the noise. He rose slowly from his chair, dimmed the Coleman, and reached for his M-16.

The noise moved up the wall to the thatched roof. A foot rustled against the *dhura*-stalk roofing. Someone was crawling along the support beams toward the mantel above the door guards. Since there was only one man on the roof and two at the door, the cat man must have had friends with him. But they wouldn't know about the inner guard. He was so engrossed in the noise that he forgot about Paul. A serious mistake. The standard move would be to snap the guard's neck with a kick, but the momentum would send the guard flying into the electrocardiogram and cause the kind of clatter that would wake the entire village.

So Paul ad-libbed.

He pinched a nerve in the guard's arm and the M-16 dropped to the floor. When the guard turned toward Paul, mouth open, ready to scream, Paul drove the wedge of his knuckles into the man's Adam's apple. He went down with little more than a gasp. Paul rolled the body under the table, then turned the Coleman down until its mantle flickered.

The next move was Piece-of-My-Heart's. He'd set the escape up. He would know that Paul had killed the inside guard. That the lights would be low enough to amplify shadows. As a hunter, he could assume all this and more. But Paul could assume a few things, too. Part of Piece-of-My-Heart's ego would say there was no sport in greasing a cripple. Maybe that's why he let Paul have the advantage of darkness—as a handicap for the wounded shoulder.

There was nothing left to do but wait.

The noise on the roof stopped. Then there was the antinoise, the fraction-of-a-second vacuum that indicated the man on the roof had leaped for the guards. A hard thump. Another steel-on-bone scrape. Gurgling. Another scuffle. Quiet. More bodies being dragged behind the clinic.

Silence.

Then the door creaked.

White moonlight spilled onto the floor in a growing slice. A shadow appeared in the light. Paul moved to a spot directly in front of the entranceway to the examination room and crouched low in the shadows.

Too late.

The shadow was inside the clinic and moving toward the entranceway. Unless Piece-of-My-Heart had taken clumsy lessons in the past few days, this wasn't him. This shadow was bulkier and, what was more telling, loped like a Yemeni. Paul held the bayonet he'd taken from the guard gently, as though it were a live bird. The shadow tripped. No, Piece-of-My-Heart wasn't involved in this escape; he wouldn't work with amateurs. So much for Paul's careful planning. The next thirty seconds would be impromptu.

The shadow hardened into a man as he moved farther into the lantern light. He spun through the entranceway to the wall where he knew the guard would be waiting. Sorry. Paul was no Yemeni. He was elsewhere.

Paul grabbed the man from behind, jerked his head back to expose the throat, and prepared to drive the blade through the windpipe. But he hesitated. This man smelled of the Highlands and camels.

"*Salaam alaikum,*" the man said through clenched teeth. He made no move to defend himself. That wouldn't have made a difference to Captain Spooky—he would have slashed the man's throat, moved into the shadows, then greased whomever blocked his way out. Paul loosened his grip on the man's hair. "Peace be on you," the man said in stumbling English.

"*Alaikum as salaam,*" Paul said. He released the man.

The Yemeni returned to Arabic. "Outside," he said. "Friends. They will take you away."

Just what Paul needed. More friends. "Who?" he asked.

"Friends."

One thing for sure: This man's friends wouldn't include Piece-of-My-Heart. So there were two options: this goatherd's friends now or the friendly face of the lieutenant from the security police at six in the morning.

"Lead on," Paul said. He followed the man through the waiting room to the door. A Yemeni soldier paced up and down in front of the clinic. Only he wasn't a Yemeni soldier. The cuffs of his army pants reached only halfway down his shins, and his fly wasn't buttoned. He walked with the bowed legs of a man who'd grown up riding a camel. The other guard's uniform fit well enough, but a dark stain sprayed down his chest like a bib. The moonlight held no colors, but the blood smell in the air indicated the stain was red.

"Who are you?" Paul whispered.

He made the palm-toward-heaven sign of the Madhi.

Rebels.

There was no time to ask how they'd avoided the guards and dogs and no need to ask why they wanted Paul. There wasn't even time to ask about allegiances and motivation. There was only time to leave. Once Paul was out of the village and in the Highlands, he would take his odds against anyone—except maybe Piece-of-My-Heart.

"Go there," the rebel said, pointing toward a clump of darker shadows on the shadowed side of the street. A shadow moved. People. "Ask for Abdullah Mohammed. An Imam." Then the rebel-turned-soldier assumed a military posture, hands at side, eyes straight ahead.

There was no movement on the street. Danger lay in the bright moon with the guards at the dock and with the men in the Quonset huts. Paul crouched in the doorway until a cloud slid across the moon, then moved with the shadow across the street. He became part of the darkness. As he moved closer to the people, they became rebels in black *'abas.* It figured that the first rebel, the tall one with the loose ends of his headcloth pulled high above his cheeks, would be the Imam. "Abdullah Mohammed?" Paul asked.

The rebel nodded toward the next person, a shorter, bulkier man. "Are you well enough to ride?" Abdullah Mohammed asked Paul in the crispest English Paul had heard since Trafalgar Square.

Paul nodded.

Abdullah Mohammed motioned with his head for Paul to follow and, crouched low, moving ever so slowly down the dark side of the street, a rebel, then Paul, then the tall rebel, then Abdullah Mohammed moved through the silky village dust and out toward the Tihama.

Someone whispered.

The fucking amateurs! Paul turned toward the tall rebel just as he asked "why" in English. In àn incredibly feminine voice. Did the Madhi recruit only English-speaking followers?

Abdullah Mohammed tried to hush the man. No luck. More whispering. ". . . six hours . . . things go well . . . the Highlands before . . ."

Suddenly, the largest Yemeni Paul had ever seen moved from the shadows. The size of the *jambiyya* raised above his head was disquieting enough, but the fact he wasn't shouting for help indicated he thought he could kill all the rebels by himself. His size indicated he might be able to do it.

If they hadn't included Paul.

The tall rebel screamed, and that answered a lot of questions. One: he wasn't a Yemeni. Two: he wasn't a he.

It was wasted effort to grab the knife-arm two-handed as they always did in the movies. It left too much to chance, and Paul's shoulder wasn't ready for a test of strength with a man that size. When Paul had fenced, he learned that the best parry was one that allowed the thrust to come as close to the target as possible—while still missing. He knocked the soldier's elbow just enough to send the *jambiyya* slicing through the outermost layer of the woman's *'aba.* It threw the man so far off-balance that his follow-through drove the blade into the dust. Even before Paul knew the terminology, he knew that no man could survive a blow to the part of the neck that drove the fourth vertebrae through the medulla oblongata. Paul used his right arm, sore shoulder or not.

The huge Yemeni lay still—except for death spasms in his arms and legs.

The woman started to speak. "Thank—"

Paul put his hand over her mouth. "Another word," he whispered, "and I slit your throat."

That she understood.

The walk out of the village only added more questions. There were no signs of struggle, but most of the lights were conveniently off, and the guard dogs were poisoned. It was too easy.

A string of sand dunes led them past Johara's grave, then to a half-dozen riding camels tied in the scrub brush. Paul wanted to look back, to take a final look at Al Rattaf and bring some of the six years along with him, but they were gone. Gone with the villagers. Gone with Johara. The time for mourning was over. First Paul had an obligation to Nuri and the convoy, then an appointment with the Madhi.

So without looking back, Paul waited until the camel knelt, then mounted, held tight with his knees as the camel stood, then bounced off into the dark mass of the Highlands.

Paul didn't know what to make of the woman, at least not after she said her name was Claudia Mallory as though the name was supposed to mean something. So he asked her who the hell Claudia Mallory was supposed to be. She did a double take then stomped away.

Despite her temper, she had saving qualities.

Even in the three-quarter moon with sweat streaking her face, she was pretty. No time for understatement. Even wearing a shapeless *'aba* and a turban so filthy it was stiff, she was exquisite. Her features were crisp and consistent in a way only years of wired teeth and generations of proper breeding could accomplish. Properly upturned nose. Thin lips. Eyes so large they dwarfed her other features.

But she wasn't a Barbie doll. She was bright, and God knows what she must have gone through to find him. There had to be a tough core under all that sheen. Somewhere. But she hid it well.

So Paul stayed away from her.

From the time they picked up four rebels who'd been left in a cave above Al Rattaf till the rebels in the village were discovered—maybe five hours—whenever Claudia rode next to him and started to chatter, he'd increase his camel's pace so the bouncing would punish her obviously sore bottom, and she had to drop back.

She finally gave up.

They traveled thirty-five or forty miles before Paul heard gunfire, volleys so distant they sounded like popcorn in a covered skillet. The fire lasted five minutes—about four minutes longer than Paul guessed it would. The camels moved at double time for the next few miles. The rebels turned into a wadi and followed its twists and turns deep into the Highlands. Within an hour, the sky above the Tihama filled with spotlight-equipped helicopters, which streaked above the sand like the mutant offspring of dragonflies and lightning bugs. Even from miles away the chopping rotor blades brought back the paddies, the corpses, and rot of Vietnam as vividly as Piece-of-My-Heart's voice had.

This wadi was an old friend. Though it had been dry for months, its undergrowth was lush. Paul had hiked it looking for specimens each year since he arrived. It snaked and dipped, then rose for twenty miles till it met the Qaria Escarpment, a ten-thousand-foot wall of volcanic rock that splintered into a thousand peaks and valleys. This Abdullah Mohammed was smart. He knew that once they reached the escarpment, nothing could keep them from their destination.

Or Paul from his.

What Abdullah Mohammed didn't know was that they weren't the same place.

The first time he had a chance to escape, Paul was off to Nuri's camp. The rebels and this Claudia Mallory woman could go anywhere they wanted. Once the convoy had been ambushed, Paul would follow the weapons back to the Madhi. Simple.

Just before dawn, a helicopter left the Tihama and veered up the wadi. A spotlight came within twenty feet of the lead camel, then swept up the canyon wall. But it wasn't even a close call. The date palms and *'ilb* trees were so thick that the helicopter couldn't have seen the rebels even if it were daylight. When the helicopter vanished over a ridge, Abdullah Mohammed led the camels from the undergrowth and up into an expanse of tallis slopes. They took shelter in a cavern camouflaged by an overhang of loose rock. It was scarcely large enough to hold both rebels and camels.

The camels hadn't even been tied down when Claudia Mallory rose to leave the cave. Abdullah Mohammed tried to stop her. A pathetic attempt. By the time she'd finished with him, he had a tail-between-the-legs look Paul had never seen on an Arab man.

She was gone too long.

When the sun edged above the escarpment and turned the sky the color of ripe peaches, Paul prepared to go after her. A helicopter would surely spot her on the barren canyon walls. But she came back into view. Limping. She sat down next to Paul, removed her turban, and shook her auburn hair down with a too-self-conscious panache. Then she stretched—a slow feline stretch—and her *'aba* pulled up above her ankle. "I stumbled into something," she said. There was sugar in her voice . . . sugar with fangs.

When she rubbed her ankle, she drew it back as though it burned. Her ankle and lower calf were covered by blisters. Let her hurt. The pain would do her good. If she didn't learn pretty quick that Yemen wasn't Disneyland, he'd end up burying another woman . . . something he wasn't sure he was up to.

Then the rebels pointed at her and started to laugh.

Whether or not she was a bitch, she was an American ten thousand miles from home and, though Paul didn't like to admit it, in a cave crowded with camels and Arabs, that meant something. "This isn't another of your schemes to talk with the 'survivor,' is it?"

Her eyes burned, but her voice was completely calm. "I can't remember the last time I met a bigger asshole," she said.

"Let's see the foot."

She ignored him. Her voice caught the fire in her eyes. "I ride all over this goddamn country trying to rescue a captured American, and after I get him out, he's worse than the fucking natives."

"The foot?" Paul asked.

Her ranting continued. "One small bomb, a hand grenade even, and this cave becomes a mausoleum. I can think of better fates than being stuck for all eternity with pseudo-Lawrence and a pack of goatherds!" When she turned her back to Paul, she brushed her calf against a rock and winced.

"If that leg gets infected," Paul said, "you may lose it."

She turned back to Paul and lifted her foot into his hand. He pushed the *'aba* up to her knee. Her exquisite knee. Blisters had already raised a quarter of an inch, and white latex from the plant remained on her skin. "What you 'stumbled into' was a plant named *Euphorbia officinalis.* Every three-year-old in

Yemen knows that means 'stay away.' " He ran his hand through his beard and smiled. "Hope the sunrise was worth it."

Claudia Mallory looked at him as though he were a drool-from-the-mouth moron. "Sunrise?" she asked in disbelief. "Wrong girl! I quit being a romantic my sophomore year. I concluded *someone* had better know the way out of this tomb in case we get found."

"I've hiked this wadi for years," Paul said.

"Which leaves me blushes and tingles all over," she said. When she rubbed the back of her hand against her forehead, it smeared the mud. Her skin was peeling, and freckles showed through the tan. And if there wasn't a colony of lice in her old *'aba,* then Paul wasn't in Yemen. He had to concede her spirit even as he wished for a little more common sense.

She winced as he touched the puffy skin around the blisters. He walked to the back of the cavern, drew some water from a goatskin, and carefully washed the latex from the burned areas. He set her foot down. "Problems," he said. "I pop those blisters, and the bacteria on your legs will seep in the sores and go wild. I don't pop them, you're through riding for a while. You'd rub them open on the camel's side."

"Can I walk?"

"You'd never keep up."

"Options?" she asked.

"A few." Paul smiled. He walked to the mouth of the cavern, checked up and down the valley for helicopters, then moved into the granite slopes, sticking closely to the shadows and outcroppings, searching, searching. He found a small green plant with fleshy fingerlike appendages, uprooted it, and took it back to the cave. He knelt down by Claudia Mallory, crushed one of the fronds between his fingers, then slowly, ever so gently, rubbed the jelly over her blisters.

"Amazing," she said. "This the legendary Balm of Gilead?"

"Close," Paul said. "The Yemenis call this *sabr.* A member of the aloe family. It will neutralize the acid in the latex."

"You know a lot about Yemen."

"I've lived here long enough."

She cocked her head to the right, opened her mouth in a childish smile, which wasn't childish at all, and stuck her tongue into her cheek. And those eyes, those huge blue eyes sparkled and burned right into his. "Where did you learn to move that way?" she asked.

"What way?"

"I'm not in the mood for similes," she said. "I just like the way you move."

"I danced for the Joffrey," Paul lied.

"And I'm one of Charlie's Angels," she said. The mud on her face began to dry, and when she squinted, it cracked and flaked. "You know about medicinal plants because you were the village medic," she said. "Were medicinal plants any help against the plague?"

"Why are you in Yemen?" Paul asked, ignoring her.

"Looking for you."

He nodded as if to say, well, here I am, then realized that was the worst thing he could do. Before she could take the offensive again, he asked, "How'd you end up with the rebels?"

"I'm really not that interesting," she said. "And I haven't lived through the plague."

"What makes you think I have?"

"The stench. The Quonset huts. The mound by the village."

"Is this an interrogation?" Paul asked.

She looked at him in amazement and shook her head. "You really don't know who I am?"

"But I have an active imagination," Paul said. "Let me guess. You're a reporter."

"Features and the like for UPI. Sometimes a thirty-second spot of PBS. You really should keep up on your reading."

"I keep a minimum of ten thousand miles between myself and the States. 'You can't go home again,' all that stuff. Somehow reporters remind me of everything I like least about America."

Claudia Mallory sat back but kept her eyes locked to his. "I'm doing a story on the Madhi."

Paul nodded toward the rebels. "I never would have guessed."

"They've spent the last week trying to convince me that this

'Wrath of Allah' business is legit. That once Allah gets angry, no science can save the target. Was there anything you could do for the villagers?"

"Stand there and watch them die."

"I need more," she said.

Paul tried to ignore her. He tried to stand, but she grabbed his hand and held it. She leaned close enough to him that, under proper circumstances, say candelabras and perfume as opposed to sweat and camel dung, it might have been sexy. The sugar reappeared in her voice. "Why won't you talk?" she asked.

Paul tugged his hand away and started to walk off.

"You're beginning to piss me off," she said.

"And you use your body like a public convenience when we both know it isn't. I've seen more subtlety from the street whores in Cairo."

She didn't slap him. He would have liked her better if she had. She drew back and shifted her weight onto her left hip. "I'll cut the nonsense," she said. "I want two things. One, are you sure it was the plague? Two, why are you still alive?"

Paul raised a hand and lifted two fingers. "One, none of your business. Two, because I've learned when to shut up."

"You really *are* an asshole!" Claudia Mallory said.

"And you walked on the sand dune where I buried my wife," Paul said. Then he turned his back on her, walked across the stones on the cavern floor, and sat with the camels and the rebels. It was a symbolic gesture, nothing else, but maybe it was enough. If anyone could understand the value of symbolism, it should have been a reporter.

XII.

The Yemeni Highlands—April 26, 1981

Claudia liked the way he moved.

Fluid, understated, like Cary Grant in *To Catch a Thief.* No, Cary had been too self-conscious. More like Baryshnikov when the spotlight was on someone else. That wasn't it, either. The medic moved like some animal that hadn't evolved yet, one with panther grace and human intent.

His description? It would have to come early in her story and really bring him to life. He was thin—wiry was a possible adjective, lithe no doubt better—and stood a full head taller than her five foot nine. He had distinct cheekbones, a short Van Gogh-ish beard, and shoulders and arms knotted with muscles.

And the man was full of surprises. She wouldn't have bought a two-dollar ticket at a thousand-to-one odds on his chances against Mickey Rat, yet their fight hadn't lasted long enough to qualify as a fight. In Vietnam, they'd have called it a termination.

God, he was eerie.

He'd gone as native as anyone Claudia had met in Yemen, but he would never look like an Arab. No matter how hard he tried, no matter what costume he wore or language he spoke, his eyes would always spoil the ruse. They were deep blue eyes, eyes that hinted he might not be all that fond of himself. Eyes that said he'd been alone long enough to ponder all the questions that didn't have answers.

Maybe she liked his eyes even more than the way he moved.

But they wouldn't play the usual games, wouldn't even make contact with hers. His eyes and head were constantly moving, and even when he entered into a conversation, he wasn't completely there. Words were secondary to staying alert. Maybe since he'd spent so much time with primitive people, he understood body language better than verbals. Maybe he had become so primitive that he'd gone completely around the circle and wasn't primitive at all. All Claudia knew was that she normally depended on her gestures registering in a man's subconscious, and Paul Kenyon saw right through them. And his wife . . .

He had some right to be angry, but the slip about his wife wasn't her fault. How could she have known that he'd taken his Bedouin thing far enough to marry one? She cleared her throat and said, "I'm sorry about your wife. Was it the plague?"

Nothing.

Maybe it would be better to bolster his ego, work on his healer image. "Mr. Doctor?" she asked.

The medic's eyes opened, made a slow round of the cavern, settled on her, and closed again.

"Any balm left?" she asked.

His eyes remained closed, but his mouth moved. "Sleep while you can," he said. "We have to make the base of the pass by midnight. That's twenty miles. It's five miles straight up the escarpment from there. On a path too thin for camels."

"My leg's on fire."

He was up. Claudia had never seen anyone make the transition from sleep to wakefulness as fast as the medic. No soft mouth. No puffy eyes. The man didn't rise in stages like everyone else she'd known, but like a time-lapse film of a plant growing . . . seemingly all at once. He walked to the back of the cavern, picked up a water skin, brought it back, and squatted next to her. He took a deep swallow and offered her one. It tasted like old goats.

"Where'd they get this?" he asked.

She shrugged. "Some well in the Tihama. Maybe twenty miles from your village."

"It's not boiled," he said. "Most of the water in Yemen will put the likes of you on her back for weeks."

The goat taste grew stronger.

Then he lifted the hem of her *'aba* up to her knees. Claudia was tempted to flirt, but the medic seemed only interested in the blisters. "You'll make it," he said. "You have tough skin for an American."

"I note a trace of disgust each time you say 'American.' "

"Only a trace?" he asked. He took a few more fronds from the aloe plant, crushed them, and smeared the jelly on her leg. What a contradiction between the warm jelly and the cooling sensation. There was even a greater paradox in the fingers that applied the balm so gently: They were the same fingers that snapped Mickey Rat's neck like dry grass.

"What's your name?" Claudia asked.

"Paul Kenyon."

"And you have an uncontrollable urge to talk."

"As long as you keep it away from the village and the plague," he said.

For now, maybe. She was patient. Whatever approach she used to loosen him up, it would have to be subtle. He didn't seem like one who suffered fools easily. "Why the Yankee-Go-Home attitude?" she asked. "I've been in Yemen more than a month without finding anything to make me turn in my citizenship."

"You expect me to be surprised," Kenyon said without looking up.

"Indifference, cruelty, misogyny, filth: the Four Horsemen of the Yemen," she said.

"Circumstance, honesty, tradition, and need," the medic said. "The same things viewed through a different lens. It's a lens that doesn't fit cameras made in America."

"You were made in America," Claudia said.

"And refocused in Vietnam."

She should have guessed. He was the ultimate dropout. It provided their first link, some common ground on which to build a friendship. "My first assignment was the fall of Saigon."

"I was gone by then," Paul said. "I was in the States having people call me a war criminal every time I wore my fatigues." His eyes were elsewhere, in a place she wasn't sure she ever wanted to visit. "I saw much too much in Nam." Then his eyes weren't moving but deep into hers. Claudia looked away. He knew more about territorial games than she imagined. "But you wouldn't know about that," he said. "I doubt you ever made it past the Embassy gates."

"I made it to the bars. The houses and dens. I met rapists, the pain freaks, the mutilators, the mass murderers. The boys who would never make it back home. I didn't see action, but I saw enough of its by-products to understand it. Where did you fit in?" she asked.

"All the above," Kenyon said. "And more." Then he shook his head as if clearing it, nodded, and smiled. "Well done," he said. "Part of the survivor's biography painlessly extracted." He looked out the cave entrance to the parch-dry mountain peaks across the canyon. "You really want to get on my good side, tell me all you know about the Madhi."

"In ten words or less?"

"Why did he hit Al Rattaf?" Kenyon asked.

"Who knows? He prophesied that Allah would destroy a village because it violated Koranic law."

"Would a Muslim marrying an infidel be enough of a violation?" he asked.

"You'll have to ask Pancho," she said. "He's the expert."

The sparkle drained from Kenyon's eyes. Evidently, he didn't have to ask Pancho anything. Kenyon looked as though he was adding a question of guilt to his long list of impenetrable questions. If he had somehow brought on the destruction of the village, it would be the focus, the hook for a story all its own. And, if she were sharp, all *her* own. It would do him good to suffer. He'd grow more vulnerable, more open . . . then she could conduct a mutually beneficial camel trade: her soft shoulder for his story.

"Were you *the* infidel?" she asked.

"The press conference is over."

"In which case you'd like nothing more than to get even with the Madhi," Claudia said.

Kenyon leaned back and stared at the cavern's ceiling. "Keep talking," he said. "I want to hear a woman's voice."

Then it was time for her life story: the Long Island childhood;

the summers on Martha's Vineyard; the Wellesley days; the sailing and field hockey. Instead, a sudden thumping of helicopter blades silenced her. She could have kept talking—the helicopter crew wouldn't hear her—but it was an instinctual matter now: instinct said to keep your butt down and mouth shut.

But Kenyon had long since mastered his instincts. He did everything backward. He raised his crouch and moved closer to the cavern mouth. Evidently, he believed the more visible a danger became, the less of a danger it was.

This helicopter didn't streak up the valley as the others had done but hovered in different locations, no doubt probing possible hiding spots. But the cave had an overhang, and there wasn't even an animal trail leading up to it. It might have been the safest place in Yemen.

Claudia hadn't counted on the camels.

In the five days she'd ridden one, she'd learned that camels were the ugliest, smelliest, foulest-tempered, most unpredictable animals on earth. Anyone who trusted a camel deserved to be trapped for all eternity with them. They bellowed and struggled every time a helicopter flew past, but their legs were bound. This helicopter hovered two hundred yards away, and the camels went wild. Squirming. Squealing. Spitting at everything within range.

No sooner did the copter begin to pull away and up the valley than a camel pulled out a knot, broke through its bindings, and dashed for the entrance. Pancho tried to stop it, but it didn't even break stride as it went over him and out into the tallis slopes.

There was a fraction of a second when everyone froze and prayed that the helicopter crew wouldn't look back and notice a pack camel stumbling through the sharp rock.

Then Claudia saw the rebels dive for their guns; she visualized the helicopter banking in a slow, graceful sweep and heading back toward the cave. A rocket exploded twenty feet from the entrance, and a rebel fell straight back, a single spot the size of a quarter in his forehead. He was nerve-dead before he thudded against the rock floor. The helicopter made a strafing run and flew so close to the overhang that its rotor-wash blew rocks into the cave. The rebels fired short bursts that bounced harmlessly off the chopper's armored undercarriage. Another rocket, and the overhang almost broke loose. If the overhang took a direct hit, the cave would be death. Slow death. Even if the chopper missed again, its radio would guarantee that three or four more helicopters would appear in minutes. There was only one chance: break for the wadi and cover.

Claudia jumped to her feet and started to run.

It was better to take a bullet in the head or back, better to have life blown away than gradually ooze out in darkness, and she was almost to the cave entrance, almost away from the squealing camels and killer rocks, when something hit her in the stomach and lifted her straight up. . . .

. . . Paul Kenyon's shoulder.

She was still gasping for breath, still trying to rub the pain from her solar plexus, when the gun ship made a strafing run, and she saw the rebels go down. All of them. Like limp pillows struck by baseball bats. Even after bits of flesh and bone were blown into the air, dust continued to kick up around their bodies.

And Kenyon hadn't fired a round.

The rebels had saved him, and he didn't lift a finger to help them. He waited until the helicopter banked for its second pass, a pass that would cause fifty tons of rock to slide over the cave entrance when he fired a short burst. Ten, twenty shots, no more.

Enough.

Glass exploded from the helicopter's cockpit, and the rotor's spinning was transferred to the fuselage. The copter began to spin faster and faster and didn't stop spinning until it crashed into the canyon wall. A cone of black, oily smoke started to rise.

Kenyon took her hand and tugged her to her feet. He dragged her from the cave and out past the rebels. Claudia wanted to stop and help Pancho. It was natural. He'd saved her life. Several times. The least she could do was help him if possible.

It wasn't.

He bled from bullet wounds in the chest and legs. There was a large pulsing gash in his neck, and his tongue drooped from the corner of his mouth. It was dust-coated. Claudia had seen enough wounded men to know Pancho wouldn't have the strength to do anything, but he took a small black box from his *'aba,* pointed it at Kenyon and her, and pushed a button. Claudia felt suddenly hot and dizzy. She staggered.

Kenyon picked her up and threw her over his shoulder. Then, instead of heading for the wadi as sanity demanded, he ran up past the cave, past the trail where she'd brushed against that dangerous plant, and toward a ridge.

It was just as well he was doing the running for both of them. He didn't tire. He didn't stumble. He ran straight up the canyon wall for at least ten minutes, then hid in some boulders. His run took slightly less time than it took for three more gun ships to come up from the Tihama and locate the smoke. They searched the canyon walls and tried to land by the rebels' bodies, but it was too steep. They hovered above the cave. About five minutes later, another helicopter, a huge two-rotored Chinook, landed in a wadi clearing. Fifty soldiers jumped out and began to search through the brush.

"You can bet another landed upstream," Kenyon said. "A third downstream. That wadi was death."

"And this ridge isn't?"

"Not for you. The CIA's in Al Rattaf. They're your ticket out of Yemen. In the morning, when the light's good and I'm long gone, raise your hands and pay them a visit. And don't hold *anything* back from then."

"No can do," Claudia said. "That man you killed in the village? That *huge* man? He never goes anywhere without a lieutenant who would like nothing better than to put me up against The Wall."

"Sloping forehead? Watery eyes?"

"How'd you know?" Claudia asked.

"We've met." Kenyon took a long glance at the soldiers far below them, then up toward the escarpment, then at some distant point to the south. "Where I'm headed requires crossing two mountains and three wadis, one of which has the steepest canyon in North Yemen. And that means crossing sideways, not following the wadis."

"Lead on."

"Your story's with the Madhi, not local bandits. . . . Once I get to Nuri's, what will I do with you?"

"Whose?"

"A friend. A *Jebeli.*"

"A what?"

"A mountain tribesman." Kenyon gave Claudia one of the hardest looks she'd ever seen. "If you blunder into any cobras or puff adders, if you forget to check your sandals in the morning and step on a scorpion, I swear to God, I'll leave you. I only have four days."

Claudia looked as disinterested as possible. "Look," she said, "I survived Laos, Afghanistan, and Uganda without your help, so don't be too disappointed if I actually survive this, too."

And they stayed half a mile above the wadi floor, crouched together under the shelter of two black boulders, while helicopters streaked above them and soldiers searched the canyon walls. They hid until the sun dropped past the mountain tips to the west, then the foothills and the Tihama, then settled into the Red Sea like a bobber being pulled under. They waited until the last streaks of red had vanished from the sky, then he took her hand and, more gently and carefully than she would have thought possible, pulled her to her feet and led her into the darkness.

XIII.

Riyadh, Saudi Arabia—April 26, 1981

A Bach sonata drifted down from the platform, through the palm trees and marble columns, past the art deco furniture and railings, past the Renaissance statuary, and out into the desert. The music had been Mendelssohn's Trio in D minor until Talāl informed his brother, Ja'far, of the composer's Jewish ancestry. Since no one else at the party was familiar with classical music, Ja'far was spared humiliation. Still, the musicians would be on a morning plane leaving Saudi Arabia. . . .

The stench of cigarette smoke, alcohol, perfume, and gossip was constant as Talāl moved from one cluster of chiffon gowns and evening jackets to the next. Butlers prowled the veranda looking for open hands to fill with martinis and Scotch—all in a country where alcohol was illegal and women were required to wear the veil. At least common women. When Talāl could stand the vulgarity no longer, he approached Ja'far, turned his back on a proffered brandy, and handed his brother a piece of parchment. The Arabic script read:

A WARNING FROM THE MADHI TO THE PEOPLE OF SAUDI ARABIA

The Prophet said, "While in the world I practiced two virtues, poverty and Holy War. Those who love me will follow these virtues."

Listen to His words, unbelievers! Allah has given to me, His Madhi, the sword of righteousness, and made it known to me that none of either race, human or *jinn,* can conquer the one who possesses it. He has named His sword Plague.

Allah brought me the sword in a vision and said, "To those who follow my words will be blessing and a spot in Paradise. but for those who doubt will be a taste of Hell on earth, the pain from which there is no escape."

On the Twenty-sixth of April at the King's Camel Race, the Sword of Righteousness will fall on the necks of those who follow iniquity, those who have given up the path of Allah for the path of the world, the House of Saud. Many will start the race. Six will not finish. See, those with eyes. Those who are blind will stumble into the torment of plague; those taken up with things of the passing life will inherit eternal fire.

Allah's miracles are His word.

My Companions being first in this world will be first in the world to come. There is no God but Allah. He is great. Amen.

Mohammed al Madhi al Muntazar

Ja'far finished reading the proclamation, looked up at Talāl, blinked, and blinked again. "Where did you find this?" he asked. The corner of his mouth twitched.

Talāl stroked his beard into a *V*, then rubbed his nose. "The wall of King Faisal's own hospital. I thought you'd appreciate the irony. It's as though the Madhi were saying 'Here, I give you the plague, now see if your Western ways can cure it.' "

"You don't believe this metaphysical nonsense?" Ja'far asked. His hand trembled so badly the ice cubes clicked against the side of his cocktail glass.

Talāl shrugged. "I appreciate style. Not only does he predict what Allah will do, but also when and where he will do it."

Ja'far called for a butler, selected a Chivas Regal from a tray, and emptied the glass in a swallow. His nervous smile disappeared with the drink. He leaned over to Talāl and whispered, "Such a disease exists, or so the American intelligence told the king." He looked straight into Talāl's eyes. "Can there be anything to it?"

"To what?"

"To this!" Ja'far slapped the proclamation as he handed it back to Talāl. "Thousands have been posted all over the country. All over the Middle East! The roads are clogged with thousands of commoners coming to the race. Three times normal! They must expect something!"

"Then you should ask them."

Ja'far leaned even closer and held the sleeve of Talāl's *thobe.* "All that time you were away, did you see anything . . . strange?" he whispered.

Talāl drew back and pulled his *thobe* from Ja'far's hand. "You still can't say 'When Talāl wore the Sufi robe.' "

Ja'far shrugged and ignored the question. "I'm asking you if you experienced anything in Punjab that would support this proclamation," Ja'far said flatly.

"If I had, I would never have left," Talāl said. "I heard talk of miracles, levitation, rooms suddenly filling with angelic choirs. . . ."

"Then you don't believe this plague business."

"While I was away I heard talk of an illness, but when isn't there talk?" Talāl placed an arm around Ja'far's shoulder and pulled him close. "You are riding in the race."

Ja'far shrugged. "Perhaps I won't."

"You would stay out because of some papers and a rumor?" Talāl asked. "Enough heads fell after the takeover of the Sacred Mosque to guarantee this Madhi will have a hard time finding converts in Saudi Arabia. And what of the camel you bought? The *omaniya* that has everyone talking?"

"Endanger myself for a trifling purse? A truck I'll give to a servant? A baroque gold dagger?"

"No," Talāl said. "Because you are a Prince of Saud. How could you keep all this without ritual and ceremony?" Talāl turned and with a sweep of his arm included Ja'far's fifty-room villa, his private golf course, landing strip, swimming pool, tennis courts, garages filled with Maseratis and Rolls-Royces.

. . . "How long could you drink this?" Talāl tapped Ja'far's glass. The ice cubes rattled. "Or go whoring in London and Cairo? Drop tradition and the people will expect you to live as you have them live."

"Still sermonizing."

Talāl smiled.

"Keep it," Ja'far said. "Can this Madhi call down the Wrath of Allah?"

"Twelve years of waiting taught me Allah doesn't trouble himself with the affairs of his creatures." Talāl took a step back, removed his hand from Ja'far's shoulder, and put it inside his own *thobe*. "Ride your camel. Win your dagger." Talāl held the microwave transmitter under his *thobe,* pointed it at Ja'far, and pushed the button that activated it. "I give you my word no god will keep you from finishing your race." Talāl laughed the suggestion off, then, after thirty seconds, turned off the transmitter. Beads of sweat had formed on Ja'far's forehead; he started to sway, looked down at his glass, blinked, and looked down at his glass again. He shook his head.

"This," Talāl said, taking the glass from Ja'far's hand and holding it in front of his face, "this is your plague."

There. It was done. The hardest of the six. If Talāl could kill his brother, he could kill anyone. But it was becoming a matter of timing. To have all six fall within minutes, the vectors inside them must be activated within minutes. He helped Ja'far find a chair (his temperature would return to normal in minutes), then began to circulate.

Most of the faces at the party were familiar, but all of them had traded traditional clothing for cummerbunds and décolletés. Even in the short time Talāl had been gone from Riyadh, things had changed. Streets were more cluttered with cars, the air more filled with planes, and the skeletons of new, sky-tall Western buildings taxed the patience of even the ground on which they stood. Everywhere were the sounds: sudden horns, the scrape of earth movers, the ghastly thump of jackhammers—sounds that could trigger his epilepsy.

Talāl bumped into a woman wearing a purple dress that

matched her eye shadow, lipstick, and earrings. Her bosom was magnificent, perfect conical breasts, and her thigh showed through a slit in her gown. She wobbled, stared into his eyes, and held out a champagne glass invitingly.

"Whore," Talāl said. He held her stare until her eyes dropped and she stumbled away. She was a bored woman. A lonely woman, rootless, cut adrift from tradition by her Western ways. Soon she would trade her drink for a child at her breast, her obscene clothing for a veil—her faith would take root and thrive in the Madhi's miracles.

Talāl continued to search for his cousins through the tuxes and gold baubles. Ja'far's suffering, the suffering of his five cousins Mansūr, Husein, Isā, Zeid, and Hasan, would be a small price. . . .

Only two men in the room wore the traditional *thobe,* no women the veil. Hasan and Isā sat in a crowded corner, gesticulating wildly and discussing the virtues of supply-side economics. Talāl held the microwave transmitter firmly as he approached them. He bumped into a butler with a tray of drinks, took one, spit in it, and threw it in the butler's face. Then he sat down across from his cousins and mentioned the advantages of gold as a hedge against inflation.

Imagine camels from all over the Middle East: black *omaniyas* from the Hadramawt; white *Shammars* from the Royal Herd; dun-colored *huteimayas* from the desert hills of Sinai. Imagine two thousand rainbow-attired men perched sun-high in their *haulinis.* Then imagine a sickly, lonely eight-year-old wandering among the shaggy legs and swinging tails while attendants who would have loved to swat him away said welcome to Prince Talāl and bowed till their turbans fell off. Now all that remained of the King's Camel Race of Talāl's youth were stinking beasts and sweating men.

Talāl walked from the white desert sunlight into the shade of a camel-hair tent the Royal Family used on such ceremonial occasions. It had been years since he'd smelled the animal sweat trapped forever in the walls and marveled that so simple a structure could so effectively block the sun. Why should there be surprise? Bedouin tents had kept Arabs alive for thousands of years, even in desert furnaces like the Rub al Khali. Just because Talāl lost his magic, why should traditional things lose theirs?

Talāl removed his binoculars from their case and surveyed the length of the race course. Timing was everything. Even now the chosen riders should feel ill, but would their pride, their tradition, keep them from dismounting and calling one of the doctors who sat idly by? They must fall in the race, not in the privacy of a hospital room. Spectacle was everything!

He looked to the point where the white sand met the sky. Thousands of Toyotas, Fords, and Datsuns were scattered across a makeshift parking lot. But there were many camels, too, and many black tents huddled amid the travel homes. In fact, there were more faithful at this race than at any since *only* the faithful were allowed to attend.

A trumpet blared. Camels and riders gathered into an enormous cluster. It blared again to give spectators a chance to clear the race course. A whisper of excitement was multiplied by fifty thousand and grew loud as a gale. There were rich and poor, young and old, from every country in the Middle East. There would be no stopping the news of the Madhi's miracles after today.

The crowd quieted. All that could be heard were the squeals and grunts of three thousand camels—then an explosion of color, noise, and movement as the camels surged forward and spread into a line a quarter mile across. The clownish heads and necks were fully outstretched, the single braided *khitamas* drooped down from the animals' mouths then rose up to the riders' hands, and there were the bobbing humps, always the hulking backs bouncing out of rhythm with the rest of the body. No matter how fast a camel ran, it always looked as though it were in slow motion, that its legs would tangle and it would fall over itself.

But they never did.

As the camels passed the halfway point, Talāl wondered if the plague would ever take effect, and the crowd's cheering grew louder, because now only fifty camels were in a position to win, and as the camels drew closer, he could *feel* the pounding of the hooves even if the crowd noise was too loud to let him hear them, and the race was two-thirds complete and nothing had happened, and then only twenty could win and the crowd grew louder and louder and the shouts turned to screams. . . .

. . . and then it was quiet but for camel sounds.

And Talāl saw why.

A riderless camel, then a second and a third, fell into a trot and dropped to the back of the race. Other camels bumped into each other, veered and stumbled as they tried to avoid trampling the white bundles of cloth that lay in their path. And in the silence, dust, and heat, only one of the camels could possibly win now, and there were a thousand yards, then eight hundred to go, and the white shape on Ja'far's black *omaniya* leaned and wobbled, and the *khitama* dropped from his hand, and the camel's head relaxed as her stride faltered, and Ja'far's robed arms extended full as he rolled back over the camel's hump and hit the ground with a thud that would have been audible if it weren't for the pounding hooves.

Then all the camels crossed the finish line. Except six. But the crowd didn't cheer the winner as happened every other year; the people didn't even run toward the finish line. Instead, a wave of people broke for the center of the course where six men lay writhing in the sand.

And though members of the Saudi National Guard formed circles around the fallen princes, though they lowered their guns and threatened to shoot the approaching crowd, they didn't shoot, of course, because what chance did a hundred guns stand against tens of thousands, so the sick princes were swallowed by the crowd. A whisper moved through the mass like a hot wind.

Plague.

And hundreds were trampled as they ran, and there were cries and shouts, then a sudden silence. Panic stopped when the people realized there could be no running from the Wrath of Allah. First one man, then a hundred, then thousands fell to their knees and, though they'd been called to afternoon prayer only two hours before, stretched into a position of full salaam again. And one voice became all voices, "Allah-o-Akbar!"

God is great!

And surely, Talāl thought, brushing the sand from his eyes and mouth, surely he is.

The plague stench gave even the hospital room's cheerful blue walls, canary tile, and white bedding a macabre cast. Though Talāl was prepared for the smell, he had to fight his nausea down. No preparation could dull the shock of experiencing total decay.

Ja'far was alive but a pasty gray. The sores on his face had burst and festered; the bed was soaked with sweat. He had been vomiting for more than an hour, but the plague stench smothered the smell of vomit. Suddenly, Talāl understood why medieval people wore dead toads and snakes as amulets, drank mercury or their own urine as preventatives: anything was preferable to this. It was a disease lifted from the pit of hell itself.

Talāl sat in a bedside chair and read the chart hanging from the bedframe: "Chloramphenicol 500 mg q 3 h IV"; then a time, 2:48 P.M., and the doctor's signature. Good. They'd administered antibiotics, which would trigger the superpromoter; the length of Ja'far's suffering would be shortened by two-thirds. There was a lovely irony: With all the expensive doctors in the King Faisal Medical City, with all the famous scientists on call, only Talāl, who knew so little, knew Ja'far wouldn't be alive to receive his 5:48 P.M. shot.

Maybe Talāl should have felt guilt.

He had expected it, but all that was present was giddiness, that childhood light-headedness that came from being naughty without getting caught. The last time Talāl felt this flighty, Ja'far and he had collected three jars of spiders and released them in the room of a tutor who was terrified of spiders. Then wedged a chair beneath the doorknob . . . then listened and laughed as the shrieks turned to whimpers. Just as that shared evil drew Talāl and Ja'far close together years before, so this evil drew them together again.

The doctors knew nothing. Nor did the Secret Police. Talāl attended the interrogation of Ja'far's attendant. Yes, the attendant said, Ja'far fell sick before the race. Yes, his chill was so strong his teeth chattered and the *khitama* shook in his hand. Yes, he wanted to dismount, but tradition demanded he run the race, and pride kept him in the *haulini.* Then the attendant's story ended, so Talāl's imagination filled in the details of the rest of the race: how Ja'far grew weaker with each stride; how he finally slumped over the camel's hump; and how, when the first convulsions hit, his arms flew straight up (the crowd interpreted it as a belated prayer) before he became unconscious and fell.

Others saw more.

A mendicant from the hills by the Dead Sea watched the Angel of Death materialize and tap each prince on the shoulder. An ascetic from Mecca saw pestilence descend in the form of a beautiful woman who gave each victim a veil. Already the new prophets fell in line to be immortalized.

The room filled with wheezing.

Talāl lifted Ja'far's wrist and took his pulse; shallow, palpitating, unbelievably erratic, it felt more like a sparrow's wings than a human heartbeat. The hand was so hot, Talāl could scarcely stand to hold it. Bones and veins showed through the skin.

Then Talāl's heart fluttered. Control, he thought. Corbin said that technically there is no disease, only toxin. You are safe. Safe. He regulated his breathing and practiced one of the low-level contemplative exercises he'd practiced for so many years in the prayer cell. His thoughts calmed. Ja'far's death would reap immeasurable fruit. It would provide a guidepost for believers, answer innumerable questions.

Talāl removed the top sheet. There was a fist-sized bubo in Ja'far's neck, a sickly blue lump with a black circle around it. There were larger swellings under his arms. When Talāl touched one, Ja'far winced and opened his eyes.

"Who?" Ja'far asked weakly. When he hiccuped, Talāl had to turn his head from the stench. "Talāl?" Ja'far asked.

"Yes."

"Kill me," Ja'far wheezed. He went into convulsions, and his body arched up from the mattress. Talāl stroked his brother's hand until the spasms stopped. He studied the clenched fists, the grinding teeth, the way the neck ligaments stretched until they looked as though they'd snap. Not beautiful, but educational. If Talāl couldn't watch this single death, how could he watch the hundreds, thousands that would follow?

When the convulsions eased, Talāl whispered, "Sleep. No talk of death now." He held up the chart and tapped it. "Antibiotics. The fever should begin to stabilize."

Ja'far breathed evenly for a few minutes, then gasped, "Worms, fat tomb worms." He moved his hand as though he were trying to shake something from it.

"Only visions," Talāl said. "Fever visions."

Again Ja'far's breathing evened. "I saw fires in the desert."

"After you fell, the crowd prayed," Talāl said. "Then they attacked every sign of the West. Trucks, cars, foreigners, loudspeakers . . ." He began to stroke Ja'far's forehead and was careful to avoid soiling his hands on the open sores. Ja'far choked. Black spittle flecked with blood appeared on the sheets. "Rest," Talāl said.

Ja'far's hand contracted around Talāl's. There was so little strength left. Talāl glanced toward the window and watched white sunlight filter through the curtains and slide across the floor. He put his hand in the light. The air conditioning made even the desert sun seem cool and impotent.

But not for long.

The spasms started again. Talāl pushed the alarm button as Ja'far twitched, jerked, and screamed . . . a thick red fluid drooled from the corner of his mouth. It was beautiful in a way, beautiful like the red of the deepest sunset or the cactus flowers that bloomed after a shower. Then the sheets blackened with urine, the neck bubo burst, and the stench became unbearable. . . . Talāl could taste it when he breathed through his mouth.

A doctor told Talāl to leave the room as nurses pulled curtains around the bed. Each of the doctors' commands, each of the suggestions carried a new tone: doubt. What good was technology against the Wrath of Allah?

Allah's Wrath was red, the red of Ja'far's drool, the red of arterial blood. And this death, this and the others, would start a red wave to wash over the Middle East and cleanse it of impurities. One more prophecy, one more public demonstration, and all Saudi Arabia would be at Talāl's feet.

As he walked from the antiseptic corridor into the pine-scented lobby, Talāl wasn't sure how long it would take for the news of his miracle to spread, or how many of the faithful would join his ranks. What he did know was that it was time to post a new prophecy, a more daring prophecy, one directed at that chief tool of the West, King Khalid.

The plague would strike in the Heart of Islam.

Mecca.

XIV.

The Yemeni Highlands—April 30, 1981

Paul watched her in the gray light to see if she was awake. Claudia shivered and reached out for him. She must have been asleep; otherwise, she wouldn't touch him no matter how cold it grew. It hadn't frosted that night—quite—but her old *'aba* wasn't much protection against a thick Highland mist and temperatures in the forties. They'd camped in the warmest spot he could find, the head of a wadi where bushes stopped the night winds and sandstone basins held the sun's warmth, but any night in the Highlands was a cold night. Period. At least it would be their last night on the trail. They'd reach Nuri's by dusk, and that meant an evening of feasts, fires, and bragging.

Claudia shivered again.

He could start a fire; it would keep her warm, and since it wasn't dark, the flame wouldn't be seen by helicopters. But there was an advantage to just lying there: he had warmth to spare. He moved tight against her. She curled, tucked her feet under her *'aba,* and they lay together like spoons.

Even in the chill, the smell of dirt and stale sweat rose from her hair. She'd never admit to such an odor once she left Yemen, but it complemented her. Paul rested a hand on her hip—it would have been nice to touch her skin, to find out if she could possibly be as soft as she felt through the coarse cloth, but that wouldn't do. He gave his hand a mental slap just as she took it and tucked it in the hollow under her chin.

"Cold?" he whispered.

No response, unlike the first two days. Bitch, bitch, bitch: How far *is* it to this Nuri's? You left the water in the cavern?

When's chow? She said *chow* as though she were saying good-bye to Marcello Mastroianni from the steps of the Uffizi.

So Paul quit the explanations and started the lessons. He led her to a sulfurous trickle of water instead of the mountain stream that ran a quarter-mile away and, instead of the roasted rabbit he planned for dinner, the entree was chameleon garnished with dry roots.

"I'll pass," Claudia Mallory had said, nose skyward. She passed, that is, until halfway through the next day's hike when she began to daintily strip bits of flesh from the lizard's flank and tail. Then a surprise: She had no problem keeping it down. It gave away her secret.

Claudia Mallory did what she had to do; she could adapt. During the second day, she pointed to a snake lying in the tallis slopes. After Paul told her it was a cobra, she began to ask *the* pertinent questions about flora and fauna: What can you bite without its biting back? She helped him gather roots for that night's meal with an amazing eye for detail. It wasn't everyone who could distinguish snake bulb from baboon root after a single day. By day three, she had killed a puff adder that hid by a boulder where she napped and, when Paul threatened to prepare it for dinner, helped him set a snare. They had shish kebab that night, rabbit interspersed with *khubz al ubaq* (she said it tasted like rampion) and wild onions. When he brought her *la'dh* fruit for dessert, she promoted him from Kenyon to Paul.

And the bitching stopped.

The air dropped fresh and cold from the ridges and whistled as it glided past on its way toward the Tihama. Claudia moved. Though Johara had been dead less than three weeks, when the new, improved version of Claudia Mallory snuggled against Paul, he became aroused—a betrayal. He rolled onto his back.

Claudia touched his shoulder, the back of his neck, and nestled in the warmth of his beard.

"Cold?" Paul asked defensively.

"I might as well be naked for the good this robe's doing me." A shiver started in her shoulders and wormed through her whole body. She rolled onto her side and faced him. "Why is it I boil in the Tihama and freeze in the Highlands?"

"Blame it on the Red Sea's humidity and a seven-thousand-foot climb. Everyone else does." Paul looked up. The sun wasn't high enough to burn through the mist, so the peaks vanished, then reappeared, then vanished as the fog moved up and down with the changing temperatures.

"Ever sleep?" Claudia asked.

"Whenever I start acting human, the people I'm close to die," Paul said.

"I suppose you won't explain that."

He dug a twig into the earth and twisted until it snapped. "There's no such thing as an off-the-record statement to a reporter."

Claudia raised her eyebrows and rested her chin on her palm. She traced her cheekbone with her index finger, cocked her head to the right, and said, "Want to start this relationship over?"

"It's an idea," Paul said.

Claudia sat up, nodded, stiffened, and offered him a hand. Then *the smile.* She could turn charm off and on like a faucet. "Claudia Mallory here. Friends call me Claudia or Claude—never 'you,' which is the best I've heard from Paul Kenyon, originally 'Kenyon,' of late 'Paul,' since I've known him."

"I'm Paul Kenyon." He stared directly into her eyes. "And I don't have many friends left."

She waited a full thirty seconds before she said, "Always the strong, silent type."

"I never had a drawing room to learn small talk in."

"Since when is the plague small talk?"

"Stop it, Claudia," he said. She stopped. Paul nodded his thanks, then began to search through the roots they'd collected the previous evening. "*Basla al hanash* all right for breakfast?"

"I never asked what that meant."

"Snake bulb," Paul said.

Claudia's shoulders and back squirmed. "There *anything* else?"

"Baboon root and the shum-shum lily."

"One vote for the lily," she said.

Paul sorted through the roots and tried to find some tender enough to chew without boiling. He handed Claudia three, then put the rest into his pants pocket.

"You haven't once, in the past week, wondered about my past?" Claudia asked.

"Of course," Paul said as he started to stand and walk away, knowing that would be more than enough of an invitation to start her chattering. And the chatter might be bait in a trap.

"Then don't be in such a hurry," she said. She took his hand and pulled him back down. "I was born with the proverbial spoon in my mouth. Private schools. Debuts. That Saigon assignment came after six months on the job. Your average reporter would have waited a lifetime for it."

"That's America," Paul said.

Claudia drew back and frowned. "Look, privilege stops at the borders of Third World countries, and that's where I go when I have the choice."

"How about this assignment?" Paul asked.

She looked rather sheepishly at him. "We were given this one. They gave us a few days for research, then our visas, and we were on our way."

"We?"

"Rick, my photographer. We were together since late seventy-seven." Claudia's voice trailed off. "We did pretty well together." She brushed dirt from a root, bit into it, and mouthed more than chewed it.

"Past tense?" Paul asked.

She turned away from him, strummed her fingers on the sandstone, and said, "Government troops gunned him down." She took a deep breath. "A mosque outside Tai'zz. Pancho set up the meeting, but he didn't mention anything about an ambush."

"I can figure out why you'd want to see the rebels," Paul said. "But why would they want you?"

Claudia inhaled. "Shit, I don't know." She exhaled in a sigh.

"Like hell, I don't. The Madhi wants his miracles advertised in the outside world."

"With Allah as a playmate, you'd think that would be the least of his problems," Paul said.

"You'd think."

"He goes to the trouble of kidnapping you, then, instead of taking you straight to his fortress, he risks your life with a sight-seeing tour. Seems a bit contrived."

"So it seems," Claudia said.

Paul leaned back on his hands and stared into the mists. They continued to swirl and blend like living, breathing cotton candy. They were amazing. During the dry months, the fog-drip supplied all the moisture in the country. Sometimes the dew in Al Rattaf was so heavy, he thought a night storm had passed through. Al Rattaf . . . a place he'd like to get off his mind. "The photographer? Were you close to him?" Paul asked.

She didn't answer, which was all the answer he needed.

"Guilt?" Paul asked.

Suddenly, Claudia's hackles were back up. "Which must be something you're pretty damn familiar with," she snapped. Her voice softened. "Sorry," she said. "Mind if I rewind and erase that?"

"No need," Paul said. "Guilt's my second nature. Some whys: The Bedouin I married wasn't a woman—always—she was sixteen. I forced her father and the religious leaders into it. The plague struck the next day." Paul rubbed his forehead with his knuckles. "The suffering was unbelievable, and whatever I did only made things worse." Then he stared at Claudia till she looked away. His voice turned cold. "I killed her when symptoms appeared."

At that, Claudia looked back at him and wouldn't turn away.

"And yes," Paul said. "Yes, I loved her."

Claudia shut her eyes and turned her head. "My turn," she said. "Rick wasn't supposed to go to the mosque. I'm not even sure he wanted to go. But he did everything I wanted. Eventually." By speaking slowly, evenly, she kept her voice under control. "The last time I saw him he was down, writhing, and the bullets kicked up so much dust around him I couldn't tell who he was." She paused. "Or *if* he was."

"Never is pretty," Paul said.

"You have a real flair for understatement." Claudia sat back on her elbows, looked into the mist and, after a few moments, began to shiver again. "You know any magic to keep a woman from freezing to death?" she asked.

"Ever eat locusts?"

"Jesus," she said, shaking her head, "have you *no* gastrointestinal pride?"

"Locusts aren't bad when you get past their crunch," Paul said. "Sometimes that takes awhile. The Yemenis call them *jarād* when they're roasted and dried in the sun. String them, wear them like a bracelet, and you can pick them off and eat them as you walk."

"What I need is an explanation of why eating locusts will keep me warm, not a lecture on entomology and local custom."

"When you're cold," Paul said, "the locusts are cold, too. Being warm-blooded gives you a huge advantage. You can move fast to warm up while they have to wait until it warms up to move fast. So as you run from bush to bush picking off cold locusts, not only will you supply us with a high protein supplement, but you will keep warm without wasting my time."

"So I collect locusts," Claudia said. She turned and walked away. When she reached the first saltbush and searched through its foliage, she turned back to him and shouted, "You really enjoyed that, didn't you!"

Paul didn't answer, but he waited until she disappeared into the undergrowth and fog before he started to smile.

The "Little Rains" were a little late. And a little early. They were a little late because they should have started in March instead of late April, and a little early because they should have appeared in the late afternoon instead of the morning. Paul heard their deep rumbling in the northeast long before thunderheads swallowed the peaks. He rose from a squat, approached Claudia, and offered her a hand up. "Time to move," he said.

"A tad early, isn't it?" Claudia asked. She pointed to the sky. "The daylight? The helicopters?"

"Ten minutes and there won't even be buzzards flying. Unless we get about a hundred feet above the canyon floor, we'll be backstroking down to Al Rattaf." Paul knelt above the ashes from the dead fire. "Mind if I borrow a piece of your *'aba?*" he asked.

"As long as you behave yourself," she said. He did, and she didn't seem pleased about it.

He cut a small circle from her sleeve, gathered it into a pouch, put some ashes in it, and tied it shut. He stood and led her out of the wadi. Before they cleared the brush, he clipped some branches from the saltbushes and added them to the ashes. Then they climbed over the loose rock and boulders until they reached a myrrh tree a hundred feet above the wadi. They sat under it.

"Mother told me to avoid trees during thunderstorms," Claudia said.

Paul cut several incisions in the myrrh tree's bark and began collecting resin. " 'Mother' was never in a wadi during the 'Little Rains,' " he said, mixing saltbush and ashes with the resin.

She pointed to the mixture and sniffed. "Pungent stuff!"

"A surprise," Paul said, knowing it would be nothing like the surprise she'd get when the storm rolled down from the peaks. The clouds looked like black mushrooms, and four seconds after lightning danced along the ridge across from them, thunder bellowed and splintered. Then rain broke over the ridge, swept across the canyon, and when it hit, it was as though someone snapped a water main above the wadi. The myrrh tree wasn't much protection; it didn't keep them dry, but it kept the rain from stinging. The tree bent, twisted, and groaned with the gusts spinning around the canyon, but it had been through it before and held fast to the rock slope. Paul turned toward Claudia. For a change she didn't say a word, just watched with her head back and her mouth open. There weren't many things that could match a Highland thunderstorm, particularly your first one.

Then there was a different roaring as the wadi filled with brown water. It rose quickly, surged beyond its banks, raced through the basins and trees where Claudia and Paul had camped, and covered the undergrowth.

It was over in a half-hour. The clouds moved off to the southwest, the winds soothed, and when the peaks reappeared, they were covered with white hail. The dust coating was swept away, and everything glistened.

"Whew!" Claudia whistled.

"That pretty much sums things up," Paul said.

"Is this spring cleaning?" she asked.

"Just wait."

They did. Within two hours, less, the water began to recede, and the canyon greened. All the stench, all the filth and carcasses had washed miles away and were settling to the bottom of the Red Sea. As the water eased back into the wadi, the basins in the canyon floor became pools.

Claudia's eyes grew. "Water!" she said. "Real, honest-to-God fresh water!"

Paul nodded.

"No bilharziasis flukes?" she asked.

"The water will evaporate before they arrive."

Claudia stood and prepared to climb down the slope. Paul took her wrist. "There *are* still helicopters, however," he said.

"Helicopters?" she said. "My first bath in a month is waiting down there, and you say helicopters!" She began to pull away.

"You'd better take this," he said. He handed her the pouch. "It's potash. The natives call it *dulūk.* It's been the closest thing to soap they've had for a thousand years."

She took the pouch, smiled, looked at him with eyes that indicated she thought she knew more than she really did, then crawled down the canyon wall.

Bits of clothing marked her descent—she was naked long before she reached the first pool. She selected a large pool, put the *dulūk* on shore, and slid into the water, just like the otters Paul had seen as a child. She splashed and went under, surfaced and splashed some more, then turned over and floated on her back. If she'd found some mussels, cracked them open with a rock, and eaten them while backstroking, it wouldn't have surprised him. Then Claudia splashed and disappeared.

With everything smelling so fresh, Paul realized he didn't. Which wouldn't do. So he stepped slowly, quietly down the slope to a pool guarded by a pile of huge boulders. He couldn't see Claudia from there. Or hear her splashing. Or squeals.

The water was cool. More than cool, *cold.* Cairo was the locale of his last fresh-water bath, and that was six months ago. The chill was so foreign, it felt more like iced satin than liquid . . . and cleaned about as well. It only hardened the dirt and grease. Instead of being covered by a thin film, he scrubbed the grime into thick swirls. Hell with it. He ducked underwater and opened his eyes—it had been years since he opened his eyes underwater without having them sting of salt. Other mountain streams came to mind. Other times. He ran out of oxygen, popped sputtering to the surface, and shook the water from his eyes and ears. Gradually, things came into focus.

Claudia sat by the pool.

Naked.

There was a huge I-told-you-so grin on her face. "You're one-hundred percent made in America," she said. "Maybe more." She tossed the pouch up in the air and caught it.

Wet hair the red-brown color of the cliffs was matted to her shoulders and back. Even at twenty feet, she smelled of myrrh. Her body was ivory except for a scattering of freckles, her pink nipples, the auburn hair between her legs, and the sunburn on her hands, face, and feet . . . and she was soft and nonchalant and full of life in a way he could never be. Paul closed his eyes and tried to shake Johara's image from his mind.

Claudia waded into the water, stopped an arm's length from him, and her smile melted into a gaze. "I'm not sixteen, and you'd be kind to say I've been recycled, but I'm here and this is beautiful and I have this peculiar interest in you." She handed him the pouch and traced a finger along the scar by his sternum.

Paul took her hand, kissed her index finger, then moved a step back. "Sorry," he said. "No can do."

"Not only *can* you do, you'd *like* to do."

"Please, not now."

Her lips curled into a pout, she put her hands on her hips, and cocked her head to the right. "Which mourning practices are you following? Christian or Muslim?"

"My own and they're not over yet." He pointed to the edge of the pool. He waited until she was on land before he said, "Here's some why.

"I grew up in the mountains and went to a high school with one teacher for all four years. I was the only one in my class to go to college. It took about two years to give up on that nonsense. I enlisted. I'd spent my whole life hunting, trapping, stalking, all the things the army wanted. You noticed the way I moved. So did they. They sent me to Special Forces school in Panama. Then Nam. I was twenty."

Claudia yawned.

Paul stopped talking.

"Sorry," she said. "I'm a TV brat . . . short attention span."

"How do you think I got the scar?" Paul asked, pointing at his chest.

"Shrapnel," she said. "A VC grenade."

"*Nada.* A present from an American."

"Intentional?"

"As can be," Paul said. "He lobbed an M-79 round into a tree where one of my tribesmen said I'd bivouacked. He was wrong by one tree."

"Tribesmen?" Claudia asked.

"Montagnards. Five hundred worked for me at one time or another."

"Why the American? Cheat him at cards?"

"Patience," Paul said, "I'm getting there." He dropped down to his neck in the water. "I didn't stay in the Green Berets long. I had this way of surviving when no one else did. Eyesight's tits on a boar in the bush. The jungle's a tent made of one-way mirrors. Charlie sees in but you don't see out. But I listened. I made no noise. Pretty soon the mirrors reversed."

"You're wandering, Paul," Claudia said.

"Others adapted, too. After Tet, when the body counts started to drop and Marines got stuck in Khe Sanh, the CIA gathered a dozen of us together, gave us carte blanche, then turned us loose in the Central Highlands to live with the Montagnards."

"So?"

"Ever hear of Captain Spooky?"

"No, thanks."

"If he hadn't given his bounty money away, he'd be a rich man," Paul said.

Claudia obviously was growing impatient. "How does all this affect us?" she asked.

"Taking bounties grew too easy," Paul said. "Someone upped the stakes. The others who adapted started going after each other. Things got messy." Paul touched the purple scar. "The guy who gave me this wasn't even good, just lucky. He hadn't even earned his label yet."

"Label?"

"A nickname. A title awarded by the grunts in the bunkers. Only the best got them. I was Captain Spooky. The main competition was Piece-of-My-Heart."

"I always had a weakness for Janis Joplin," Claudia said.

"He had a weakness for human hearts . . . and a special way of killing: a piano-wire garrote. It is useless at more than an arm's length, which gives you an idea how good he was. It was more than a garrote in his hands. It didn't merely strangle, it decapitated."

"Sounds charming."

"I saw him in Al Rattaf. The competition is still on."

Claudia shrugged. "So? You're Superman. He'll never find you. And if he did . . . look what you did to Mickey Rat."

"He isn't Mickey Rat. He'll find me. He's *that* good."

"No one could follow our trail," Claudia said.

"No one else. Maybe if I was alone . . . ? Shit, I'm not even sure of that anymore." Paul turned from her and looked up at the cliffs. "Here's the crux: There have been only two women in my life with faces and names, and both are dead—because of what I am and what it's made me. And because they softened me just enough to get themselves killed."

"If that implies I'm number three, I'm flattered."

"You're not 'you' anymore, you're Claudia." He looked back to her. "And you're beautiful. If this were New York, you wouldn't even look at me." Paul waited for her to say something, maybe even contradict him, but she remained silent. So he turned from her, scooped out a handful of *dulūk,* rubbed it in to his face and beard, and bathed.

Claudia waded out to him.

"I like the way you move," she said. Paul tried to speak, but she covered his mouth with her hand. It tasted of myrrh. "Besides," she said, "only a monkey can wash between his shoulder blades." She took the pouch from him, asked him to turn around, and with brisk, impersonal strokes, began to scrub his back.

"What's this Nuri like?" Claudia asked as they walked along a ridge of sharp volcanic shard and prepared to descend to a path.

Paul had put off the inevitable discussion far too long—at least she'd provided him with a starting point. "Nuri's the real thing," Paul said. "You two should really hit it off."

"How so?"

"Ever wear a veil?" Paul asked.

"*No!*" she said.

"We'll be his guests. That has special meaning in Yemen."

"It means misogyny," Claudia said.

"From the moment we step inside his walls, we jeopardize his tribe. Yet his hospitality will be endless. We can't offend him."

"The *we* meaning *me,*" Claudia said.

"You weren't asked to come." Paul thought it was an excellent point, but for some reason she didn't look guilty. Strike one. Time to retreat and regroup. He climbed a huge boulder and looked to the south for Al Asil, Nuri's village. A single ridge blocked the view. And the sky . . . All that remained of the storm were frayed bits of clouds, which swept over the mountains on their way to the Red Sea, then Ethiopia. The winds followed the surest escape route. It was tempting to join them. The sun broke from behind a cloud, and Paul had to shield his eyes—it was only a hand's width above the highest peak: two hours till dusk. Fortunately, it was only an hour to Nuri's. Also unfortunately. The veil business had to be attended to. Now. At least he could ease into it. "Speak any Arabic?" Paul asked, moving down off the boulder.

"A smidgen," Claudia said. "I've been in and out of the Middle East enough to learn survival phrases: 'How much you asking?' 'Where's the john?' Tidbits like that."

Paul rubbed his temple. "Why is it you make me think you're holding back?"

She shrugged.

"Nuri doesn't know a word of English," Paul said, "yet I *know* you two won't have any problem communicating."

Claudia stopped in mid-stride. She plopped down on the flat surface of a rock. "The sadism in your voice is hardly reassuring," she said. "If this is going to be round two of the veil thing, let's have at it." She crossed her legs in a lotus position.

Paul squatted across from her and picked up a handful of pebbles. "As a Jebeli chieftain," he said, "Nuri has had more wives than you can count on one hand, yet has never had a serious conversation with any of them. And doesn't want to. God, Claudia, he's light-years past being opinionated. He's . . . he's . . . well, he's Nuri." Paul shifted his weight from his left leg to his right. "The only female faces he's seen belong to children, close relatives, and whores. You're not any of those."

"Thanks on the last one," she said, "but no veil."

"As a woman, you rank a distant third in importance after his male friends and camels."

"Still no veil," she said.

Paul suddenly stood up. "Then we stay here. In the cold. Without a fire. And eat raw snake."

"Why not stamp your foot," Claudia suggested. "Or pound your chest?"

"I won't insult a friend."

Then she changed strategies. It was not fair. Her voice grew soft and her big eyes just slaughtered him. "Aren't I a friend?"

"Jesus, Claudia! If this were the States . . . !"

Her voice acquired a heavy coating of frost. "That means no, I presume." She stared right through him.

"It means yes." Paul caught a sense of pleading in his voice. He tried to erase it. "Here the veil means protection, respect."

"So now it's for my own good!" she said. "Give me your knife!" He handed it to her, not entirely sure whether she'd try to return it to its sheath or a point somewhere below his sixth rib. She knelt, cut a wide strip from the bottom of her *'aba,* and tied it over her nose. "I suffocate, I'll haunt you."

Paul agreed with a nod. Why was the sense of impending doom greater now that he'd won an argument with Claudia then when he'd lost? Even now, veil up to the bridge of her nose, her lower face covered in utter surrender, the spark in her eyes gave serious doubt as to who was in control.

When he offered to help her up, she accepted with a feigned helplessness that was infuriating. They walked over the sharp volcanic shards and, within ten minutes, intersected a path that had been hewn from the mountain a millennium ago. It was a Jebeli path, and there were no switchbacks despite the steep incline. The mountain slopes were terraces—step after step of thin soil carted by hand from the plateaus. With terracing, *dhura* could be grown at eight thousand feet. They topped a final ridge, and across a gorge and up a thousand feet sat Al Asil, which followed the crescent-shaped peak of Jebel Saba. Many of the three- and four-story buildings leaned over the precipice.

When Claudia and Paul were a quarter-mile from the gatehouse, village sounds poured down the path: children laughing, dogs barking, a squawking chicken caught up in the torrent of feet. A wave of boys broke through the gate shouting, dancing, and waving their *jambiyyas* high above their heads.

"They don't take scalps, do they?" Claudia whispered. When the boys recognized Paul, they called out "Al Rish" and surged close, but he held out his hand and they respectfully backed away.

A goatskin drum thumped.

There was a line of men at the fringe of the village: a small line; only half the number that would normally take part in the *moqāb,* the ceremony of welcome. Children scattered into the buildings as the line of men wheeled in a slow, sinuous war dance that followed the drumbeat. The men shouted battle cries and fired their rifles into the air. Nuri stepped out from the line. Paul told Claudia to stay put. He walked toward Nuri and they met halfway and embraced. The storm had done nothing to ease the stench of Nuri's collection of noses.

Paul looked down at the bag. "Soon it will burst," he said in Arabic.

"When I heard your village had died, I sent some rebels to their Paradise with no way to sniff the Madhi's arse," Nuri said. His voice lacked its normal sparkle. He held Paul at arm's length and looked hopefully into his eyes. "The quail?" he asked.

"I buried her," Paul said.

Nuri embraced him again and whispered, "Then we will sacrifice a goat for her. Later. When our weakness won't affect the children." He turned and looked at Claudia. "Or women?" He walked toward her. "Is this a mare in a man's clothes or a gelding in a veil?" he asked, walking tight circles around her.

"She's American," Paul said.

Nuri nodded as though that explained everything.

"She dressed as a rebel to help me escape," Paul said.

"One with fire!" Nuri snorted in Claudia's ear. "The wilder the mare, the better the ride!" he said.

"That one would throw you," Paul said.

"Bah!"

"You've never met Claudia," Paul said.

Nuri tried to pronounce her name. Though he mouthed each syllable carefully, the foreign arrangement of sounds tied his tongue in knots. "Even the name mocks me!" he said. He looked at her hair and the curves that could be seen through the *'aba.* "Refined lines. An exquisite mane! Now she has a new name: *Saqlāwi.*" Nuri laughed and thumped Paul on the shoulder. "Nuri ibn Sha'lan thrown by a *saqlāwi*? Never!" Then he leaned over and whispered, "By the Prophet, I like the lines on this one. Will you sell her?"

Paul would have paid admission to see Claudia and Nuri

square off across the language barrier, but . . . "She's not mine to sell," Paul said.

Nuri gathered his eyebrows and stroked his beard. "She broken?"

"Not by any standards that you'd comprehend."

Nuri pointed his finger toward the village and shouted, "Then we'll give her to my wives! They'll teach this heathen to be a woman for you!" Then Nuri sighed. "Since I can't have the pleasure of breaking her for myself." He took Paul by the arm. "Come."

Nuri's house sat on the highest point in the village, a virtual aerie. As they walked up the rock-cluttered street, two men forced a camel to kneel in an open lot by the cliff. One gave the animal an armful of *dhura* stalks to eat. When the camel lost interest in everything but food, the other man snuck up and brought an ax down between its eyes. Before the camel's death spasms ceased, other men appeared with knives and began the butchery. Children reappeared, ran up to the carcass, and ran back to their homes carrying organs or large chunks of raw flesh high above their heads. The blood drained out of the animal, pooled into crevasses in the rock, then dripped over the cliff. Buzzards appeared. And the flies.

It was fifteen degrees cooler inside. Nuri shouted for a wife, and a small, hunched shadow dressed in an indigo robe and veil came from the woman's quarters, took Claudia by the arm, and led her through the door. Something was wrong. Claudia left without a word.

Nuri called another name, and a taller, stouter figure came through the door. Nuri scolded the woman for not having coffee prepared, then waved her away. Nuri leaned over and whispered, "Wife number four. She's new." He sat back in a cushion and a huge expanse of white teeth appeared through his beard: a smile. "She is as strong as I am . . . almost." Nuri laughed. "That is why she is my favorite!"

When she reentered the room, she carried a stand, a brass coffee pot, and some dried camel dung to serve as fuel for the fire. "A guest! Boil the water three times!" he commanded.

"Have you been boiling all your water since I've been away?" Paul asked.

Nuri shrugged. He pulled up the bottom of his *'aba.* A guinea worm wound halfway around a matchstick protruding from his shin. "I have medicine," Nuri said. "I stole it from a government truck. It's for the children."

"And the old children?" Paul asked.

Nuri shrugged. "The worm is a trifle." Then he was quiet for thirty seconds, the longest extended stretch Paul could remember. Something was bothering him, but as host, Nuri couldn't bring up problems on the day of Paul's arrival. It would be an inexcusable breech of hospitality. The first day was only for salutations, the second only for entertainment, and on the third came time for discussion.

He needed some help. "Excuse my heathen ways," Paul said. "There are matters of such importance that they can't wait to be discussed."

"Why must things change?" Nuri asked. "There is a new storm in the Highlands, but he washes nothing clean."

"The Madhi?"

Nuri nodded. "The prophecies. First the soldiers, then your village, then the camel races, and now . . . now the Saudi king," he said, scratching his head, searching for a name.

"Khalid?" Paul asked.

"Yes. That one. When the young men heard the prophecy of the village, then heard of Al Rattaf, they rode to the Tihama for proof. None came back. If this Saudi dies, all will join the Madhi."

"At his fortress?"

"No one goes there. He has camps in the villages, caves in the wadis." Nuri nodded toward Paul. He smiled ironically. "Where there are Madhists, there are no infidels."

"The slaughter's begun already?"

Nuri nodded.

Paul looked out the window into the night. "Are there enough men left to take the convoy?" Paul asked.

"I would not sell guns to one who kills your quail and steals my men."

"And my debt?" Paul asked.

"Bah!" Nuri spat. "Stay with me, you and your mare."

"The government would destroy your village to get me."

Nuri smiled. "It's a dangerous world," he said indifferently.

Paul's voice grew cold. "Even when you converse with Allah." He stroked his chin and nodded his head slowly. "Who's to say how long this Madhi will live?"

Nuri's smile grew wider. "You'll visit him?"

"It would help repay many debts."

Nuri jumped to his feet, groaned, and began a vigorous war dance, which grew gentler with each step. He sang of the sweetness and joy of revenge, then began a softer, more introspective verse about how the days of men pass like the Highland rains. When he finished, he stood above Paul. "We go together."

"I go alone," Paul said. "The visit requires silence. Johara was my wife."

Nuri was familiar enough with Paul's tone not to take the argument further. Instead, he walked over to a wall decorated by weapons, took a small, curved dagger from a hook on the wall, and handed it to Paul. "It's many generations old. It has many stories to tell. Let it tell another."

"There is one problem left," Paul said. "My plan was to follow his men back when they took the weapons."

Nuri sat back on the cushion, smiled indifferently, and shrugged his shoulders. "I am a Jebeli," he said. "The mountains speak with me."

Paul edged forward. "Where is he?" he asked softly.

"You'll find Bustān al Kaf Maryam on the hidden shelf of Jebel Ash Shu'ub. And the graves of the men who built it."

Paul exhaled deeply. He sat back on the cushion and looked toward the ceiling. Spiderwebs full of flies hung from all the corners. "There is much to do in three days. Many young to treat," Paul said. He touched Nuri's shin with his toe. Nuri winced. "And some old."

"And the mare?" Nuri asked.

"She will want to follow me. Keep her for a week after I'm gone, then take her to the Tihama and convince a fisherman to sail her to Ethiopia. There is a colonel named Mussallim Hasan at T't'o who owes me many favors."

Nuri's smile continued to grow. "And what if your mare hears from my wives of my potency and doesn't wish to leave?"

Paul laughed. "In that case, my brother, I can only wish you luck."

XV.

Al Asil, Yemen—May 1, 1981

Claudia looked out the back window of Nuri's home. The Red Sea was far out of sight, but ground fog streamed up from the valley so rapidly that it must have been pushed by a humid air mass. She sighed and tried to take a breath of the frosty air. Impossible; the veil pulled tight against her nostrils. If she had such a hard time breathing in the Highlands, how could the Tihama women keep from suffocating in all the heat and humidity? Claudia lifted her veil, took a breath deep enough to last for a while, then walked back to the pillow where she'd slept and sat down.

The veil was the least of her problems. She'd come to terms with what it symbolized while still in New York, and when you came right down to it, the veil wasn't any worse than going around dressed like a man, which was the only alternative. She'd planned to spend a few days in purdah to research a behind-the-veil angle for a feature story, anyway, and had Paul to thank for arranging it so unobtrusively.

Of course, he didn't have to know that. Let him think that purdah was the most humiliating experience of her life. Let him think that only her infinite loyalty made her put up with this. The time in the woman's quarters hadn't been fun and games—preparing broiled goat's head was hardly her forte—but there were things about Nuri's wives that she found attractive. No sooner had Claudia joined the women than they gave her a long, sheer *qamis* to replace the *'aba* from Tai'zz, and offered to plait her hair. And they taught her ways to sidestep the veil. While they couldn't join in the men's conversations, there was nothing to keep them from listening—and since Claudia was a guest, she received the best spot, the spot nearest the doorway, and learned the most valuable information on earth: the location of Bustān al Kaf Maryam. Getting there remained a problem but not her major problem.

Her major problem was Paul.

He was strange. Period. In some ways he was as barbaric as the sheikh who tried to buy her, yet in others Paul was the most human male she'd ever known. The moment in the wadi when he put love ahead of lust was something special—something she hadn't seen a man do since puberty.

Claudia turned to the sound of footsteps. Haifa, Nuri's oldest wife, walked through the doorway, helped Claudia to her feet, and led her through the curtains into the men's quarters. Paul and Nuri lounged on floor cushions while the wives prepared a morning meal of yogurt and dates. Paul's grin indicated that he found Claudia's veil a whole lot more entertaining than she did. Just wait, she thought, things always even out.

"You've survived," Paul said. He looked at the *qamis* and the plated hair, and his grin widened to a smile. "Thrived, actually."

"When in Yemen . . ." Claudia said.

Paul drew back and eyed her suspiciously. "Is that Claudia Mallory behind the veil?" he asked.

"Let me take it off so you can make positive identification."

The smile melted from Paul's face. "Nothing I can do about that," he said. "It would cause a rebellion in Nuri's harem, and when I took you outside . . ."

"Where?" Claudia interrupted.

"Nuri will allow you to be my nurse. For the children, naturally."

"Naturally," Claudia said. "And the women?"

"There won't be any," Paul said. "They'd rather die of disease than disgrace. I'm a man."

But Claudia wasn't—something Nuri seemed too preoccupied with. He stared at her as though he'd paid to see a strip tease. It was time to establish some personal boundaries—while Paul was still nearby. She briskly raised the middle finger of her left hand. Nuri acted as though it were part of some routine: first the finger; then the veil comes off; then the *qamis;* then . . . He laughed, clapped, and sputtered some Arabic nonsense about stallions sniffing mares. Claudia's natural comeback involved knives, castrations, and geldings, but she didn't use it. No sense letting Paul know how much she understood. As it was, he was watching her eyes too intently.

"What was that all about?" she asked.

"He says he likes women with spirit," Paul said, smiling.

So much for reliable translations from Kenyon. There was, however, one word she had to know. "What's a *saqlāwi?*" she asked.

Suddenly Paul was suspicious. "Why?" he asked.

"Every time it's mentioned, there's a huge finger pointing at me."

"It's Nuri's nickname for you," Paul said. The humor in his voice grew soft. "One of the pure Arabian breeds of horses. The one known for beauty and refinement. Legends say the Prophet Mohammed himself chose the first *saqlāwi.*" Paul paused. "He's partly wrong."

"About the beauty or refinement?" Claudia asked.

"The *saqlāwi* isn't supposed to be strong," Paul said.

Not the most elegant compliment she'd ever received, but she'd take it.

Paul offered her his arm. They emerged from the building onto the street. Mountain peaks surrounded the village on all sides, and there was enough steam remaining from the thunderstorms to form fog pockets on the ridges. The peaks looked like earth-covered seedlings sprouting through snow. The sun was so bright that vapor sizzled. Claudia shook her head to help clear the dizziness.

A huge stone cistern squatted in the village square. Children splashed, goats waded and bathed, and a tawny dog lifted his hind leg to add a yellow stream to the already discolored water. Claudia nudged Paul and motioned toward the dog.

Paul tightened his grip on her arm. "Ever see a 'Fiery Serpent'?" he asked.

"No, thanks."

"Drink any water from that cistern, drink any standing water that hasn't been boiled, and I guarantee you'll be winding a yard-long parasite from your shins."

Claudia stared at him as hard as the veil allowed. "Look," she said, "I'm no fool, and we're gonna have nothing but problems as long as you keep confusing me with one."

She couldn't tell anything from his nod, but before they continued, he chased the dog away from the water. The "hospital" was a one-room stone hut near the edge of the cliff. It had huge windows—a necessity as there were no lanterns. Boxes and crates were scattered all over the floor—some of the stacks reached the ceiling. Paul searched through them until he found a cache of cartons marked with red crosses. He removed some hypodermic needles and cotton swabs from one, a bottle of alcohol from another, and some small vials from a third. He held the vials up to the light. "Shit," he said.

"Problems?"

"Goddamn Nuri only stole this stuff because he thought it was nitroglycerine and he could blow something up with it." Paul shook his head, popped his breath, and rubbed the back of his neck. "It's gonna be a long day."

"Always the optimist."

"Three-fourths of these solutions are antimony compounds, tartar emetic, and the like." Paul made a nasty face. "Possible side effects include hepatitis, cardiac arrest, nephritis—sure, it kills parasites, but it's so strong that if you get sloppy and drip some, it takes off skin . . . and the side effects . . ." He whistled, then looked out the window. "None of what's on today's program will be pretty."

"With the exception of this morning's walk, I haven't seen anything recently that is," Claudia said.

Most of the crates were from a United Nations relief shipment, so there were plenty of cots to assemble, IV stands to erect, and a variety of drugs to arrange on a table by the window. The sun was bright enough to highlight specks of dust as they swirled with Paul's movement. Claudia wondered why she was noticing common things in an uncommon way. Maybe it was something in the air. Or continuous exposure to the Madhi's supernatural song and dance.

Maybe it was Paul.

Her heightened imagination lasted until the patients started to arrive. And it wasn't pretty. She cleansed burst guinea worm tumors with alcohol and brine, saw the eggs of bilharziasis flukes in the watery feces of a four-year-old, and felt the swollen abdomen and emaciated arms that signaled Kala-azar on a boy who looked five but turned out to be twelve.

So what if it was far from pretty? It was nothing like what she'd seen in the dungeons in Uganda, nothing that could make her turn away. And here she could do something. Paul said that prompt treatment could drop a ninety percent mortality rate to less than five percent. That was *something.* Besides, most parasites weren't *that* contagious, and since Paul didn't find any of the bad bacteria, cholera, typhoid, leprosy, and the like, she felt quite secure.

And useful.

Claudia would have liked to fill in more of Paul's biography, but there were too many doses of niclosamide to distribute, too many pustules to lance, too many doses of tetracycline to administer.

Then a boy of six was carried into the building by his father.

The boy was shaking, drenched with sweat and, judging from his smell, had spent most of the morning vomiting. Paul told the father to leave, then lay the child on a cot, removed the boy's clothes, and probed his abdomen. His temperature was 105°. "You're looking at a malarial paroxysm," Paul said. "If I wasn't as familiar with the symptoms as I am—say I was you, for example—here's what I'd look for. High temperature. Increase in pulse and respiration rates. Believe it or not, enough parasites can develop to clog capillaries."

Paul took Claudia's hand, moved it across the boy's abdomen, then pushed down.

"Jesus," Claudia said, feeling a huge lump, "I hope *that's* no parasite."

"It's his spleen—only three times normal size. The liver, kidney, and bone marrow are affected to a lesser degree. It's even worse from his point of view," Paul said. "The thirst never quits, all pain is endlessly exaggerated, and the nightmares, the visions . . . well, they're light-years beyond anything a healthy mind can conjure up."

"Why the special interest in malaria?"

"Because you'll see more malaria this time of year than any other disease. Here's an equation for you: standing water plus mosquito eggs equals billions of vectors." Paul turned and walked toward the medicine table. "Besides, I know where the kid is at. I've had malarial relapses since Vietnam."

"Twelve years?" Claudia asked.

"An even dozen. And they haven't gotten more pleasant. During the last attack about a month ago, I imagined that *P. malariae* parasites were dining on my brain. It almost took me out." Paul removed some tubing from a carton, took an IV bag from another, and rolled an IV stand over to the boy's cot. "He won't be able to keep oral doses down so, despite the risk of liver damage, I'll dissolve 600 milligrams of quinine in 300 milliliters of glucose solution and feed it to him intravenously over a half-hour." Paul wrote the instructions down on a piece of paper. "Once things stabilize, you can start him on chloroquinine phosphate orally. . . ."

"Why is this starting to sound more like a lesson than a demonstration?" Claudia interrupted.

Paul's initial response was to pull some hairs from his beard. His sheepish look appeared again . . . this time it wasn't cute. "You never know when it might come in handy," he said. "Ever give shots?"

"I had a diabetic roommate in college."

"Then you're years ahead of where I started," Paul said.

It was past time for him to explain what was going on, but just then another child, a pre-purdah girl, limped into the room. Paul looked up from the IV stand and smiled. "She's all yours," he said. "At least till I'm through administering this."

Judging from the smell of this young lady, she hadn't been

outside during the storm. No sense procrastinating. Claudia placed her hand on the girl's forehead. "She's burning up!" Claudia said.

"Look for tumors, swellings, cysts, and the like."

The girl's hair seemed fine—greasy but without lice. Certainly no tumors. No problems behind the ears. Or the neck. Claudia grabbed the girl under the armpits to turn her around. And stopped. Something was wrong. Very wrong. The lymph nodes were swollen. Claudia started to whistle as she pulled the robe down to the girl's waist. Enlarged lymph nodes. Red. Tender. Claudia didn't want to look any further—her mouth grew so dry from fright, she couldn't whistle. After she'd moved the robe past the girl's waist, Claudia stopped thinking. There was swelling in the girl's groin, and worse, the inside of her thighs were scaly and black.

Plague.

And she'd touched the girl—for all she knew, at that instant some flea was biting her and giving her . . . she touched the girl and . . . If this were the Madhi plague, all preventatives were useless—Claudia was dead. She tried to get her breathing under control, then gathered enough air to talk. "*Paul!*" she said.

Her tone must have been convincing because Paul left the malarial boy and came running. He looked down at the girl then, without so much as a blink, dropped to his knees and examined the discoloration and swelling. When Claudia took his hand, it wasn't even trembling. "Plague?" she asked softly.

Paul sighed. Loudly. "Filariasis, Claudia," he said. "At least probably." He touched the girl's leg. "It's acute but not chronic. We can help."

Claudia struggled to breathe. "I need air."

"And the girl needs help. First the girl, then the air."

When Claudia stood, the room spun. Slightly. She grabbed his shoulder to steady herself, breathed deeply, glanced at the door, then walked toward the medicine table to get some drugs. "All right, Dr. K.," she said. "Now what?"

Again he proved himself a very unpredictable man. Instead of shouting instructions as the situation demanded, he approached her, removed her veil and threw it out the window, then kissed her gently on the lips. He moved back an arm's length. "The *Merck Manual,*" he said, pointing to a book on the table. "It's about time you learned how to use it."

And though Claudia wasn't sure why, she had the feeling he was right.

It had to happen sooner or later, so when it happened sooner, Claudia was grateful. She just didn't need any more suspense.

The malarial boy slept on a cot while Paul adjusted the drip rate on a glucose bag. The other patients were gone. Until tomorrow. Claudia sorted through medicines, restacked some crates, then washed in surgical scrub and stood in front of the window—partly so the breeze would dry her, partly so sunlight could silhouette her figure through the *qamis.* She caught Paul staring, and smiled when he turned back to the valve on the tubing as though it were the most fascinating thing on earth. Patience, she thought, some games require purring instead of clawing.

Then it began as it always began: He looked at her with a face all too serious for the occasion, then swallowed as he said, "Claudia." On the surface, it sounded like the name he'd said a hundred times in the past week, but his tension shattered the word into pieces.

Claudia kept her mouth shut.

He cleared his throat and started over. "Claudia," he said again, more smoothly, in more determined fashion.

"The name sounded better when you choked on it," she said.

He stood there looking lost for the first time since she met him, then shrugged his shoulders and exhaled. "Nothing," he said. He turned back to the IV with a sheepish shake of his head.

"Paul, feel like a walk?" Claudia asked.

"Thought you'd never ask."

A final check of the patient, and Paul and Claudia walked through the door and down the pathway that led away from Al Asil. There wasn't much but rock in the high country, but Paul knew his way around. He found a hollow where some tamarisk had snared just enough soil to survive. Some butterflies danced in the wind, a yellow bird scolded them from a tree limb, and a hawk wheeled and dived through the updrafts. They just stood there, watching the hawk and smelling the fresh air.

It was obvious that the next move would determine the outcome of this game, and Claudia wasn't about to leave it to a rookie. "Paul," she said, the tension in her voice a surprise even to her.

He reached over and ever so gently touched her neck. She trapped his hand against her shoulder and nuzzled it, and when he reached beneath her *qamis* and found there was nothing there but Claudia, they shuddered together. And laughed. The *qamis* slid from her shoulders noiselessly.

The tamarisk needles were sharp. Claudia said she wouldn't mind being on the bottom, but Paul said no, his skin was tougher, which is what she hoped he'd say, freedom of movement being urgent, and she showed him about leverage, and he said "Slow down," and she said "Enjoy," and he said "Thanks," then something she couldn't understand. The second time, it was Claudia's turn to say things she didn't understand. By the time they finished, neither of them had much to say.

For the next little while, there was nothing but a softness, quiet. Claudia couldn't believe that anyone's heart could pump as loudly as Paul's, and when she gathered enough energy to explore his body, she found muscles she didn't know existed. She traced a muscle that crossed his thigh and fastened behind his hip. "Where'd you get that?" she asked.

He sighed as if to say, do you *really* feel like talking, then, when she continued to trace it, said, "From walking uphill instead of taking elevators or escalators."

"No, Paul."

"Sorry," he said. He kissed her on the eyebrows, the eyelids and lips as a form of truce.

Claudia countersigned by kissing the scar on his chest; she would have loved to run her tongue along the scar on the inside of his thigh, but she was a little too tuckered out and a little too sore to chance the consequences. "You've really been through the meat grinder," she said.

"Several times," Paul said. "Several times." He looked into her eyes, then straight up into the sky. And it didn't look as though he were searching for a hawk. He pointed his finger at her as if searching for the right words, yet knowing all the while that they didn't exist. He wouldn't say anything like I love you, Claudia knew. He just wasn't the type. Too bad. "And I'm about to go through the meat grinder again," he said. "I have no intention of taking you with me."

It was a lot closer to I love you than Claudia expected. She put her hand on the back of his neck, and he rolled his head over and over, caressing it. "Dummy," she said, "I don't need your protection."

"Not from most people you don't, but against the Madhi, yes. Shit, *I* need it from him. And Piece-of-My-Heart? Well, he isn't a person. I saw the games he played on a mammasan with his garrote. He took off a lot more than her head." Paul took Claudia's hand. "Ever been shot?" he asked.

"At," she said.

"That doesn't count."

"Then no," she said.

"Stabbed?"

"No."

"Then it isn't real. It's *Dawn Patrol, From Here to Eternity, Sergeant Rock* comics. It's not your fault, it's cultural. I saw a fifty-year-old colonel charge a bunker like he was John Wayne at the Alamo, and grunts crawl into VC tunnels like they were rides at Disneyland. They were dead before they found out they could die."

Claudia tried to interrupt, but Paul was having none of it.

"You already mentioned your photographer, but he doesn't count. He was an image at fifty feet, no more." Paul tightened his grip. "If you'd smelled his blood, maybe. If you'd held his guts in your hands, still only maybe. If they were your own guts, then for sure. But that's one experience you don't need. Which is why you're going to stay here even if I have to tie you up."

"Going somewhere?" Claudia asked.

All of a sudden, Paul let loose of her hands and began to gesticulate, opening his hands as if pleading. "*Pleeeeeeese* cut it out, Claudia!" he said. "I've watched your eyes when I talk with Nuri. Your reactions tell me you're good at Arabic nouns, weaker at verbs, and don't know shit about declensions. You know where I'm going."

She gave up the ruse in a shrug. "And your trying to turn me into Florence Nightingale isn't a sham?"

"Not completely. Every treatment I've begun takes ten days to two weeks to take effect."

"So I stay here and keep your meals and bed warm while you're out in the mountains playing Captain Spooky," she said. "Who do I contact with complaints about casting?"

"The security police want me. Bad. Bad enough to hit Al Asil if they find out I'm here. They have no love for Nuri, anyway. He fought on the wrong side of their civil war and has been using their convoys as a personal commissary ever since."

"How about me, mister?" Claudia asked. "My career? My shot at an anchor desk? My debt to Rick? *Me?*"

He raised three fingers, one at a time. Finger one: "You'll save lives if you stay." Finger two: "You'll get us both killed if you tag along." Finger three: "This way I'll know where to come when I'm finished."

"I know, I know, I know," she said. He was three times right, and that made no difference at all. "You talk as though *when* wasn't *if.*"

Paul ignored her. "I only have a few days left. Just enough to show you how to use the needle, oral drugs, and administer some tests."

"You want me to forget about the Madhi?" Claudia asked. There was real disappointment in her voice.

"I'll tell you all I know when I get back."

"If you get back."

Paul looked away from her. His eyes settled on a large-leafed plant with blue flowers. He bent down, picked a flower, and wove it into the plaits in Claudia's hair. "It's not supposed to grow this high up," he said.

Claudia looked at the orchidlike petals and white-gold stamen. "So fragile," Claudia said. "I've never seen anything like it."

"A *shauk al ajus.* Only for special people."

He leaned over and kissed her. And put a hand on her breast. Claudia was distant at first; she hadn't said enough—at least not the right things. Up to that point, she considered herself a master of good-byes, but now that one worthy of the Brontë sisters arrived, she'd gone flat. A word master without words. But as soon as the hurt was forgotten, as soon as the disappointment was lost in motions far less complex than repartee, she realized there was nothing left to say and this was, after all, the only thing they could do.

XVI.

Al Asil, Yemen—May 4, 1981

Paul snapped the AK-47's slide mechanism back and forth to be sure he'd assembled it properly. The crack of metal against metal hurt his ears; he'd grown too old for the sound and the memories it held. He turned the automatic rifle over to check the bolts attaching the metal stock. Tight as a drum. There was a time in Vietnam when he'd carried an AK-47 (it was easier to strip ammunition off dead VC than to make the dangerous trip back to Khe Sanh), but it was more than a decade since he'd used anything but his Mannlicher and machine pistol. He pulled the trigger, and the firing pin clicked. Crisp and new. In fact, the entire gun was stiff. Nuri had stolen it at . . . well, he wasn't sure anymore, but it must have been somewhere near the South Yemen border, because the gun was packed in Cosmoline, and the markings on the crates were from Russian factories.

Nuri handed him two bandoliers filled with clips, and Paul buckled them on. Nuri tugged at Paul's black *'aba,* then straightened the black turban. "They look better on you than the monkey I took them from," Nuri said.

"It's a good thing I'm used to wearing a dead man's clothes," Paul said, sarcastically scratching his nose.

"We all wear a dead man's clothes," Nuri said. He took some ashes from the fire and rubbed them into Paul's beard. "No blond Anglos fight with the Madhi." He scooped some red-brown mud from an earthenware jar and smeared it on Paul's skin. "Now you will be able to walk up and kiss the Madhi . . . before the knife finds a home." Nuri paused and smiled. "Don't kiss him for too long, or you may want to prod him with that," he said, pointing at Paul's groin, "instead of that." He patted the dagger in Paul's waistband.

The air was heavy and cool with the moisture that would settle and become morning dew. The peaks were silver with moonlight, and a single cloud brushed beneath the moon and left a shadow as it crossed the valley from ridge to ridge. The cloud would be Paul's only companion. The thought made his eyes narrow and his face draw tight.

Nuri stared at Paul. "I will protect your mare," he said.

"It's not her," Paul said. He pointed at the cloud. "I was out there alone already. The cloud took me back a dozen years." He glanced at the entranceway to the women's quarters. "Claudia doesn't fit with all that came before her."

Nuri spat. "Thoughts of that mare will get you killed." He pointed out the window. "It's a hunter's moon. There's no place for women in the hunt. Women are different, a different game, a different thrill."

"I'm not sure if what I feel is thrill or fear. I'm not even sure if I know where one stops and the other starts."

"Thrill starts with revenge."

"And fear when you start to care?" Paul asked.

"Care when there's time to care," Nuri said. "For you, now, it's revenge. Think of your village, of your quail."

Nuri was right. Softness would get him killed. Him and maybe others. This hunt was like all the rest, only the game was a little bigger. The hunter's moon seemed to heighten his senses—Paul heard movement in the women's quarters, someone turning over. His eyes widened and he turned toward the sound.

"Go to her quickly," Nuri said. "Then be gone."

"Into your harem?"

Nuri shrugged. "You are my brother. My wives have me. They will wake for no other man." Then he laughed.

Paul slung the AK-47 over his shoulder and held Nuri at arm's length, trying to etch a permanent picture of the Arab's face in his memory. But the coals in the grate scarcely glowed, so the face was only sparkling eyes and teeth trapped in a tangle of dark hair. So Paul concentrated on the smells—the sour yogurt in Nuri's beard, the camel-dung ashes hovering in the room—to form his pictures.

"Enough," Nuri said. "We are not women." He pointed to the nose bag hanging on the wall. "Now go, and don't come back until you have something that now belongs to the Madhi." Then Nuri turned abruptly away, sat on a cushion, and stared into the embers. He wouldn't move till morning. Women and children would run to the roof to catch a final glimpse of a friend disappearing into the mountains, but emotion was for women. Warriors preferred a clean break. If Nuri ibn Sha'lan were to behave as a woman, then surely the Jebeli world was lost.

But Paul wasn't Nuri. He stared a final time at the huge silhouette by the fire before he entered the women's quarters.

It wasn't hard to find Claudia. She still smelled of medicinal scrub, and only she tossed and turned on her layer of pillows. Still, she was only an outline: most of the room's moonlight puddled like mercury beneath the *qamis* hung in the window as a curtain.

How would he look to Claudia in half-sleep? As a monster creeping from the fringe of a nightmare? A shapeless shadow among other shapeless shadows? Neither was the image he wanted to leave her with. He squatted next to her. "Claudia?" he whispered.

Her first words weren't audible, the slurred language of dreams.

"Paul," he said.

She reached out with her left hand—to where he'd lie if they'd just finished making love—to where he wished he was. He smiled. It was impossible to feign *that* particular movement. He ran a finger across her lips so she wouldn't speak. "Don't wake the others," he said.

"That you?" she asked. Her words were as puffy and swollen with sleep as her eyes must have been.

"There's not much time," he said. He slipped a piece of paper into her hand. "The name of someone in Eritrea who can get you to Cairo."

"What?" she mumbled. "When?"

"If I'm not back in ten days, I won't be back. Go to the wadi where we bathed if anything happens." He put some rials under her pillow. "Money for a *dhow* trip across the Red Sea. Nuri will help." Before she could say anything else, before she could weaken him further, he kissed her, closed her eyelids with a fingertip, then slid through the back window and into the moonlight. He stayed in the shadows until he left the village—and some of his old skills must have remained, because not a single dog woke.

Paul sighted the AK-47 first at the morning star, then at the outline of a peak that must have been at least ten miles away. There was security in the heft at his shoulder, the kind of security he hadn't felt since the plague. He'd take the Madhi out with a single bullet. From a distance. He didn't want him to become a man, grow smells, a voice. Just an image. When Paul lowered the rifle, his shoulder throbbed. The wound hadn't healed completely, but it was getting stronger . . . just as long as he didn't get careless and rip something out, he'd be okay.

Once he was clear of the village, far enough away that the dogs wouldn't waken, he shoved a clip into the rifle and, with a jerk, snapped the rifle to his shoulder. Still fluid, plenty fast. As he left the path and climbed toward the top of the escarpment, he startled a pair of ravens, which fed on a large, indistinguishable carcass. They cawed as they flew away, then looked back at him with a warning not to join their feast. Maybe the cawing was to invite him to a later meal.

With Paul as main course.

Hardly the best of omens.

He laughed them off. It was night, there were shadows, and he was Captain Spooky. What were omens to him?

XVII.

Al Asil, Yemen—May 8, 1981

Claudia sat on the table next to the clinic's only window and took a breath that should have been beautiful but wasn't. A touch of night chill remained, and sunlight capped the peaks like snow, but she wasn't buying any of it.

She might be able to forgive Paul for leaving her with that malodorous bandit, maybe even his exiting in the middle of the night, but never, never would she forgive him spiking this story. But she was a patient woman; things would even up.

Maybe it wasn't entirely his fault. She'd been the one to turn all cuddly and available. This time she paid a high price for her addiction to bare skin and nuzzling, but being left to play Snow White to four dwarfs, Paul's inpatients, was too much. She nicknamed the children Sleepy, Happy, Grumpy, and Dopey for reasons that had more to do with the medications they took than their genetic makeup.

Claudia shifted her weight and took another breath. It was crazy. What she really needed to sort through her emotional mess was a week of uninterrupted monotony. Just time for a walk would have been nice, but there was no free time. The lines for oral medications formed early, the children were a constant chore, and no doubt by noon she'd be up to her armpits in antiseptic delousing a new patient.

As the sun rose, red light slipped down the eastern slope of the escarpment. A solitary peak stood out on the horizon. It was rough, distant . . . like Paul. What she wouldn't give to run her tongue along his lips. He'd taste of salt and when she touched him . . . Jesus H. Christ, with all the men in the world, why did she have to fall for a cowboy-turned-Arab? It would be easier to stroll up to some cliff, grab onto her nose, and cannonball into eternity. If he got killed, she'd never forgive him.

There was a knock on the door. It creaked open, and a round face with dark brown curls and an olive complexion peered into the room: It was the girl in the moon, her face was that plump. Claudia smiled. She could use some female companionship. As the girl walked inside, she shied away from the catheters and tubing. Maybe she thought they were part of some enormous spiderweb. The girl's face was sour, but Claudia's charm turned it into a smile. As soon as the girl seemed comfortable, Claudia removed the girl's clothes. There were no rashes or external cysts. No abnormal swelling. There was some tenderness in the abdomen, but that could be the result of anything from amebiasis to too much yogurt. Since there wasn't enough information for a diagnosis, Claudia decided to keep her for observation.

Grumpy, no, make that Happy, started to chatter, the traditional signal for the start of morning rounds. Claudia dressed the girl, took a rectal thermometer from a jar of alcohol, shook it down, rolled Happy over, and eased in the thermometer. She signaled for him to stay put, then walked to the medicine table and picked up the jar of quinine tablets.

There was a rock slide somewhere far down the valley.

Correction: The steady thumping was far too mechanical for rocks. It sounded more like a lumberjack convention—a thousand axes falling on a huge log. The noise faded, then grew louder again. When Claudia stuck her head out of the window, the sound vanished. Maybe the altitude was playing tricks with her hearing.

She turned back to the quinine.

The chopping started again, only this time much louder. Then she knew what it was. Rotor sound. She dropped the jar with a crash and ran into the street just as a dozen helicopter gun ships popped over the rim of the cliff.

There were kids all over the street, some playing with sticks and rocks, some splashing in the cistern, but *none* diving for cover. They probably didn't even know what helicopters were.

Claudia shouted. The trance shattered and the children scattered. Some rolled under ledges or hid behind stones. Some ran for home. A boy tugging on his sister's arm ran toward a two-story building in the middle of town. They arrived at the doorway at the same time as a line of dust puffs. The bullets danced down the street and out of the village.

The children fell in a red spray. The girl curled into a broken fetal position while the boy lay motionless on his stomach.

And without thinking, Claudia sprinted into the street, dived, and slid on her upper thigh and hip. The back of the girl's head was gone. The boy was alive—barely; his mouth twitched when a fly landed on it.

Now that Claudia was out there, what was she going to do?

She tried to turn the boy onto his back, but something began to slide from the gash. She eased him back down. The air buzzed with insects, and flies coated the wound. When a second chopper bore down on the village, automatic rifles poked out of the windows, and bullets bounced off the helicopter's undercarriage. There wasn't time to panic or think, just time to move. Maybe. Claudia pressed the boy to her breast and tried to run, but she tripped over her *qamis* and the bullets kicked up a ridge of dirt, and there wasn't time to stand, so she half-crawled, half-crabwalked, wishing like hell she could drop the child and save herself. It was like one of those dreams where the harder she struggled the slower she moved, and a bullet cracked within a yard of her head as she rolled through the door with a bone-jarring crash and looked up at the ceiling.

The rafters were covered with a red film, and her eyes stung so badly she blinked. She touched her tongue to her lips. Salt. Iron. She followed the blood back up her forehead until she found a half-inch gash in her scalp, which was probably the result of a rock splinter. She tried to pinch it closed and, when that didn't work, took a gauze compress and applied direct pressure.

The kids were screaming, and who could blame them? People were dying in the street, the wounded boy was groaning, and Claudia's wound looked a lot worse than it was. When they started to go outside, Claudia shouted for them to get away from the door before they got their heads shot off, and though they didn't understand English, they *understood,* and scurried back behind the safety of the wall.

Claudia wiped the blood from her face and, in her softest purr, coddled them with sound, coaxed them back into a corner where they would be safe. Relatively safe. Then she found a first-aid chest and dragged it up to the wounded boy. His eyes were glassy and distant. He moaned. The shock was starting to wear off, and pain would follow. Incomprehensible pain. Claudia lifted his head into her lap and gently stroked his hair. What to do? What to do? She had five minutes, maybe less.

The boy looked up at her serenely, as if to say she was the doctor; she would help him. Jesus. There wasn't anything an M.D. could do. How could she? . . . She tried, anyway. Claudia ripped away his robe and tried to cleanse the wound, but the organs were all chewed up—there was dirt throughout the abdominal cavity. Though she knew it was useless, she poured sulfa on the wound, then took three battle dressings and, one at a time, stretched them tight over the gash.

He began to writhe, and there wasn't any more she could do, and maybe she'd only made things worse and the boy would die in agony and . . . she noticed the Syrettes of morphine.

She could let him sleep.

She injected three, no four, Syrettes into his arm, then propped his head up on some compresses and watched his eyes cloud and close. Without arguing the morality of her decision, she gave him three more Syrettes, then lifted the dying boy onto a cot, closed his eyes tight, and kissed him on the forehead.

A roar.

A rocket swished past, exploded, and the building across the street crumbled. Dirt and shrapnel poured through the window. Claudia waited until the dirt settled, then pinched her wound shut and applied sulfa powder. How could she protect the children? She glanced around the room. The crates! Adrenaline gave her the strength to drag and push, pry and stack the heavy crates into a four-foot-high barrier around a corner of the wall. She pretended it was a fort like the ones she used to construct in the woods behind her house. One by one, she lifted the children behind the barricade and told them to sit down.

She was about to climb in herself when she heard a deeper, louder thumping from down in the valley. She ran to the window and looked down the street, past the mountain ledge. Two helicopter transports escorted by a C-47 cargo plane droned steadily up toward the village. She'd seen a C-47 like that in Nam. It was equipped with computer-synchronized Gatling guns, which, she remembered from the Army propaganda pamphlet, put a round in every square inch of an area the size of a football field in less than a minute. The pamphlet called it "Puff the Magic Dragon," but the Marines were the ones who saw it work. They knew. They called it "Spooky."

Claudia knew it was death, but she couldn't stop watching it until it was over the village. Then the Gatling guns opened up; they drooled fire, and the village was swallowed in a cloud of dust and chipped rock. Claudia rolled back across the floor and was face-to-face with the gut-shot boy. His eyes were fogged over. "Spooky" made two passes, banked away, and the helicopter transports started their descent. Small-arms fire from the village started again. Helicopters thumped down in the village square. More small-arms fire—the Yemeni soldiers had disembarked.

Claudia had seen enough World War II movies to know the scenario for taking a village: cover the windows; creep up to a building; lob a grenade through the door; then, while dust still hung in the air, burst through the door with machine guns blazing. Idea: Arrange the IVs, the vials of medicine, and the Red Cross boxes conspicuously around the dead boy so there would be no doubt that this hut was a clinic.

When she had finished, Claudia dragged the metal table across the room, pulled it up the crates, climbed into the fort, and wedged it above the fort like a roof. Then she huddled the children beneath her and waited. Gunfire moved closer. Bullets thudded into the clinic's wall. Several grenades, their explosions muffled by buildings, rumbled.

Something scratched the wall by their door.

Claudia started screaming "*Salaam alaikum*" so loudly that the children began to cry. She didn't know whether the scream or crying saved their lives, but no grenade rolled in.

Someone crawled across the floor toward the crates. When Claudia looked into a gap between the crates and table, a grenade clutched in a fist appeared. "Don't you dare!" she shouted. She jumped up, bounced her head off the table, and reopened her wound.

She was dizzy but not so dizzy that she wasn't aware of the silence. Blood stung her eyes. Claudia wiped the red from her eyes, tried to focus, and wished she hadn't.

When the blurred images finally merged and she could finally see, she wanted to crawl back into the fort with the children and hide. She was face-to-face with the grotesque lieutenant from Tai'zz.

And she didn't like the way he smiled.

The lieutenant had two soldiers guard Claudia, left, then after the village was secured, radioed that she be brought to him. The street was marred by rocket and grenade craters, the walls pocked by bullets. Surviving villagers had been herded into the square . . . there weren't many left. The dead were stacked by the cistern. Claudia saw a blue *qamis* among the bodies. It was Haifa's. She must have been caught in the Gatling gun's field of fire. Lateefa, Nuri's youngest wife, was there, too. And many of the children she'd treated. Too, too many for her to look any longer.

The soldiers took her to Nuri's hut and nudged her inside with their M-16s. The lieutenant sat on a cushion where Paul had sat not a week before. The lieutenant's eyes still watered, only now he was dressed in combat fatigues. He touched the cushion across from him, and the soldiers pushed Claudia down. He handed her a tarnished mirror and smiled as she tried to clean the blood from her face. "I warned you to be careful of shadows," he said. "Highland shadows in particular can be hazardous to one's health."

Claudia was tempted to mention Mickey Rat but decided not

to show how much she knew. Let the lieutenant do some fishing; he might make a slip. She pointed to the blood on her face. "The vice-consul in Tai'zz would love to see me looking like—"

"Stop!" the lieutenant shrieked. He smiled when Claudia jumped. There was the slightest quiver at the corner of his mouth. "Your government thinks you are dead. Kidnapped by Madhists and killed." He paused and offered her a date from one of Nuri's bowls. "I filed the report myself."

"You were at the mosque?"

"We are not all goatherds," he said, fingering a date pit. He stood, walked across the room, took a dagger from a peg on the wall, unsheathed it, and ran a finger along the blade. "May I call you Claudia?"

Maybe it was time for some sugar. "Why not?"

"Yes," he said. His voice was as cold as a draft from a catacomb. "Why not?" Then his sadist's smile again. "How did you find your way to the lair of this mountain bandit?"

"The Madhists," Claudia said.

"Nonsense. We found the rebels who took you. Sadly, none were in condition to provide us with information."

"The helicopters were yours, too?" Claudia asked.

He bowed slightly.

"Three of us stayed in the cave," Claudia said. "When they realized there were too many patrols to escape, they brought me here."

"The Madhists traveled fifty miles cross country to find succor with an animal who would slit their throats? Unlikely."

Claudia felt unexpectedly protective of Nuri. "If he heard you call him an animal, you'd be sniffing that date through a hole in your face."

"I'm familiar with his proclivities," the lieutenant said. "Why is it that I'm not trembling?"

Her voice grew soft. "Where is Nuri?"

The lieutenant crashed the dagger into the table and shouted, "What will it take to convince you that the time for games is over! We no longer trade information! I ask! You answer!"

Claudia nodded.

"You were brought here by an American killer named Kenyon. He works for the Madhi and this bandit. Only the medic could have escaped the trap in the wadi. He's not with the dead. Where is he?"

"If you know the medic," Claudia said, "you know he's not the type to chat with strangers. He didn't say five words to me the whole time I knew him."

"A whore knows ways to get what she wants." The lieutenant's voice softened, a snake's hiss. "You wished to see the Madhi."

"And still do," Claudia said. "The medic said no." She dropped her voice into a purr. "Maybe you'd say yes?"

"We have played long enough." The lieutenant wiggled the dagger free from the table and called for the guards. One took Claudia by the arms, the other by the legs, and they spread-eagled her across a cushion. The lieutenant's face was a foot from hers. "Fortunate, is it not, that the bandit kept his knives sharp."

It was a bluff. Everything the man had done with her had been a bluff. "If I knew more, *anything* more, don't you think I'd tell you?"

He didn't seem to hear her. "It finally comes down to discovering how familiar you are with pain," he said. He smiled and sat on her stomach. "Why is it I think you'll tell me what I wish to know very quickly?"

It was a bluff. All bluff. She looked into his face and smiled. Then he did the unbelievable. He grabbed her left wrist, forced her fist open, and dragged the dagger across her fingertips.

Her hand exploded.

But she wouldn't scream; she wouldn't give him that satisfaction. She tried to dull the waves of pain by regulating her breathing, but she could scarcely draw a breath. When his face came back into focus, she realized it was a good thing she hadn't screamed: he was smiling, enjoying her pain. "Why would I hold things back? What's in this for me?" Claudia asked.

He paid no attention to her. He snapped his fingers, and one of the soldiers handed him a bag. "If this were Tai'zz," the lieutenant said, "I'd have special tools and there would be little trouble ferreting out your lies. Sometimes it takes a subject days to die."

He took salt from the bag and, one fingertip at a time, crushed it deep into the slices in her fingers. Claudia tried to squirm free, but the men holding her were far too strong. Her eyes filled with tears, and she bit down on her lip until she tasted blood.

The lieutenant sat back and smiled, then leaned over until his face was three inches from hers. "You are full of surprises," he said, "but you *will* talk." He motioned for the guards to hold her tighter, then sat on her breasts. She couldn't breathe. "Please tell yourself that you won't break under the pain. It is a lie, of course, but you will last longer."

Claudia closed her eyes and tried to concentrate on Paul's face, the gentleness in his hands.

"There is a question that bothers me," the lieutenant said. "And who is better to ask it to than you?"

He paused, waited for a response, but Claudia wasn't in the mood for repartee anymore.

"What would a woman," he asked, "a woman who had been beautiful her entire life, do if she suddenly weren't beautiful anymore? Say she was treated to the traditional punishment for a whore: her lips slit and torn so they would never heal? Or better yet, if one were to take a lesson from the bandit? What would this woman do if she had no nose to powder? If she had only a hole in her face with which to smell the world?"

It wouldn't do any good to panic or scream, Claudia knew that, but it didn't make any difference. She tried to scream, but with no breath, there was no noise . . . a shriek in a void.

"And what if someone took this woman to a house of prostitution in Tai'zz?" the lieutenant continued. "She would be too ugly to take normal clientele. She would have to beg lepers, those who took pleasure in pain, for a single rial to mount her so she wouldn't starve or . . ." The dagger lowered toward Claudia's face.

Someone called.

Claudia wasn't sure who it was, because her mind screamed

even if her voice couldn't, but it was a voice that held memories of security and friendship. Suddenly the dagger eased away. The lieutenant quieted and leaned back. He trembled with frustration. The voice grew louder. When its timbre, its resonance, finally registered, she started to cry. From joy. She blinked the tears from her eyes, turned her head, and saw, quite literally, the most handsome face she had ever seen. Not handsome in a Robert Redford or Burt Reynolds sort of way. Quite the contrary. The head was balding, the beard was thick and wiry, and she couldn't see the eyes because of sunglasses. Mix the features together, however, and they had a single saving quality.

They belonged to Rick Hodges.

XVIII.

Bustān al Kaf Maryam, the Yemeni Highlands— May 8, 1981

The mountain threw distinct shadows across rocks the color of rusting daggers, green terraces of onions and garlic cut step by step into the slopes and down into the valley. Above only narrow goat paths wound up the summit, and the tallis spilling off the peaks seemed undisturbed.

Jebel Ash Shu'ub seemed the last place on earth to find a fortress.

Even when Paul stood on the arête directly above the overhang, the fortress was invisible. No wonder there were rumors that Allah protected it! But drill and dynamite scars in the rock, a broken bulldozer's tread, and the numerous, level spots large enough to land helicopters stuffed with supplies showed Paul that Allah was pretty familiar with modern construction techniques.

The fortress itself was an architectural wonder, a three-dimensional lesson in Islamic art. Its ten-foot-high walls were etched with arabesques, and the axis of the courtyard pointed north, toward Mecca, as the Prophet demanded. A domed minaret jutted from the northern wall, and there was a three-tiered fountain in the middle of the courtyard, but the real wonder was the three-story building. It was supported by hundreds of slender columns and hidden in the deepest shadows of the overhang. In the late afternoon, when the sun dropped far enough in the west, the columns looked as fragile as a spiderweb. The Companions slept among these columns and called it their "sanctuary," their resting place beneath the Madhi. And the sanctuary was as much of the building as the Companions ever saw; the top two floors of the building were off-limits, with an eternity in hell promised to those who trespassed. Paul was amazed to find out how little the Companions knew about their Madhi . . . he kept his distance from mortals as befitted the successor to the Prophet. They saw him five times a day—to lead them in prayer—and he never descended from his balcony.

Paul had seen his outline just once: when the Madhi appeared in darkness to lead the predawn *Fajr,* the first prayer of the day. Paul could have killed him then. If Paul didn't want to discover how the plague worked. If he never wanted to see Claudia again . . . if the Madhi were assassinated by a gunshot, not even Captain Spooky would be able to escape. It would have to be a silent job, a job done at arm's length.

Paul glanced around the fortress. Strange, he wanted to be there, yet he didn't. There had been so many battles on so many different sides that he just couldn't separate the "us" from the "them" anymore. These Companions of the Madhi's really weren't much different from the grunts he'd known in Nam. Granted, grunts didn't pray five times a day or debate genealogies of the Prophet, and they sure didn't follow regulations that required abstinence of any kind, but they were the same where it counted: the eyes.

Example: the young Jebeli ten feet away leaning against a column. His innocence was gone. There was no spark left, no verve, just *know.* Those eyes belonged on a ninety-year-old instead of a teenager. When Paul first arrived in Vietnam, a platoon sergeant walked up to him, took an inventory of his eyes, and said, "Hundred-eighty pounds on the hoof." Paul had butchered enough cattle to understand what the sergeant was getting at, but it wasn't until five days later, as Paul hid beneath the corpse of a buddy while the VC played knife games with the wounded, that he *knew* anything.

The Jebeli caught him staring.

Paul tugged the turban down, pulled Nuri's dagger from its sheath, picked up a flat piece of granite, spit on it, and began to resharpen the already sharp blade. The more time Paul spent with his eyes down, the safer he'd be. There was no dye that could turn his blue eyes Arab-brown.

A white-robed muezzin walked from beneath the minaret's dome and his long, plaintive call announced *Zohr,* the early-afternoon prayer. Soon the Madhi would appear. He had to appear. To forget prayer was a sin, and as the Prophet said, *salaat* in company is twenty times better than *salaat* alone. The Madhi's routine formed the blueprint for Paul's plan: While the Companions prayed in company, he would visit the room behind the Madhi's balcony alone.

There were ten parts to *Zohr,* each of which took an average of thirty seconds. Five minutes. Enough.

While the Companions stopped disassembling rifles, cleaning mortars, arguing theology, and clustered around the fountain in the courtyard, Paul slipped through an archway shaped like a Byzantine dome and into a stairway. The building was cool, and condensation gathered on the stone. By the time the muezzin's call to prayer faded into the cliffs, Paul was on the second floor. The Madhi began his chant—Paul peered through a window and saw a tall, black-robed man in a white turban. The Madhi turned toward Mecca, and the Companions joined him. "Allah-o-Akbar!" the Madhi called in a deep baritone.

The Companions dropped to their knees and stretched into full *salaat.* "Allah-o-Akbar!" they sang.

There was something eerie in the way the sounds rebounded off the walls and overhang, as though the sounds of the call were eternally trapped and chorus after chorus of words would pile atop each other. But this wasn't the time to study acoustics. Paul crept from the stairway into a corridor. It was long and dark, lighted only by the gray sunlight trickling in through crescent-shaped tracery. He flattened against a wall that intersected the next hallway, checked for guards, and sprinted to the next stairway.

"*Takbur-e-Tehriema . . .*" the Madhi began.

"*Takebur-e-Tehriema,*" the Companions echoed. They'd started the *qayem,* the prayer's third step. Paul had two, maybe two and a half minutes left. As soon as he reached the third floor, things became different. There were smells, Western smells. Gin? Vodka? The thought of the Madhi being a closet alcoholic normally would have been hilarious. Normally. God, were there rotten eggs? Actually, the smell was like sulphur and brimstone. Maybe the iron gates to hell were located somewhere on the third floor.

". . . *Wa-to-Aala-Jaad-o-Ka,*" filtered in through the windows. Two minutes. No more. No time to look for hell just yet. He ran until the hallway became a tunnel. Not a tunnel but the hallway narrowed till it touched his shoulders, and the ceiling dropped so low he had to crouch to avoid scraping his turban.

Then the turns began.

Right angles, left angles, turns that seemed like loops in the darkness but probably weren't—a sudden straight section that turned back on itself. A dead end. He tried to retrace his steps, found the straightaway again, but hit another dead end . . . and the chanting outside stopped.

"*Allah-o-Akbar!*" He knew the final chant was a shout, but the stone walls were so thick, they sounded like a whisper. Paul tried to run while feeling his way with his fingertips—the floor tilted away from the wall and gave the illusion he was walking upside down.

Move faster, he thought, faster. Light. Not much but light. It grew brighter, and Paul started to run, and the corners were cramped and the floor tilted, but that didn't stop him, and suddenly he was out of the maze and into a room . . . and he couldn't stand.

He tried to stand but he couldn't, so he fell to his knees and tried to shield his head and face—the Madhi's sword would be sharp.

But it didn't fall.

Paul waited until his head stopped spinning, then looked up. The room was like no other in the world. Sparse wasn't the word for it. Or Spartan. Early Prayer Cell was the closest he could come. There was a bare stone floor, and in the middle an elevated prayer carpet.

A glint.

Paul blinked, stared at the walls, and as his eyes adjusted to the amplified light, he realized the walls weren't walls at all but reflections. Mirrors. Hundreds of mirrors, rectangular mirrors, circular mirrors, mirrors of all sizes, some tilted at one angle, others at another, some reflecting off the ceiling. *That* was why the mirrors looked like walls: They were positioned to reflect off the ceiling. But why?

One thing for sure. The Madhi had disappeared. He wasn't out on the balcony, and he certainly wasn't in the room. The mirrors revealed every corner and niche. Soon Paul could stand, so he walked. The prayer carpet was exquisite. The arabesque in its upper left corner was among the most elaborate he'd ever seen. More surprises. A radio hidden in the base of the carpet's platform. A door in the back of the room, which explained where the Madhi had disappeared to. Paul wished he had more time to explore. There had to be a secret to this room, a secret that involved the Madhi's power, but the late-afternoon prayer, *Asr,* was only two hours away. Which meant there would be two hours to find the Madhi, find out about the plague, and take a present for Nuri . . . it would be the last trophy Paul would ever take. He walked to the door, opened it, and was greeted by the smell of sulphur and alcohol. So hell lay that way. All the answers to his questions lay at the end of the corridor amid fire and brimstone. Paul would spend his season in hell after all.

XIX.

Al Asil, Yemen—May 8, 1981

Claudia's adventure had ended just like those of John Wayne and Maureen O'Hara, Bogie and Bacall, and just about every other movie she'd ever seen: The hero gives the heroine just enough rope to hang herself, then appears just in time for the rescue.

Rick rummaged through a pack by the window. He pulled a bottle of Jack Daniel's black label from beneath some shirts and pants. "Drink?" he asked.

"No thanks."

He unscrewed the cap, took a deep swig, wiped its lip on his shirt, and handed the bottle to her. What the hell. The whiskey burned at first but mellowed considerably by the time it reached her stomach. "So what's happened in the past three weeks?" he asked.

Claudia looked out the window and remained silent. It wasn't hot—for Yemen—but fear and pain made her sweat. She went into a mental glide and imagined . . . what, she didn't know.

"What happened?" Rick asked.

. . . the floating scenes in her head still didn't make sense.

"Still with us?" Rick asked.

"Sorry," Claudia said. "The torture wasn't the worst part of the day. I knew most of the bodies in the street as people."

"I don't mean to be pushy," Rick said. "There's not much time."

Claudia wondered why she wasn't happier to see him. Her sidekick returned from the dead to save her life. He was tanned, healthy; why wasn't there an urge to wrap her arms around him? "You look pretty good for being dead," she said.

Rick dipped a rag into the bucket on the floor, scrubbed part of her face, squeezed out pink water, and whistled.

Claudia wanted to be alone. To think. To mourn. Maybe a hard look into the Highlands would help her regroup and relax. She stood and took a step toward the window, but Rich grabbed her robe and pulled her back down.

"I expected a more enthusiastic welcome," he said.

The worst day of her life, and Rick's ego was bruised because she didn't pat him on the head. She touched a fingertip to her lips and brushed it across his mouth. "For now," she said. She rested her chin on her hands. All she could visualize were the boy and how helpless she had been. It was a perfect occasion to start crying: a soft shoulder, a sense of relief, and the loss. Instead, she looked at Rick. "How?" she asked.

"How what?"

"How did you return from the dead and arrive here just in time to save me? And how did you get this?" she asked, gesturing around the room.

"Shouldn't I be questioning you?"

"No," she said in a tone that indicated she meant it.

He shrugged. "Where should I start?"

"Try your resurrection."

He frowned and shrugged again. "You saw me go down."

"Saw you!" she shouted. "I almost was shot going after you! I was the one who talked you into going. I was responsible. I walked away. Jesus, the last three weeks taught me a new meaning of the word *guilt.*"

Rick pulled the khaki shirt from his pants. His lower back was covered by a gauze bandage, "That put me down," he said. "A flesh wound. It entered above the kidney and exited through the love handle."

"You were writhing the last time I saw you."

"I didn't say it was painless," he said. He pulled down his shirt collar and touched a bandage on his neck. "This one saved my life. It knicked the fourth vertebrae and knocked me out. They didn't notice I was alive until after they saw I was Anglo—therefore valuable. I woke up in a stinking infirmary with flies crawling up my nose."

Claudia tried to speak, but Rick covered her mouth with his hand. He walked to the pack, removed an extra shirt and a pair of safari pants, and handed them to her.

"Why?" she asked.

Rick pointed to her clothes. "If all that blood came from you, this would be a monologue," he said.

She took the clothes and the bucket into the women's quarters, washed the blood from her body, and put the clean clothes on. Then she walked back into the men's quarters and sat across from Rick. She started to ask him how he'd arrived in Al Asil, but he put his hand over her mouth, then walked his fingers up the bridge of her nose, across her forehead, and along the part in her hair until he found the wound. "Head," he said, pointing to his lap.

Let someone else play doctor. She'd had her chance and failed miserably. Rick cleaned the wound, applied something that hurt like hell, then put on some bandages. "A gash like that would normally be worth five stitches. The bandages will have to do until we get back."

He pointed to her clothes. "On you, even baggy looks good."

Claudia wasn't going to be sidetracked any longer. "How did you arrive at just the right spot at just the right time?"

"You always were persistent," he said.

"Brushing flies from a nine-year-old's guts does wonders for tenacity."

Then Rick's face assumed a hangdog look, a look she'd never seen on him before. "Number two is simple," he said. "And it incorporates number three. I'm five grand richer."

"The lieutenant?" Claudia asked.

Rick nodded.

"Did he offer you the money in a Koran?"

"No. A *Time* magazine."

Claudia exhaled as she shook her head. "What about the story?" she asked. "*Our* story?"

"Jesus, Claude, I woke up on a stinking cot with flies buzzing all over the place, my back and neck thumping like hell, and Lieutenant Bu-jahl—"

"You're not on a first-name basis?"

Rick ignored her. "Bu-jahl told me that the consulate was informed that I died in an ambush. As soon as I could walk on my own, he gave me a guided tour of the dungeon."

"Sounds familiar," Claudia said.

"Only *I* knew there was no chance of someone arriving to get me out." Rick sniffed, then scratched his hairline. "The first cell we came to had a man who'd been half-eaten by rats. He was still alive. I said no thanks, so when Bu-jahl pulled out a magazine stuffed with thousands, I offered the man my hand."

"He doesn't have much imagination," Claudia said.

"Not in bribery, but he's a genius when it comes to torture. I've seen the results of his work on rebels. Most unpretty. He gets what he wants."

"Not from me he didn't."

Rick threw up his hands. "Claudia, Claudia," he said, shaking his head. He must have been pretty frustrated to revert to her real name. "He wasn't using pain on you. He used psychology. Those scratches on your fingers are a joke."

"I didn't laugh."

"You wouldn't have either if you'd seen what he can do to a human body with a white-hot crowbar." He shook his head again. "Pain's only one way to work on you. Let me guess: first he threatened disfigurement, then sexual humiliation."

Claudia sighed. "I'm *that* transparent?"

"You've never played by these rules. Go easy on yourself."

A gust of wind blew dust through the window—there was still blood in the air. Claudia breathed deeply to fight the nausea. "If you hadn't arrived when you did, I'd have told him anything."

"So would anyone else," Rick said. "Example, this is the deal I struck: I write the stories, he edits them and transmits them to Cairo via telegraph. It's still the only way to get information out. Since it's my byline, the home office knows I'm alive. Which makes life safer. Bu-jahl calls me when things are going to break."

"Why did they break over Al Asil?"

"The security police heard the bandit was selling arms to the Madhi. Things have changed since you disappeared. The rebellion is for real. The plague has made the Madhi legit. Tribesmen are lining up for the opportunity to become martyrs in the *jihad.* They swarmed a garrison outside Hoedida . . . only air power kept them from taking it. Last week, Bu-jahl was ten feet from a trip to heaven via the Molotov Cocktail Express. The strategy's changed. The government decided to hit the rebels in the Highlands before the rebels can hit *them* in the cities. I was photographing the effects of 'Puff the Magic Dragon' when I heard that Bu-jahl was entertaining an Anglo woman. I came running."

"I'm glad."

"I've tried everything. The Madhi's story is dead—at least from his angle. There's just no finding out where he is. Every copter in the Middle East is after him with no luck. They've even called in help."

"Which explains the CIA," Claudia said.

Rick looked startled, then frowned. "Where did you get that?"

"There was a survivor in the plague village." Claudia didn't fight the sexy smile that spread across her face. "I got to know him pretty well."

Rick didn't seem terribly happy about that.

"He said the CIA was crawling all over the plague village," Claudia said.

"Which could supply us with a way out of Yemen should we choose to part company with Bu-jahl."

"Hardly. The medic said it would be safer to bribe some fishermen. That one of the CIA people is a crazy."

"What else did you get out of him?" Rick asked.

"That the plague's for real. That there's no cure. That he's found enough inconsistencies in the story to be sure that Allah has nothing to do with it."

Rick moved his body back onto an elbow, then squirmed until

he became comfortable. "Unless someone finds this Madhi pretty soon," he said, "it won't make much difference whether Allah's in on it or not. Madhist rebellions have started in Oman, Saudi Arabia, next might be Egypt . . . then who knows?"

"Shit."

"Not eloquent but succinct," Rick said. "And if you think Bu-jahl is nasty, you should see a village of infidels once the Madhists finish with it. There isn't enough left for the crows."

Claudia stood and walked to the window. The Highlands were clear and bright, and the air so clear, she could see the mist hovering above the Red Sea. Paul was out in the mountains somewhere. Alone. Against thousands of rebels. If he was still alive. Scratch if. He was still out there. The sun was high enough that the browns, reds, and grays of the rock were as sharp as a Hopi painting . . . alone. How could she help Paul? Their relationship could certainly use some evening up—and he could use some help. "How do the Madhists treat nonbelievers?" she asked.

"We haven't found enough of one left to be sure."

"They treated me well."

"You're Claude, their ticket to the outside world," Rick said.

Claudia gazed back toward the mountains, then scratched her nose. "You know any Yemeni soldiers?" she asked.

"I've had the same driver and helicopter pilot for three weeks."

"Can they be bribed?"

Rick laughed. "Bribed? Without the greased palm, the wheels of this country would rust solid overnight."

"How much to get a helicopter?" she asked.

"That depends on where to, what for."

The smile returned. Claudia ran her tongue over her lips and tapped her fingers on the floor. "I have a thousand bucks in rials. Is any of your bribe left?"

"All of it." He leaned forward and shared her smile. His eyes grew big and bright. "What are you on to?"

Claudia kissed his cheek. "The Madhi angle isn't dead," she said.

"Let loose, Claude; what did this medic put you onto?"

"Not the medic, his Jebeli friend. He claimed the mountains talked to him."

"Well, what did they have to say?"

"That if you can convince your helicopter pilot that a trip to Jebel Ash Shu'ub is worth six thousand dollars or less, we have an exclusive interview with the Madhi."

"You sure?" Rick shouted. "You *dead* sure?"

"The medic was sure enough to risk a cross-country trip to get a shot at him," Claudia said.

Rick sat back and beamed. "That's sure enough for me." He scrambled to his feet and said, "It may take awhile to get things organized. I'll get back as soon as I can." Then he ran out of the building.

Without even stopping for a kiss.

That fast.

There was nothing wrong with that, of course; he should have left. There were bribes to arrange, money to gather—strange, he hadn't asked her for the money Paul had given her. Well, she could wait. Masses of helicopters landed and took off. A lot more took off than landed. Claudia thought Rick would be back in thirty minutes—an hour at most—but he wasn't, so when the second hour became the third, and the sun was almost to the point in the sky where it suddenly slipped behind the peaks (sometimes it dropped so rapidly she could swear she heard it plop), Claudia began to sense something was wrong, that she might have missed something.

Like her helicopter ride, maybe.

But Rick wouldn't dare leave her behind, particularly not with Lieutenant Bu-jahl still lurking around the village. Sure, Rick would be tempted by the solo byline, but the rebels didn't want Rick; they wanted her. Besides, Rick wasn't *that* big an asshole.

But he didn't come back.

Period.

So Claudia got angry. Then, atop being angry, she grew hungry. She knew where Nuri's wives kept food, but Nuri's was now Bu-jahl's, and she wasn't *that* hungry. And since Bu-jahl hadn't visited her, she concluded that Rick's quarters must be off-limits.

For some reason. And no hunger was great enough to make her risk an encounter with that man.

The pack. It would be stuffed with junk food and supplies.

She knelt down by it, untied the top flap, and began to search. The top layer contained half a package of Fig Newtons, a deck of cards, and a thin, flat, unbelievably sharp knife that she slipped into her calf pocket. It might mean protection later.

There were yo-yos in the bottom of the pack. Leave it to Hodges to bring three yo-yos when one would have been plenty. Claudia took them out and spread them across the floor—they were a ticket back to childhood. There was a Duncan Imperial, red with gold lettering; the legendary, top-of-the-line Black Beauty; and one that must have been a family heirloom . . . it was old, wooden, and so overused that only dark brown stains remained of what once must have been the finish.

She hadn't played with a yo-yo in years.

Claudia stood, looped the Imperial's string around the middle finger of her right hand, tested it for balance, let it roll from her palm, and was amazed at the speed it snapped back.

It actually hurt.

When she tried an Around the World, a move which had taken most of her ninth year to master, the yo-yo hit her on the head and almost reopened her gash.

The Imperial was not for beginners.

Maybe the antique was. It was made of hard wood, maybe maple, was light, and unusual only in that it was shaped more like a pentagon than a circle—five small indentations carved into each half. Judging from the knife scars, it was hand-carved. If Rick was working on a new design to revolutionize the industry, he'd made only one mistake. It didn't work. She couldn't find a loop to attach to her finger.

The string *had* to be in there somewhere. She tried to dig it out with a fingernail, but the groove was far too narrow for that.

It was old enough that it must have been repaired more than once. Maybe it came apart. She twisted on the halves one way. Nothing doing. Then the other. It moved. Slightly. She twisted and pulled, and the yo-yo snapped neatly into two pieces, one for the palm of each hand. It was amazing how the indentations corresponded to each finger.

Wrong.

Something was very wrong. There wasn't a finger loop. The string was welded to the middle of each half. When Claudia spread her arms, the string didn't tumble down but remained in tight, shiny coils. Then she realized that the string wasn't really a string, and the toy wasn't a toy at all.

It was a piano-wire garrote.

XX.

Bustān al Kaf Maryam, the Yemeni Highlands—
May 8, 1981

Blue light from the ceiling lamps flooded the corridor. It was fluorescent light—which meant electricity, therefore generators—but there was no chug of motors or smell of diesel fuel. The thick stone walls smothered sound. After fifty feet, Paul came to a door, opened it, and entered a vestibule. Then there was another door, a metal slab so solid it could have come from a treasury vault—its handle was a foot wide and shaped like a spinning wheel. And he couldn't budge it. He twisted and pried, used his shoulder for leverage, but nothing happened. There had to be a release somewhere. Paul stepped back and looked for something, a lever or loose rock, and found a metal plate in the floor. When he stepped on it, an iron door slid down from the ceiling behind him. There was a vague whistle as the atmosphere changed. His ears popped.

He was in an airlock.

Maybe he should have tried the line Ali Baba used to open the forty thieves' cave . . . instead, Paul waited for the pressure to stabilize, then tried the door handle again. The wheel spun noiselessly. He pushed and the door opened. And what was on the other side seemed less believable than the *Arabian Nights:* a laboratory. . . .

. . . sparkling yellow floor tiles, white walls, negative pressure ducts, fans spaced equidistantly in the ceiling, movable glass cabinets, Bunsen burners, individual lab carrels. Black signs with red lettering dotted the wall: DANGER: CONTAINMENT AREA; DANGER: RADIOACTIVE MATERIALS; CAUTION: BIOHAZARDS.

The smells were not of this world—or at least any world Paul had been in since college chemistry. Sulphur. Ammonia. A whiff of camel dung or stagnant water would have been nice . . . to remind him he was still in Yemen.

There were whirring centrifuges, racks of test tubes, petri dishes filled with gels of various colors . . . but no Madhi. Time to check the rest of the doors. The one that read CULTURE CONTAINMENT AREA wouldn't budge. No surprise there; a red light flashed above it. The next door opened to a cloud of freezing steam—a walk-in refrigerator. The conference room was empty, and so was a bathroom with shower and flush toilet. The door marked J. CORBIN—GROUP LEADER was slightly ajar, and a hollow sound, perhaps a knee bumping against a metal desk, filtered through the opening. Paul eased the dagger from his belt and pushed the door.

A man dressed in a black *'aba* sat behind a desk, his feet propped up; the cloud of cigarette smoke above his head drifted toward an air-conditioning vent. A turban cloth lay on the floor next to a pair of sandals—he now wore jogging shoes. His face was perfectly balanced, a cold, almost ghostly beauty. His profile was a duplicate of a Roman senator's bust, only he'd replaced his toga with the Madhi's robe.

"If I had guessed you'd be chatting with Allah," Paul said, "I would have guessed wrong."

The man started—slightly—and looked up. He glanced at his robe, almost smiled, then let his eyes follow the contours of Paul's face. "CIA or the medic?" the man asked in crisp English.

"I *was* the medic."

There wasn't any fear in the man's eyes, and whatever surprise surfaced was under control. He looked more inconvenienced than anything. "I've expected you for weeks," he said. "Though hardly under these circumstances." When he began to stand, Paul motioned him back down with the dagger.

"I assume the *J* before Corbin doesn't stand for Jesus," Paul said.

"Jacob."

"Doctor?"

"B.S., Biology, Harvard, 1948. Ph.D., Biochemistry, M.I.T., 1952," Corbin said. He paused and looked at Paul's *'aba* and turban. "You don't seem surprised by the facilities."

"Only that they're in Yemen," Paul said. He sat in an orange swivel chair, pulled it up to the desk, leaned forward, and moved the dagger toward Corbin's throat. "Talk."

"No need for that," Corbin said, nodding toward the dagger. "I have a low pain threshold." The voice was too calm, too rational, too controlled.

Paul pulled the blade back. "How does it work?"

"The P-4 lab?"

"The plague."

Corbin ran his fingers through his flowing white hair and left brown makeup streaks. He glanced at the clock, then at the door. "I have a diagram in—"

"Try to open that desk," Paul said, "and I'll have to look elsewhere for my information."

The hands eased away from the drawer and returned to the top of the desk. Corbin took a deep breath; he whistled as he exhaled. "How much do you know about recombinant DNA research?"

Biology 101, or was it *Time* magazine? Sequencing. Restriction enzymes. Amino acids shaped like spiral staircases. *Confusion.* "I've been there," Paul said. "Many moons ago."

Corbin strummed his fingers impatiently on the desk—the noise professors once made when Paul arrived during office hours for extra help. "Genes make you what you are," Corbin said. "Your blueprints. They're made of DNA. How that DNA is ordered determined that you'd be a human being as opposed to say . . . *Yersina pestis,* the bacteria you call plague." Again the eyes started to wander; again they settled on the clock.

"Two hours till prayer time," Paul said. "I've been here long enough to know there'll be no visitors till then."

The eyes came back to the conversation. "We've discovered enzymes that can split DNA," Corbin continued, "and others that can rejoin it. Thus we can insert new strands of DNA, change the order of things as it were."

"You can take parts of rats and put them in cats," Paul said.

"Useless child's play," Corbin said. "The challenge is to alter existing creatures in a useful way. We redraw blueprints. If living things can be compared to computers, we reprogram them."

Paul leaned back in his chair, scratched his nose, then ran a hand through his beard. "Which tells me nothing," he said.

Corbin took a cigarette from his desktop, offered one to Paul and, when Paul refused, struck a match. "What do you know about *herpes simplex?*" He lit his cigarette, inhaled, and let the smoke escape through his nose.

It was a disease, but Paul had never encountered it in Yemen—no, where was it—*bingo!* Those VD movies in basic training. Symptoms: blisters on genitals and elsewhere. Contagious as hell. And one extremely notable feature: no cure. Once you had it, you had it. But it was time to learn about Corbin, too, so Paul kept quiet.

Corbin didn't have much patience. He paused ten seconds, no more. "It's a virus. It lays dormant in a human indefinitely until something, a food, illness, sometimes even sunlight, triggers an eruption. Then fever blisters appear."

"I know," Paul said.

Corbin looked at Paul with uncertainty. Good. "We used *herpes simplex* as our vector," Corbin continued, "the material into which we spliced the DNA coded for plague toxins. Instead of the blisters caused by *herpes simplex,* buboes, discoloration, tachycardia, rales erupt. Death follows."

"An unstable bacteria?"

"I said nothing about bacteria," Corbin interrupted. "I said a strand of DNA, which is coded to produce plague toxins."

"Why put poison in someone's system if an illness, the sunlight, some goddamn accident can trigger—"

"You're oversimplifying," Corbin said. "Since we create the strand, we can program it the way we want. No chance for 'accidents.' This DNA is sensitive to only two triggers: a chemical that doesn't occur in nature, or an abrupt rise in body temperature."

Paul sat back and began to rock. Jesus. An incurable disease that lay dormant indefinitely, wasn't contagious, and could be triggered at any time. "Amazing," Paul said.

Corbin feigned a bow. His eyes were perfect, perfect and grotesque. There was emptiness in their perfection, no room for passion or remorse.

"Specifics?" Paul asked.

"If you'd let me use—" Corbin reached for the drawer.

"Hands above the desk," Paul said.

Corbin closed his eyes. His fists clenched, then relaxed. He breathed evenly for a few moments, then said, "Your assistant, Ali Abdul—"

"Ali worked for you?"

Corbin nodded.

"Where is he?" Paul asked.

"Recently deceased," Corbin said. "He planted the vector in your village well. The qat you distributed was treated with the chemical trigger."

Paul had given each leaf, each stem with a smile . . . like the angel of death. He breathed deeply and let the air escape slowly, ever so slowly, through his mouth. "Why am I alive?" he asked. "Ali spoon-fed me the water. I chewed enough qat to last a month."

"Which is why you interest us," Corbin said. "There are control mechanisms. We hope to postpone the Apocalypse, not create it." He took a drag from the cigarette. "The vector only survives in a fluid environment between seventy-five and one hundred and two degrees."

"Only water?" Paul asked.

"Or drinks served at room temperature or warm yogurt . . . any number of things. But the protective protein coat lasts only for a week unless it integrates into a body . . ." Corbin sat back and scratched behind his ear. "You said 'spoon-fed'?"

"I was out. Malarial paroxysm."

Corbin tapped his temples, then sat back. "A fever above one hundred and two?"

"I said malaria."

"Your temperature inactivated the vector," Corbin said. "No

plague DNA, no plague symptoms." Corbin shook his head, covered his face with his hands, and massaged his forehead. "We should have let the security police keep you . . . and avoided the present problem."

"There's another problem," Paul said. He rolled the dagger in the palm of his hand. "The children too young to chew qat. Twenty or so. In the clinic. They were dead when I got back."

Corbin was silent.

"No time to run out of whys," Paul said. He touched the dagger to the tip of Corbin's nose.

Still silence.

Paul pushed until blood trickled down into the corner of Corbin's mouth. "Your village was the testing ground. We had to know everything before we could take the vector out of Yemen. There was data to collect. Tests to run."

"Ali wrecked the radio to buy you time."

"The security police aren't the type to help us collect samples."

"And the children were your guinea pigs," Paul said. "You force-fed them the qat, sat back, and took notes." He moved the blade from Corbin's nose to his throat.

And for the first time, there was panic in Corbin's voice. "How long have you been in Yemen? How many incurables did you treat each week? How much leprosy? How many starve? If we win, the money that now goes for guns will be turned into food and medicine. . . ."

Corbin's voice faded as images rolled through Paul's mind, connections made at a level deeper than consciousness: the *'aqil*'s house; the mushroom rock; the Night of Entrance; the qat; and they all merged in Johara's face and spun and spun and spun . . . and fell into place. "One thing more," Paul said. He could scarcely gather the strength to talk.

"Before what?"

"Say you were infected by the vector," Paul asked, "but never ate the chemical or had the sudden temperature rise?"

"You'd never know you'd been infected," Corbin said.

"How long would you live?"

"Indefinitely."

The images melted in the tidal pool, and Johara's reflection superimposed on his own. Paul had killed Johara twice. First when he forced her to eat the qat, again with the poison ring. When he began to talk, his voice wasn't human anymore. "It's no longer a question of whether you're going to die," Paul said, "but how long I choose to take."

Corbin's eyelid twitched. His lips drew tight across his teeth.

"I owe more people than I can possibly repay," Paul said. "Only one place to start: detaching the Madhi's nose from his face."

Corbin went for the drawer, but long before he could withdraw the small pistol, Paul had slammed the drawer on Corbin's wrist. A scream. Paul twisted Corbin's free arm behind his back, then brought the dagger to the bottom of his nose. "I'm not the Madhi!" Corbin shrieked.

"You have unusual taste in clothes," Paul said.

Corbin's eyes seemed to sort through the pain. He quieted. He tried to regulate his breath as he stared at the desk top.

"No time to stop talking," Paul said. He pushed down harder on the drawer.

Nothing from Corbin but a grimace.

"There's another option," Paul said. "I used it in Nam. I start by chopping off your hand. You talk, I squeeze down on the wrist like a tourniquet. You live. You stop talking, I let go of your wrist, and red stuff squirts all over the place. . . ." Paul raised the heavy dagger above the point where Corbin's arm disappeared into the desk drawer.

"Mecca!" Corbin shouted. "Khalid!" He started to shake violently.

"Who will do it?"

"Oh, Jesus," Corbin wailed. When he started to black out, Paul slapped him back into consciousness.

"Who," Paul asked, pushing the drawer in farther.

"I'm only a scientist!"

"Who?" Another push. A bone cracked.

"He has freedom to move!"

"Who?" Paul asked.

"Talāl! The Madhi!"

"He moves where there is a prediction?"

"The microwave trigger is only good at ten feet!" Corbin screamed.

"How could this Talāl get to King Khalid? The PLO has been after him for years."

Just a moment's hesitation from Corbin, and Paul kneed the drawer. A loud scream. "Arafat doesn't belong to the Saudi Royal Family!" Corbin's voice started to trail off.

"And this Talāl does?"

"Talāl ibn Saud. A prince." Paul eased up on the pressure. Corbin sighed. A cough caught in his voice. "Who else could afford this?" Corbin asked, motioning around the lab.

"Khalid wouldn't take a drink from the Prophet himself," Paul said.

"He doesn't have to," Corbin said. "We invented a topical. Plague DNA grafted into plantar's wart virus. A drop on the skin. A day for integration—"

"When?" Paul asked.

"Today . . . this evening."

Then it was time to move on, on to the radio in the mirrored room for a short broadcast to the Saudis. "When I let up on your wrist," Paul said, "if the gun appears, you're out one hand."

The gun didn't appear. Paul took the turban cloth from the floor, tied Corbin tightly to the chair, then turned the chair upside down and pushed it under the desk. He took the pistol from the drawer and slipped it into his *'aba,* then looked down at Corbin. "For the life of me, I don't know why you're still alive," he said.

Paul walked back into the lab. It was time to limit the escape routes. He found several lengths of pipe and wedged one into the wheellike latch on the Culture Containment room. But did he really want to contact the Yemenis and the Saudis? Just one call and the Madhist rebellion was finished and, with it, a chance for stability and peace in the Middle East. Just turn his back, walk down the corridor, and not stop till he found Claudia. Khalid would die, the rebellion would spread from Yemen to Saudi Arabia, and . . . fuck it. The Madhi was an illusionist, no different from any of the others . . .

. . . and Paul didn't like his style.

Paul took a length of pipe with him and ran up the corridor to the steel door. He pushed the release, turned the handle, and slipped into the airlock. After he closed the door, he wedged the pipe into the handle. A further precaution. Even if Corbin escaped from the chair, this would be as far as he got. The air pressure equalized. As soon as the iron slab raised toward the ceiling, Paul knew something was very wrong. Faint pops, distant thudding—gunfire—battle sounds muffled by two doors and a stone wall. He sprinted up the corridor, opened the door, and rolled into the mirrored room. There were patches of shattered glass where ricochets bounced off the balcony into mirrors. Paul crept across the floor and peered into the courtyard.

There was a war going on. And not a small war. There were no breaks in the small-arms fire. Helicopters wheeled in under the overhang, fired rockets, and strafed the courtyard. The minaret took a rocket in the dome—and collapsed in a roar. Two, three small helicopters, Loaches hovered above the courtyard and poured fire through the open windows. A Loach bore in on the balcony, hovered for an instant as if looking for someone, then wheeled away without firing.

Paul couldn't wait for the Yemenis to consolidate their forces . . . Khalid might be dead by then. Paul crept back to the radio and turned it on. Again a Loach streaked toward the balcony. Now, Paul thought, if the Yemenis haven't blown the transmitting tower . . . He slipped on the headphones:

> SOS—SOS—SOS
> King Khalid in danger—
> Saudi Prince Madhi—carries plague toxin—
> Intercept Talāl Ibn Saud—
> Repeat—Intercept

The rotorwash of a helicopter swirled dust around the

room—and it was a permanent rotorwash; it blew shattered glass aginst his foot and lifted the *'aba* above his head. He paused the standard ten seconds, then began the broadcast again:

SOS—SOS—SOS
King Khalid in . . .

A line of bullets whizzed past Paul's head and exploded into the transmitter. Molten lead and sharp glass tore his hands and face. Paul rolled from the set, drew the pistol from his waistband, tried to wink the blood from his eyes, and when the helicopter pulled away, the rotor sounds were replaced by an eerie voice, the half-spoken, half-sung verse to an old song: "It Had to Be You."

An M-16 pointed to Paul's head and motioned for him to throw the pistol away. The handgun clattered in the broken glass. Paul's eyes moved from the campaign boots up to the tiger-striped fatigues up to the face. A beard. Sunglasses. Piece-of-My-Heart.

"You're awfully slick," Piece-of-My-Heart said. "Here I hunt the Madhi for months, and by the time I arrive, you've collected souvenirs."

"He's not here," Paul said. "Try Mecca. About to fulfill a new prophecy. Thirty more seconds and I would have put a stop to him."

"Khalid's only part of our game. You know that." He glanced down the corridor. "The gene lab?" When Paul did a double take, Piece-of-My-Heart smiled. "Shit, yes, we knew, but we didn't know where. There's been a strong black market in gene-splicing materials for half a decade. We traced some to Yemen. What would these goatherds do with restriction enzymes? Use the crates for goat pens?" He laughed but held the rifle perfectly still. "The scientists?"

"Detained," Paul said.

"Then it's time we got down to it. They can wait till I'm done with you." Small-arms fire roared outside. Paul heard a chugging motor, the scraping of a broken helicopter rotor, then an explosion in the courtyard. "I had a chat with your friend, Claudia," Piece-of-My-Heart said. "She sends her best."

"You took Al Asil."

"Used to be a scenic little burg." A pause. "Don't worry about her. No one's gonna hurt old Claude. She's enough to make a man turn in his game bag. Almost."

"Which makes you her photographer."

"She's a morsel, but such a child . . . and such loose lips—"

"And Nuri?" Paul asked.

"The bandit?"

Paul nodded.

Piece-of-My-Heart unbuttoned one of his thigh pockets, withdrew Nuri's nose bag, and removed a nose covered by still-coagulating blood. "He told me to give you something to remember him by." He tossed the nose at Paul's feet. "My, but he was loyal. A whole afternoon of Bu-jahl's crowbar games, and not so much as a peep."

Paul tried to keep Nuri's image from his mind. It would bring rage, and with rage, mistakes. "You've a game in mind?" Paul asked coldly.

"Just death," Piece-of-My-Heart said, "just death." He glanced at the blood on Paul's face and hands. "You're sixty, seventy percent healthy? Plenty." He motioned toward the prayer carpet with his M-16. "I want you away from the broken glass."

More bullets bounced off the ceiling. More mirrors shattered. The sun slipped beneath the rim of the overhang. Still two hours till sunset, three to darkness. Too long to do him any good. When the slanting rays hit the mirrors, the room glowed with a strange aura. It was incredibly bright. Piece-of-My-Heart squinted, blinked, and motioned for Paul to stop. He threw Paul a wooden disk—two parts connected with piano wire.

Piece-of-My-Heart took an identical garrote from his pocket. "The original plan was to arm you with the Spit. Poetry, you must admit. I brought it along from Al Rattaf, but I had to leave it in the bandit camp. Claude was in the room." He frowned, grinned, then the muzzle motioned for Paul to move . . .

. . . when Paul stepped onto the carpet's upper left corner, the world exploded in light. Paul instinctively rolled . . . a burst of M-16 fire filled the spot where he had been. Mirrors shattered.

When he looked up to see why Piece-of-My-Heart had missed, he couldn't see anything. Piece-of-My-Heart? He couldn't even focus on the hand three inches in front of his face. First, it suffered funhouse distortion, then went up in flame, then disappeared in darkness. Directions? He knew which way was down—barely—its opposite was up. The others were scrambled. No sense crawling. Noise would attract Piece-of-My-Heart.

Paul could wait. He squatted for a day, longer in the bush without moving, scarcely breathing . . . but now he didn't have a day. Already the battle was slowing. When it stopped, Piece-of-My-Heart's playmates would arrive and decrease the already poor odds. Paul crawled carefully, feeling for any broken mirror that would make a fatal noise. He paused to listen for breathing. . . . Piece-of-My-Heart couldn't be more than ten feet away, but there wasn't a sound.

As Paul edged forward, his hand began to take form . . . glass splinters . . . the fingers were perfectly outlined. He pulled back and the hand dissolved in chaos. He moved forward. A fingernail appeared. Then a knuckle. Again he pulled back. He was in front of a broken mirror. Where the mirrors were shattered, there was no distortion. Paul froze—and listened.

Silence.

If Paul were Piece-of-My-Heart, he'd squat by a broken mirror and wait for anything, a hand, a foot, preferably a head, but anything to emerge from the chaos. Then . . .

Who knew? Piece-of-My-Heart could be at an arm's length and waiting. What to do? What to do?

Illusion.

Of course! The room was an illusion, like all the Madhi's miracles, a controlled illusion. Controlled. Then the secret of the room was to find its control.

The carpet.

The motor had engaged when Paul stepped on the carpet. The Madhi held audiences from the carpet . . .but how to get to the carpet without getting clotheslined by Piece-of-My-Heart? Less firing outside. Ten minutes left, maybe less.

In slow, painful movements, Paul eased across the floor, carefully feeling for the shards of mirror that would indicate the distortion-free areas in the room—the dead zones, if he blundered into one. Splinters. Paul felt one way, then the other. The glass had sprayed from the right. Paul went left.

More glass.

More groping.

The platform.

Where was the control? Where . . . The motor had started when he touched the upper left corner of the platform. Keeping hold of the thick wool carpet, he crawled to the lower right corner, then moved onto the platform and saw a world of shadows.

Ringwraiths.

It was a world of neither darkness nor light, but a flickering blend of both. But a world with direction. The mirrors weren't chaos anymore but a yellow-red wall. There was a black hole in the room, a shadow whose head turned from side to side, always listening, always waiting. The shadow fell to all fours and crawled as Paul had crawled, smooth as liquid, feeling for glass, edging for the prayer carpet.

Nam thoughts.

The first man Paul had killed crept toward him that way, crept through the bush in a semidark jungle afternoon, and Paul squatted quietly, wondering, could he, could he kill another? . . . but a dozen years had passed and with it the doubt.

Piece-of-My-Heart was five feet away now, closing like a plane on radar . . . three feet . . . Nuri in the fire's glow.

Paul leapt, but Piece-of-My-Heart was fast and moved both hands up to his throat before the garrote pulled tight. Piece-of-My-Heart shifted one way, then another, trying to throw Paul off-balance, but Paul *was* balance, and Paul had debts to pay, and the piano wire quickly cut through the skin, sprayed blood, hit bone, but no problem, because Paul knew the wire game—he slid the wire toward the joints, wiggled it slightly as he hit tendons—and sliced right through, one at a time, and the fingertips were on the floor now, and the hands spurted and beat on Paul's leg, but the wire was in the throat now, cutting deeper and deeper, and the spasms started, the jerking, the gurgling as blood poured into the lungs, and Paul slipped on the blood, but he didn't fall, and the quivering started . . .

. . . and stopped.

And Paul stopped. The gunshots quieted. Scarcely any time. Paul dropped the body and crawled back on the platform. Where there were *on* switches, there had to be *off* switches. Back to the upper left corner. He pushed the arabesque, and the whirring motors stopped. The flashing chaos settled back into the wall. The radio was done. So was Khalid. So was Piece-of-My-Heart. His head hung loosely from his body from tendons . . . a nightmare doll.

Grappling hooks clanked over the edge of the balcony. It would take the soldiers thirty seconds to crawl thirty feet and enter the balcony. Paul took the M-16 and some extra clips, then sprinted toward the maze—and hoped no one would be waiting for him at the far end.

They weren't.

The Companions had retreated to the upper level of the building and paid no attention to the additional black *'aba* sprinting down the corridor. Loaches hovered outside and poured bullets through the windows. Paul zigzagged to the back windows. To the shadows. Bullets chipped the native rock above him. He moved to a ledge outside the window and jumped ten feet to a second-floor ledge, then another leap to the ground floor. Some snipers saw him, and the rocks chipped at his feet, but he was in the shadows now, and the shadows meant safety. He ran for some boulders—they marked a goat trail that weaved through the gaps in the overhang toward the summit of the mountain. And Paul became the mountain goat. Fast and sure, sticking to the darkness, he was on the highest arête by the time the moon had peaked and was into the next valley by dawn.

But he didn't stop for rest. There was no time. Claudia was three days away . . . and she was with that psychopath Bu-jahl.

XXI.

Mecca, Saudi Arabia—May 8, 1981

No sooner had Talāl left his room and wedged into the stream of people on their way to the Sacred Mosque than a muezzin called early-afternoon prayer. Everyone dropped to their knees and opened their hearts to Allah. Despite the sour stench that rose from the massed bodies, despite the fact he found the posture required for *salaat* painful, despite the infinite care he had to take not to bump the ancient Koran he held in his briefcase, Talāl was as cheery and alert as any time since childhood. The reason was simple. Several hundred thousand people from all over the Middle East, fully ten times the number who would normally be in Mecca this time of year, had gathered together to scrutinize the Madhi's miracles. Next week, once Khalid was dead, the crowd would swell by ten times again, only then they would gather to pay homage to the true Madhi. Uniting the entire Moslem world was no farther away than the Koran at his side.

The sun was high and white, and the flat heat seemed to radiate as much from the gray-white mountains and buildings as the sun. Dust itched his nose, and the rays felt so sharp, they could have been rain stinging his face.

After the muezzin and the crowd joined together for the final call of "Allah-o-Akbar," Talāl rose to his feet, brushed off his white *thobe,* and glanced around. Mecca was the holiest of holy cities, a spot where only Muslims were allowed entrance. It was the spiritual heart of Islam. It was here that the Prophet Mohammed had been born, here that the archangel Gabriel descended with the revelation of truth that there is but one God and he is Allah, here that Mohammed purified the Ka'ba, the black-robed shrine within the Sacred Mosque, by overturning the idols and promising to worship only Allah.

Two years before, three hundred and fifty of Talāl's followers had been killed in an attempted takeover of the Sacred Mosque; it was only fitting that the Madhi should perform a great miracle here.

Perhaps the only thing more noticeable about the crowd than its smell was its excitement. The visitors were of all races, all Islamic sects, and though the tones of the conversations differed, only one name was on all lips: the Madhi. Talāl brushed past a man in peasant rags who had missing teeth, enormous ears, and open sores on his face, then squeezed between two elegant Orientals who argued the respective merits of the "Miracle of the Camel Race" and the "Miracle of the Disbelieving Village," and reached out to a wall of mud and rough stone. He ripped an onion-skin parchment covered by Arabic script from the wall. Despite the hundreds of Saudi National Guardsmen who arrested anyone distributing Madhist prophecies, despite swarms of security police in brown *thobes* and headcloths who attempted to stop any conversation mentioning the Madhi, copies of the latest prophecy appeared everywhere:

THE MADHI'S FINAL WARNING TO THOSE WHO IGNORE THE LIGHT OF MIRACLES

Brethren:

I write this final warning because I am a humble servant of Allah and, knowing that you are the same, believe you cannot have heard of my prophecies and miracles or else you would have joined me.

Allah has given me His sword of righteousness, the plague, so that I may convince my enemies that He will destroy all those who oppose me. Satan has put the love of the West into my enemies: the love of wealth, the love of technology, which appears to make life's pathways easier but paves only the pathways to hell. Beware: The life of ease and pomp cause hypocrisy to spring up in the heart like rain causes the bitter herbs to grow.

The Saudi Khalid, a sinner who affronts Allah with his claim to be king of Islam's heartland, is among the bitterest of these herbs. Today he will enter the Sacred Mosque for prayer. Tomorrow his soul will enter hell's boiling pitch.

Brethren, if upon reading these words you still don't believe, meditate on the creation of heaven and earth. Meditate on the miracles I have shown you. While there is still time, meditate on Allah's Wrath.

Pass on these words to those who have not heard. While Allah's patience is as infinite as His mercy, it is not extended to those who disobey His will.

Know that all things are in the hands of Allah. Leave all to Him and rely on Him. There is no God but Allah. He is great. Amen.

Mohammed al Madhi al Muntazar

Talāl handed the parchment to an ascetic-looking man who said he was from Cairo, then eased his briefcase away from the man's arm. Even with the briefcase for protection, he had to be sure nothing ruptured the Koran's protective membrane, so he stepped under the arched mud gate of a cemetery, snapped open the briefcase, and felt the hook with his gloved hand. Though the ancient leather appeared to be sheathed by a protective cover, there were actually two covers. The inner one was plastic and the outer one a membrane that would dissolve when touched by the oils on human skin. Between the covers was a thin coating of clear liquid—the plantar's wart virus into which the gene coded for plague toxin had been grafted. Talāl would open his briefcase, tell the guards of the book's value and fragility, then be cleared for the King's Pavilion. Talāl would approach King Khalid, take the book in his gloved hand, and offer it to Khalid. The king would smile at so rare a gift, the outer membrane would dissolve, the plague vector would touch Khalid's skin, and tomorrow, when Talāl had breakfast with the king, he would hold a small black box beneath his *thobe*. . . .

Khalid's death would be the signal for the thousand Companions hidden outside Mecca to seize the Sacred Mosque and capture the *ulamas,* the teachers who were the final authorities on Islamic law. Either the *ulamas* would declare Talāl Madhi, or there would be new *ulamas.*

Talāl closed the briefcase and returned to the street. He stayed in the shadows—though the temperature in the sun approached 103 degrees, it was ten degrees cooler in the shade. He remembered a childhood shortcut. He walked into an alley, passed some of the smooth cement buildings that were the new Mecca, and turned into Al Mas'a, Mecca's largest bazaar. Though many of the buildings were new, the smells were rich and ancient: spices, dried food, incense. There were shops for prayer rugs, religious literature, places to buy *thobes* and headcloths. Talāl squeezed past a crowded corner and looked up . . . seven minarets rose from the gray-green marble of the Sacred Mosque. He quickly looked to his left, hoping to see Jebel Khandama, the largest of the bare mountains surrounding Mecca, but a multistoried building blocked the way. When he was a child, each trip to the Sacred Mosque had been magical, and the sight of Jebel Khandama recalled that magic. As soon as Talāl was declared Madhi, all buildings that obstructed the view of the mountains would be torn down.

And it was all so simple.

He couldn't help it. He had the urge to gloat. Why not talk to a commoner? A commoner would give him a sense of the masses. He picked a shop in an old building, a shop that sold prayer rugs and religious artifacts, ducked as he walked through the open door, and paused to let his eyes adjust to the light. There were thread-worn carpets of red, gold, and blue hanging from the walls and crammed into stacks in the corners. The display case was long and waist-high; it contained religious books and ancient scrolls. A shadow entered through a rear door and became a man. He looked carefully at Talāl's clothes, then into his eyes. He smiled. "Can I serve the rich visitor?" he asked.

"Your best?" Talāl asked, dismissing the carpets on the walls with a wave of his hand.

"For special customers," the shopkeeper said, "there is always special merchandise. Come." There was a wheezing in the man's voice. He motioned for Talāl to follow and led him down a bare white hallway and into a small room with no windows. He flipped a light switch on the walls. The room burst into color from the rugs on the wall. The shopkeeper opened his arms and slowly circled as if he were unveiling a treasure hoard or a sumptous feast. He sat back on his heels and smiled.

"Your best?" Talāl asked.

The man looked insulted. "There is none better," he said. There was dust floating in the air, and the man wrinkled his nose as though he might sneeze. He walked to a wall and began to stroke a maroon-and-gold carpet as though it were a favorite pet. "This one," he said, tracing a finger along its arabesques, "only five thousand rials."

Talāl felt the carpet's weave. Loose. Thin. Shoddy. "Are you a man of faith?"

The man almost jumped in surprise. The insult returned to his voice. "You will not find a better five-thousand-rial carpet in all—"

"I wasn't questioning your honesty," Talāl said. "I asked if you were a man of faith."

"None is more faithful." Talāl couldn't judge the tone in the man's voice but concluded he wasn't smart enough to be sarcastic.

"What do you think of this Madhi?" Talāl asked.

The shopkeeper moved his lips and made a slurping noise. He rubbed his nose and moved to another carpet. "Note the attention given to—"

"Have you no fear of Allah's Wrath?" Talāl interrupted.

"These holy ones come and go," the man said. He turned back to the carpet. "Note the gold thread—"

"They say this Madhi performs miracles," Talāl said.

The shopkeeper picked at the hair bristling from his nose. "Would he give me a house by the gulf? Would he send my sons to school in America? He would do nothing for me." Then he smiled and raised his hand in a gesture that indicated a brilliant idea. He took a key from the folds of his *thobe* and, in movements that were more ceremony than function, unlocked a large tamarisk chest and opened it. "Only for those with traditional tastes," he said.

Talāl was becoming angry. He had given orders for most of his life under the assumption they would be obeyed. Now this camel-herd turned mercantilist avoided a simple question. "Aren't miracles enough for you?" he asked.

The shopkeeper threw up his hands as though he couldn't believe that a man with such breeding could be so naive. "What do I care who rules Saudi or Yemen or America or—"

Talāl's first instinct was to strike the man, but he pulled back. "That one," he snapped, pointing to a green carpet with white-and gold weaving.

"A man of exceptional taste. Seventy-five hundred rials."

When Talāl took a wad of rials from inside his *thobe* and laid the money on the rug, the man acted as though he were insulted Talāl hadn't made a counteroffer. He rolled up the carpet, and Talāl tucked it under his arm, walked down the hallway, out through the door, and into the bazaar. These mercantilists were disgusting. A glint distracted him. He looked up at the lines of windows stacked up the side of a modern hotel, up past the roof to a small patch of blue sky trapped between two buildings.

Progress.

He squinted and looked again. The glint hadn't come from the windows but from something atop the roof. Something moving. Perhaps a rifle barrel.

Cries came from the crowd. Men in uniform were struggling through the massed bodies, trying to get to the Sacred Mosque. There was a thumping of rotor blades. Two helicopter transports swept over the bazaar and hovered above the mosque. Ladders dropped from their hatches, and a steady line of soldiers crawled down into the mosque. Clusters of soldiers appeared at all the gates and stopped the crowd from entering.

Talāl drew back into the shadows.

He heard bolts snap on automatic rifles. The crowd tried to move back from the mosque but were trapped by a second group of soldiers that encircled the bazaar. Soldiers with olive-drab uniforms and red-and-white-checkered headcloths. Saudi National Guard.

The Madhi's miracles would have to wait.

Talāl stepped into the bazaar and, just for a moment, tried to move against the stream of people flowing toward the mosque. It was impossible. They were being herded down the bazaar by armored personnel carriers. Only by using his briefcase as a battering ram was he able to fight back to the alley by the store where he'd bought the carpet. Others poured into the alley, trying to escape being crushed by the crowd. Talāl climbed three dried mud steps and looked out toward the mosque. A national guardsman was distributing sheets of paper to men in brown *thobes,* the security police. The paper sparkled in the sun: photographs. The security policemen began to rip headcloths from men and hold their faces next to the photos. It wasn't hard to guess whose face they were looking for. The muscles in Talāl's throat contracted. He had witnessed the beheadings after the last failed takeover of the mosque, the blood blossoming from the shoulders, the crowd-noise, the jerking torsos.

Even his status in the Royal Family would do him no good.

There was an escape route through an alley directly across the bazaar, but there was no chance to get there unless he walked on heads. Besides, the bazaar was merely a larger trap. He was trapped by his own followers.

The only chance was to disappear. For a price, the mercantilist would help him . . . if he could get to the shop. Literally crawling on top of heads and shoulders, he moved the thirty feet to the shop entrance. Once he slipped between two bodies and was almost trampled but clawed his way up. He rolled in through the door and sat his face toward the glass counter. As soon as the sunspots eased into the gray light of the shop, Talāl looked for a place to hide his briefcase.

"There is madness outside," the shopkeeper said.

Talāl nodded and swallowed. He tried to catch his breath. He looked straight into the man's eyes. "What would you do with a house on the gulf?" Talāl asked. "Would your shop seem empty if your children were in America?"

The shopkeeper shifted his shoulders and smiled. "The soldiers are looking for someone, no?"

"Are there places here to hide?" Talāl asked.

"For there to be so many soldiers, for them to be so inhospitable, the man they search for must be most important."

"You deal in antiques, in religious artifacts," Talāl said. He stood, opened the briefcase, picked up the Koran in his gloved hand, and held it out to the man. The shopkeeper walked suspiciously toward Talāl, took the Koran, carefully studied the cover, then opened the book. Already the membrane would be dissolving and the plague vector integrating into his system.

"I have never seen one so fine," the man said.

"Take off the cover; feel the leatherwork." The man removed the cover and handed it to Talāl, who discarded the cover, then his gloves. The proof.

"Five hundred thousands rials?" the man asked.

"It couldn't be bought for twice that," Talāl said. Then he put his hand on the man's shoulder. "It is yours."

"The man for whom the soldiers search must be very rich." The man put his hand on Talāl's back.

"There are more Korans," Talāl said. "And money as endless as grains of sand. You will never work again."

The shopkeeper unlocked the display case, put the Koran inside, and relocked the counter with a gentle pat. "Perhaps my rich guest would like to see my storeroom. There are many crates and baskets there."

Talāl didn't bother to glance over his shoulder and see how close the soldiers were; he merely followed the shopkeeper. The shopkeeper would be paid in full. Once Talāl escaped, he would send a Companion back to visit this shop . . . a Companion with a microwave device in the folds of his robe.

The shopkeeper led Talāl to a cool, dark room. He took off the lid of a crate and helped Talāl inside. "Each month you will receive a box with a special Koran inside," Talāl said. "You are a rich man."

The man smiled, blinked, and replaced the lid on the crate.

It was as dark as a tomb. As death itself. Talāl would wait till night, take some blackface from the man, exchange his *thobe* for a beggar's rags, and crawl through the alleyways and *suqs.* He had spent most of his youth in Mecca. He knew all its secrets, all its passageways. Once outside the city, he would climb Jebel Khandama and find his Companions in the volcanic wastelands to the north. The timetable would be altered but not destroyed. If he could time Khalid's death during the annual pilgrimage seven months away, the effect on Islam might even be greater.

He heard voices in the hallway. Talāl tried to flatten even farther into the crate, knowing full well that he couldn't disappear through the bottom. His heart began to race. But everyone had their price. Talāl was sure he had found the shopkeeper's. The talking stopped outside the storeroom. Talāl listened to see if the shopkeeper could steer the soldiers away.

"Rich friend!" the shopkeeper shouted. "This soldier tells me that King Khalid himself wishes to find this very important man. The king's wealth is as vast as the stars!"

Footsteps tapped across the floor and stopped right next to the crate. Someone lifted off the lid. It took a moment for Talāl's eyes to even the weak light of the storeroom. A man wearing a brown *thobe* and white headcloth motioned for Talāl to stand. He squinted at the photograph, looked carefully at Talāl's face, looked back at the shopkeeper, and put down the picture.

Then he drew his pistol from its holster, pointed it at Talāl's nose, and smiled.

XXII.

Al Asil, Yemen—May 8, 1981

Claudia was alone for the first time in her life. Not alone as in having no date for Friday night or in sentenced to bed for misbehaving but *alone* alone. She'd run out of guides, run out of men to pick her up when she fell. Whatever saving there was to do, whatever nastiness had to be done, she was the only one left to do it.

If she could.

It was useless to speculate. All the fantasies in the world wouldn't affect whether she could kill Bu-jahl.

She sat up on the cushions she carefully piled in the middle of the room and tried to keep from panicking. All of it, her entire life, the who-withs, why-fors, where-tos, and how-longs depended on how she reacted to the next face that came in from the darkness.

Maybe it would be Paul. How sweet that would be, but no way; there'd be no lithe medic walking through her door in the near future if, as a result of her naiveté, at all. And Rick was no more, as it turned out, never was. The man she called Rick was a werewolf, a shape changer, a Halloween ghoul named Piece-of-My-Heart. To stand a chancc against a liar, a killer that good, she'd have to learn a lot in little time. If she learned anything less than all about him, she'd be mistake-prone—in his league that meant dead.

The only face left was Bu-jahl's. It was hardly her favorite with its hairless cheeks and sloping forehead—in fact, the only one that terrified her—but it was the face she hoped to see. If she played him correctly, he was information. She couldn't out-quick or out-muscle him, but she could certainly outthink him.

Claudia walked to the window as she had every five minutes and looked up and down the street. The breeze smelled of night. There was laughter from the buildings that housed soldiers, moaning from the corrals that held prisoners. A woman screamed over and over and over. Claudia ran back to the pillow and lay down, shaking with terror.

Talking from down the street. Then outside her door. Talking and insane laughter. The oil lamp's flame flickered as the door opened and Bu-jahl walked into the light. Alone. Good. The visit was for pleasure instead of duty, and no matter what "pleasure" meant, the odds were better.

"The Gates of Paradise open for those with patience," he said. He smiled fatuously and paused as though he expected a comeback. But there'd be no comeback just yet. Tonight, every word must be measured, controlled . . . Claudia's life depended on it. Bu-jahl nodded at her silence as though he'd won some initial skirmish. "Allah is just," he said.

Now for the opening of her play, a play in three acts. Act One: disgust. "Isn't He, though," Claudia said sarcastically.

He twisted his head and squinted. "Perhaps the comparison is jaded," he said. "Or perhaps compliments mean little to one so lovely."

"Who but a goatherd would compare my legs to a gate?"

Bu-jahl started as though he'd been punched. He clenched his fists, but quickly, too quickly, regained his composure. It wouldn't be as easy to regulate his moods as she hoped. Ice touched his voice. "Perhaps you would explain this goatherd? Perhaps it means boorish? Stupid? Perhaps uneducated?"

"Perhaps," Claudia mimicked. "Only a goatherd would ask."

His eyes turned flat and cold as a snake's, and he picked at the bristles that stuck from his nose. "Then perhaps I will tell you what a she-goat is. It is one who thinks she has power she doesn't have. One who thinks she is safe when there is no safety."

Claudia was scared, but it wasn't time to *act* scared—yet. She had more, much more, to learn. Claudia would have spoken, but fear would crack her voice—and fear was for later, her means of seduction. Disgust now. Fear later. "With Rick around," she said, "I'm safe enough."

"Rick?" Bu-jahl laughed. "Who is this Rick? Rick the CIA assassin? When we found him, his head hung from strings like a marionette."

Claudia felt nothing for Rick. He'd vanished when she found the garrote. His death meant only one thing: Paul might be alive. But he wouldn't be back. At least in time. Claudia had more to learn. Quickly. Time to begin Act Two: a shift from disgust to betrayal . . . let Bu-jahl see a weakness that wasn't there. "Assassin?" Claudia let her voice crack.

"You said a goatherd is stupid. Here is stupid. You thought he was assigned to you. Nonsense. You were his cover. When your government wished another country agitated—or wished for agitation to stop—you would receive an assignment. Of course, you thought it merely fortuitous that the Afghani Amin died while you were in Kabul, and that El Salvadoran bishop—"

"Romero?" Claudia asked weakly.

"Yes, that one was shot while you attended his mass." When Bu-jahl sensed doubt in Claudia's voice, he moved closer. She instinctively tucked her legs beneath her. "You think you came to my country to cover a rebellion. Nonsense. The Madhi agitated my country for years. We couldn't find him. There was no one your Rick couldn't find. Now your country has a new biological weapon and some scientists, and the Madhi agitates no more."

When Bu-jahl moved to the edge of the cushions, Claudia shivered. A bad move. She had to take the offensive again. "Since Rick worked for you," she said, "it makes complete sense you ambushed him at the mosque."

Bu-jahl laughed again. "The CIA man follow *my* orders? Nonsense. It was I who followed his. Peculiar, you must agree, that your *'abas* were white while the rebels' were black. Strange, surely, that no bullets came close to you. White glows like fire in a starlight scope. The American scientists in Tai'zz were CIA sharpshooters. Rick took few chances."

"Then what about his wounds?"

"When we talked in Tai'zz, I mentioned a *hadith:* 'What is, is not as important as what appears to be.' One may put bandages anywhere."

Claudia's head started to spin. And this was no time for weakness or indecision—either meant death.

"He was the puppet master, you the puppet," Bu-jahl continued. "But there are times when even the master must be free of strings. He needed time to interrogate the rebels—your 'capture' at the Imam's execution gave him time. When the plague broke out, things became urgent. He needed to sever strings with you completely to command the search. Fortunately, Abdullah Mohammed gave you a note and new plans developed."

"Even Pancho worked for you?"

"Indirectly," Bu-jahl said. "A lovely irony, a Madhist providing our means to find the Madhi. We kept you imprisoned to increase his hunger. We followed you to establish your cover. When he became reckless, we delivered you at the mosque." Bu-jahl took a small metal disk from his pocket and tossed it to Claudia. "The *'aba* your *photographer* handed you at the American consulate had many bugs, yes? This one was electronic."

Claudia threw it against the wall.

He smiled, then pouted his lips like a small child. "The villages where you stayed? The wells where you drank? The cave where you slept? The rebels will use none of them anymore." He moved directly above her and smiled a gargoyle's smile. "I watched you enter the village. I watched you crawl through the shadows." He giggled. "I could have touched you."

The thought sent shivers down Claudia's back. She heard a rat scurry in the next room—there were rats everywhere in Yemen—and . . . she snapped back from a slide into confusion and fear. "Then why did Mickey Rat try to use a dagger on me?"

"I know of no Mickey Rat," Bu-jahl said.

"The dungeon. Your corporal."

Bu-jahl ran a fingertip from behind her ear to the tip of her chin. Claudia didn't have to feign a shiver of disgust. "Corporal

Sadid. Hah! You have a quick eye for others' faults. Mickey Rat. That is good." He leaned over her. "How could we plan for the rebels' incompetence? The Madhi has ears everywhere—only Piece-of-My-Heart and I knew of the bug. Sadid heard noisy rebels. If the medic hadn't killed him, I would have." He patted Claudia's cheek. "Sadid was a friend. Since the medic is dead, someone must pay for his death."

When Bu-jahl sat on the cushions, Claudia eased away from him. She listened for the guards. How much could they hear? Their talking sounded like a whisper. The shadows in Bu-jahl's face were exaggerated by the lamp's flame—his smile held hatred, lust.

"All the rebels needed to do was hide!" he shouted. "How could the pilot *not* see the escaped camel? How could he *not* fire at rebels who run into the open?" Bu-jahl paused and glanced at Claudia's eyes. He leaned forward. "It was our good fortune the medic was competent. We landed troops in the wadi so he wouldn't grow suspicious."

"Then why go after Nuri?"

"The bug hadn't moved in a week. We knew it wouldn't lead us to the Madhi. We had to risk that you could. It cost us many lives not to bomb indiscriminately. We didn't know which house you were in."

"A puppet," Claudia muttered.

"Rather a goat with fancy ribbons," Bu-jahl said. "A sacrificial goat. The goatherds were the medic, the Madhi, and the killer. Now there are no goatherds left—only you and I." He grabbed her leg. His fingers were like worms or small snakes, so thick with muscle and fat that Claudia could scarcely feel bone. It was time for the final act: terror. And it would have to be controlled terror, or she would die. Slowly. Far too slowly.

An insect, she thought. He's only an insect. She closed her eyes and breathed deeply. "Now?" she asked.

"Now we are atop a mountain a hundred miles from the nearest American consulate. There are guards outside who have been told to be hard of hearing. It is a goatherd's custom for his wedding night, The Night of Entrance." Then his shark's smile.

Claudia started to glide into a panic again. She needed to concentrate—she needed pain for a ground. She squeezed her hand until the blood welled up thick and rich. He was something, but whatever it was, it was not human. The pain gave her clarity. She looked for his weapons. He wore only a pistol. He abruptly let go of her, walked to the corner, removed the revolver from his holster, placed it on a table, and returned to the cushions.

"There is a new game," he said. "The gun, for you, is hope. Hope that if you reach it you will be free. And you will. The guards know that noises, *any* noises, are part of the game. Reach the gun and *bang,* I am dead. And you are free. That knowledge should make you strong, playful." He weaved like a snake in the flame and giggled a high woman's laugh. "There will, of course, be obstacles."

Claudia had no intention of leaving her cushions. She didn't go for the gun but the oil lamp instead. She leapt straight up, grabbed the burning wick, and the room went dark.

But not as dark as it should have.

Moonlight poured in through the window and, in the fraction of a second it took to see if the guards reacted to the noise, Bu-jahl had her by the waist. Like a practiced wrestler, he used her strength against her. "Excellent," he murmured as he tried to flip her onto her back. "Perhaps you would have fared better in darkness. Too bad about the moonlight."

Claudia struggled to stay on her stomach. Which was what he expected. Which was what he wanted. He wasn't the type for passion; he wanted only power. The more the mouse struggled, the more of the cat he'd become. And the less he thought— He punched her in the kidney. When her concentration shattered, he flipped her on her back and pinned her shoulders to the cushions with his hands. They were incredibly powerful. She couldn't budge.

The more she writhed, the wider his grin spread. She relaxed just an instant to regain her breath, and he forced his knees between hers and spread her legs so far apart that they hurt.

Fight down the panic, she thought. Keep the panic under control or he has you. He wasn't pure animal yet. There was still some reason, still some thought.

He let up, probably to give her hope, but instead of crawling for the pistol, she grabbed his hand and bit down on his thumb joint. She felt it pop between her teeth. He jerked his hand from her mouth, bellowed, and slapped her twice, three times, *hard.*

She brought her knee into his back; he raised up, and she tried to crawl from beneath him, tried to act as though she was going for the pistol, but his weight smothered her. She made it to the edge of the cushions. Then, with a power that truly terrified her, he ripped out the front of her pants, ripped all the way around, till all that remained were the legs and panties. He lifted her straight up and threw her down under him.

His fly was open.

When he let go of her hands, she dropped them to her groin for protection. She could see his eyes now, eyes rolled back in ecstasy, huge, metallic eyes, and insect's eyes in the moonlight. His lips curled back and rippled over his teeth. One at a time, he began to pop the buttons on Claudia's shirt.

She lost it.

She went after his eyes with her fingernails, ripped through his eyebrows and across the bridge of his nose. He screamed and slapped her away, then clasped his hand around her throat. He could have broken her neck instantly—if that was what he was after.

All along Claudia had known he was after something else. He wasn't interested in quick death but pain.

Pain for ecstasy.

His hands worked carefully at her throat as he lowered his groin to hers. First there was air, then no air. He allowed her a deep breath, enough to keep her senses screaming, then the hands would tighten. She tried to knee him in the groin, but his thighs were too quick, too practiced, and deflected the blows. And when he laughed, when his high giggle moved into a shudder from deep in his throat, Claudia reached under the pillow and brought out the knife.

Don't look. Keep struggling. If her eyes wandered or her tension slacked, he'd notice and she *would* be done. She blinked and squirmed, rolled her tongue across her lips. . . .

With both hands tight around the haft, she started the knife at her breasts and drove it up, up through the Adam's apple, up through the trachea and arteries; the point hit something hard, probably the spinal column, but she kept jabbing up, up and the knife point slid to the side of the obstacle and out the back of his neck. Like a cheese cutter gliding through Brie.

And the hands around her throat loosened.

And Bu-jahl's eyes didn't show fear or shock or even the first glaze of death . . . just surprise, endless surprise. Then the fingers left Claudia's throat, and he leaned back and looked at his hands as if scolding them for failing him, then turned his head sideways. The knife's hilt was flush against his throat; the point protruded a good two inches beyond the back of his neck and gleamed in the moonlight. His hands locked around the handle, and just for an instant it looked as though he contemplated pulling the knife out. When he opened his mouth to yell for help, no sound emerged, only blood. A wave of blood. He turned from Claudia and began to crawl for the door.

But Claudia was strong, Claudia was damn strong, because if he made it to the door, there'd be a roomful of guards, and there'd be no time to set them up as she set up Bu-jahl, so she grabbed his ankles, pulled his legs out from under him, crawled up on his back, and covered his head with a cushion.

And all of a sudden Bu-jahl was the mouse and she was the cat, and where were his strong hands and brawny shoulders? And his insect's eyes? And sadist's laugh? Where was that high-pitched voice that ordered the childrens' deaths, and Haifa's, and Pancho's and . . . She bounced up and down on the cushion, his shoulders and back . . .

. . . up and down . . .

. . . up and down as hard as she could, but he kept writhing and struggling, and the fucker wouldn't die, he just wouldn't die.

A soldier looked in. There was no surprise in two bodies struggling, but Claudia lowered her head to be sure he wouldn't see who was on top.

A twitching passed through Bu-jahl's body, a violent series of jerks that almost caused her to throw up. But that day was past; Claudia was strong, and the body beneath her had tried to rape her, to kill her, but she'd killed him instead, even when no one else had been able to. She stayed on Bu-jahl until the quivering stopped and his hands curled up on the floor.

Claudia was weak-kneed, and she didn't think she had the strength to stand up, much less drag Bu-jahl's body into the women's quarters, but she did it anyway. She withdrew the knife from his throat, cut away the pant legs that had fallen around her ankles, and used them to wipe the blade clean. Since her original plan hadn't included getting her clothes torn off, she had to do some ad-libbing. The insects would devour her if she escaped into the Highlands naked.

And she couldn't use Bu-jahl's clothes . . . his shirt was blood-soaked, and his bladder had emptied into his too-large-anyway pants. So she crawled back to Rick's pack, took the extra shirt and pants, a canteen, some water-treatment pills in case she couldn't remember locations of the fresh springs, several packages of breakfast bars, a spool of thread, and some clean socks. Then she stuffed Bu-jahl's pistol into the front of her trousers, the knife into her calf pocket, and checked Bu-jahl's pockets for money. A couple hundred rials. Hardly enough to bribe a fisherman to take her across the Red Sea. Perhaps she'd have to . . .

No sweat.

She had time to think, time to plan, and so what if things had changed, there was no telling what she might figure out by the time she reached the Tihama. But first she had to reach the Tihama.

She looked out the back window, checked for soldiers and dogs, and when she saw none, she climbed over the windowsill and onto the ridge above the cliff. The fall was two hundred feet. Straight down. So what? So what if her hands hurt and her legs were weak; she had hours.

Slowly, carefully, one hand, then one foot at a time, she crawled down the granite embankment. A foot wedged into a crack while a hand kept balance on a ledge. She rested twice, then three times, perched on an outcrop to eat a breakfast bar and, within three hours, was running on a ridge that dropped toward the valley. No bloodhound could follow her *that* way, and it would be days before they picked up her trail. If they picked it up at all. By then she'd be three valleys away, sitting under a myrrh tree above a very special wadi. She knew how these soldier-types thought: They'd scour all the valleys dropping toward the Tihama, waste gasoline in their stupid helicopters. Hadn't Bu-jahl said anyone could hide in the Highlands? Only a fool would go straight for the Tihama, and she was no one's fool anymore.

Besides, she had a date to keep.

So what if Bu-jahl said the medic was dead? He hadn't furnished any specifics. And Paul had this unusual way of showing up when he was least expected. And though she couldn't be sure from the way he acted the last time she was with him, Claudia concluded he might even come back from the dead to have her scrub his back in a certain wadi pool.

XXIII.

Riyadh, Saudi Arabia—May 15, 1981

How different this final cell was from the prayer cells of Talāl's youth. Instead of the stink of greasy straw, mildew, and age, the suite where he was kept prisoner had a television set, a private bathroom, meals whenever he requested them, and, perhaps most notably, armed guards who kept him from leaving. It was almost as though part of King Khalid's sentence was intended to make Talāl spend his final days surrounded by Western squalor.

Talāl walked across the blue pile carpeting, past the rubber trees and palms standing in pots, past the Monet hanging on the wall, and sat on the couch by the window. Once the Royal Palace had the finest view of the desert in all Riyadh. Now there were high-rises everywhere. Some of the newer buildings seemed to scrape the sky. Gas stations, fried chicken outlets, Quonset huts housing laborers had replaced the city walls, the groves of date palms, the black Bedouin tents. The old ways were vanishing with the sands that swirled out from the Empty Quarter and scattered over the Persian Gulf. In reality, all that remained of tradition was the palace grounds: the gardens, fountains, pavilions.

Even they were changed. A thousand soldiers were stationed around the palace. There would be no Companions sneaking through the shadows. No wave of black-robed men on camels sweeping in from the desert to save their Madhi.

Though the trip from Mecca to Riyadh hadn't taken long—perhaps two hours—Talāl's appearance before King Khalid's *majlises,* Talāl's trial, was even shorter. The CIA gathered evidence and were more competent than expected: the sources of Talāl's money were uncovered; his officers in the National Guard were arrested; and his Companions in the wasteland outside Mecca were attacked from the air and destroyed. The image of F-16 fighter bombers napalming men on camels seemed too large a contradiction in terms to be possible. But it was possible. Perhaps it was the image that best captured what was happening to the Middle East.

Khalid hadn't even looked up as he read the charges. When his eyes finally met Talāl's, it was to ask whether the charges were true. And what could Talāl do? He was a prince of the Royal Family. Tradition was all that linked him to the past. Tradition was honor. Talāl nodded.

Then Khalid had said, "Saudi justice is swift and final." Those words had only one meaning: Talāl's head would fall.

It was agreed that all family matters would be kept from the public eye. Talāl would die in a small garden on the palace grounds. He'd be spared the stench and degradation of a crowd, the shouting and singing of songs, the tearing of his *thobe* into souvenir strips, the waving handkerchiefs trying to catch flecks of spurting blood. Instead there would be soldiers. Some cousins to hold his arms. Respectful silence.

Talāl wouldn't whimper or vomit as he had seen others do. He was a prince. His tradition would give him strength.

If he were going to panic, it would have happened by now. Even when the barber arrived to shave his neck, Talāl remained calm. Lather floated in the water bowl like islands. All the dishes—in fact, all the utensils but the razor blade—had been gold, as befitted a prince. The razor was so sharp against his spine, it tickled . . . almost. The barber had been gentle, and Talāl helped him by stretching and turning to ease the glide of the blade. There must be no hair left to slow the stroke of the scimitar, or the beheading might take more than one stroke. Talāl gave the barber a gold ring as he left. Talāl kept one ring, a ring for the headsman, to assure the stroke would be swift, final.

A doctor arrived and offered sedatives, but Talāl refused them. There were too many things to learn to try to comprehend them with half a mind. He tried to imagine the scene: The sun would be unbearably hot, and the *khamsin* wind wouldn't smell of sand and camels but of gasoline fumes and fast-food outlets. And there would be flies. Millions of flies. He hoped one wouldn't land on his nose, distract him, weaken him, and cause him to break.

No. His will was too strong.

Still, he had questions. Would there be a block? Would he feel splinters prick his throat at the moment the scimitar touched his neck? And pain? Would there be pain?

Talāl sat back on the couch. Already he had the muscle contractions in his throat that prevented swallowing. Similar contractions had been reported in most of the condemned during the French Revolution. Drool coated his lips and slid onto his beard. He picked up a book on the Reign of Terror, one of the many books he'd read on beheading in the past week, and opened it. Most of the experts said beheading was painless, humane. Dr. Guillotine himself hypothesized that the slice would feel like a cold breath on the neck—no more. Surely once the spinal column was severed there could be no pain.

But how long could the brain live when separated from the body?

French doctors conducted experiments to find out. They would arrange a series of questions with the condemned, and hope the severed heads would blink in sequence as answers. Some said the experiments were successful. There were stories of severed heads that mouthed the Lord's Prayer; other stories told of how Charlotte Corday's head grimaced with embarrassment when it was held before commoners, still others of how Robespierre . . .

It made sense physiologically. There would be blood, oxygen trapped in the brain. Until the oxygen was exhausted, the brain would remain alive, alert. For how long? Two minutes? Three? They would be incredible minutes! Talāl prayed that the concussion wouldn't knock him out.

Then he understood.

Finally he comprehended the wisdom behind what the *ulamas*

had taught him so many years before . . . the lessons of the great learning in great suffering and how killing was the most intimate act. Finally Talāl realized that the only suffering which mattered came from within, and the only killing that held great truths was his own.

XXIV.

The Yemeni Highlands—May 15, 1981

Paul was afraid she'd left for Ethiopia until he smelled the roasting lizard. God, how she could adapt. He had stood on the ridge, looked for smoke, and seen nothing. He watched the trail descending to the wadi for snapped twigs and loose rock. Nothing. She even filled the holes where she uprooted snake bulbs and baboon roots.

Only the meat smell gave her away—and then only at a hundred feet. Paul crept to a boulder, crab-walked to a salt bush twenty feet from the camp fire, and flattened. Sharp rocks jabbed his side, but he hardly felt them. Claudia knelt by the coals and turned a spitted lizard, jabbing it with a stick to see if it was done. Nope, her expression said, still raw. She turned some bulbs she had roasting on rocks by the fire, then stood, returned to a flat piece of shale, and sat down.

Her pants and shirt were dirty but untorn. Her face was soot-covered and her hair matted with grease. Somewhere she'd found a blue *shauk al ajus* blossom to tuck behind her ear.

She was beautiful.

Paul didn't want to frighten her by standing up or shouting, so he said "Claudia" as softly as he could.

She didn't jump. She closed her eyes when she heard his voice and kept them shut for at least ten seconds. When she opened them, they continued to blink. "You're early," she said. Her voice cracked. "Dinner won't be ready for another fifteen minutes."

Paul stood, walked into the clearing, and squatted across the fire from her. He picked up a twig, poked the lizard, and said, "Closer to ten."

"I don't want the main course raw," she said.

Paul measured the distance from the coals to the spit with his thumb and index finger . . . it was the right distance for roasting. "At least it won't be charred outside, raw within."

"Trial and error," Claudia said.

Paul laid the M-16 against a rock, picked up one of the hot snake bulbs on a stick, then took a bite. "If I had known this would be more than one course, I would have brought wine."

No repartee from Claudia.

She reached over the fire and sizzling lizard and ran her fingertips over the scabs on his face. . . . She paused on his chin, then reached for his free hand and felt the gashes. "The meat grinder pretty tough?" she asked.

"No worse than expected."

The softness in his voice must have gotten to her. She sat back on the rock, turned away from him, and tried to regulate her breathing. But she didn't regulate it enough, because when she spoke, she quivered. "I almost got you killed."

"How could you know who he was?" Paul asked. "The competition is over now. There's no other way it could have ended."

Claudia swallowed, then sniffed. "He could have killed you."

"But didn't."

Claudia inhaled, held her breath, then let it escape in a shiver. "He played me for a fool."

"Why not let go?" Paul said. "You've earned it."

"Not yet," she said. "When we're in Cairo. When I make sure you're all in one piece—then I'll have earned it." She bit her lower lip. "And not until."

Paul looked down the ridge toward the wadi. The sandstone basins were almost dry—a white scum line on the rock marked where the water had come up to their chins. He pulled the stiff *'aba* away from his sticky skin. "How about running me a bath?" he asked.

"You'll have to take a rain check," she said. "No sense taking the parasites with us." When she turned back to him, the tears that gathered in her eyes jarred loose and ran along the sweep of her nose, followed the curve of her lip, then trickled into the corner of her mouth. She ran her tongue along her lips. "Salty," she said.

"Mind if I taste?"

"Surely you jest," she said.

He stood and walked to her, sat down on her rock, cupped his hands behind her head, touched her lips with his, searched for her tongue with his own, felt the liquid warmth of her inner mouth, the smoothness of her teeth, then nibbled on her upper lip as he pulled away. "Couldn't find any salt," he said. "Let me try again."

After a third try, his head started to spin. He rested his forehead in his palms and rubbed his eyes.

"When was the last time you slept?" Claudia asked.

"For more than a couple minutes?"

"More than an hour."

"Six days," he said. He blinked and tried to shake the dizziness away. "Maybe a week. One helluva long haul." He leaned back on his elbows and watched the high clouds sprint out toward the Red Sea. "My killing Piece-of-My-Heart left you without a protector. I knew I'd find you dead when I got to Al Asil, but I was going to be sure that Bu-jahl had hurt his last person."

"He has," Claudia said.

"From what the soldiers said, that's an understatement."

"You know?" Claudia asked.

"I borrowed an army uniform, sneaked into camp, and chatted with the soldiers. All they could talk about was how this Anglo woman had *done* Bu-jahl, slipped down a cliff, and escaped."

"They don't give up. There have been four, five helicopters searching the wadi every day."

"But not for you, Claudia. They *have* given up." Paul leaned toward her and put his hand on her shoulder. Her greasy shoulder. He smiled. "The way the Yemenis see it, no woman could survive in the Highlands for a week. The army's in the north cleaning up on the Madhists. These helicopter flights are checking for strays." He kissed her neck. "We're home free."

"Not quite," Claudia said. "I gave the bribe money to Rick." She took the lizard from the spit, sliced it in half, and gave part to Paul.

"Home free," Paul said. "I've spent six years in a *dhow.* I'm Al Rish, after all. I hunted sharks. Two days to the Tihama, a night or two in the Red Sea depending on the winds, and we'll be eating the people's food with Colonel Hasan."

Claudia handed him a canteen. "The water's from the clear spring on the ridge," she said. She watched him drink. "I never bothered to ask how a Marxist ended up owing you favors," she said.

"I fought with him, for him, in Eritrea." Before Claudia could interrupt, he touched a finger to her lips. "After you've killed enough," he said, "you find out all sides are the same."

She shrugged, reached down, unbuttoned her thigh pocket, and removed a double-edged knife from its sheath—the Spit. Paul took it from her. "Where did you get this?" he asked.

"Rick's pack." She frowned. "Looks like you've seen it before."

"We're old friends." Paul turned the knife slowly in his hands, felt the perfect balance, the way the handle's indentations molded to his palm and fingers. And he grimaced when he thought of the quivering sensation as it slid between vertebrae. "Will you do something for me?"

"You have to ask?"

He handed it back to her. "Walk to the ledge. Take it with you."

She rose slowly, then hesitantly weaved through the sharp granite rocks, through the stand of cactus and *Euphorbia officinalis,* and stopped near the edge of the cliff. "Now what?" she asked.

"Throw it as far as you can."

"How will we slice the lizard?"

"Just pitch the thing." She rolled her eyes, wound up, and threw it—like a girl, all arm and no back, her body flailing one way, her legs the other, and somehow, barely, the Spit flew out past the ledge. Paul held his breath and waited to hear it clatter on the rocks below, but there was nothing, nothing but the wind's hissing. As she walked back, Paul couldn't help smiling. The silliness of her motion, the solemnity of her act—somehow the opposition seemed just right. "I thought you were a natural at everything," he said.

She blushed. She actually blushed. "I never learned how to play baseball," she said.

"You couldn't have done it any better," Paul said. He took Nuri's dagger from his robe, bent over, and sliced thin strips of meat from the lizard. They ate dinner in silence.

Once the utensils were rubbed clean with sand and Paul returned from the spring with a canteen of water, Claudia sat down and pointed toward her lap. "Head," she said.

Paul lay down, used her head as a cushion, and looked up into her face. It was sun-blistered, streaked with dirt, but the eyes sparkled.

"You're not interested in my story?" he asked.

"It can wait." She ran her fingers through his hair, then massaged the back of his neck. "Sleep," she said.

He rolled over and looked at the escarpment—the clouds spilling over the peaks were red with long rays. But he couldn't sleep. He lay quietly with his eyes open for an hour and watched the interplay of shadow and light make animals of the wadis and ridges. A rogue elephant. A crocodile. A slithering snake.

A crunch.

Paul turned over and saw Claudia pull something from a string, put it in her mouth and chew. When she noticed him watching, she picked off another and held it out to him. "Locusts," she said. "When they're roasted and dried in the sun, the natives call them *jarad.*" When Paul shook his head, she put an insect in her mouth and bit down. "Not bad when you get over the crunch," she said, pointing toward the salt bushes. There, hanging from threads, were hundreds, maybe thousands of dried locusts.

"You planned to *feed* the Yemenis if they found you?" Paul asked.

"No," Claudia said. Suddenly all the traces of her smile were gone. "I planned to stay here till you showed." She began to massage his temples. "Now shut your mouth and *go to sleep.*"

With that, he shook his head in amazement, ran a finger across the dirt on her face, winked, then rolled over and closed his eyes.

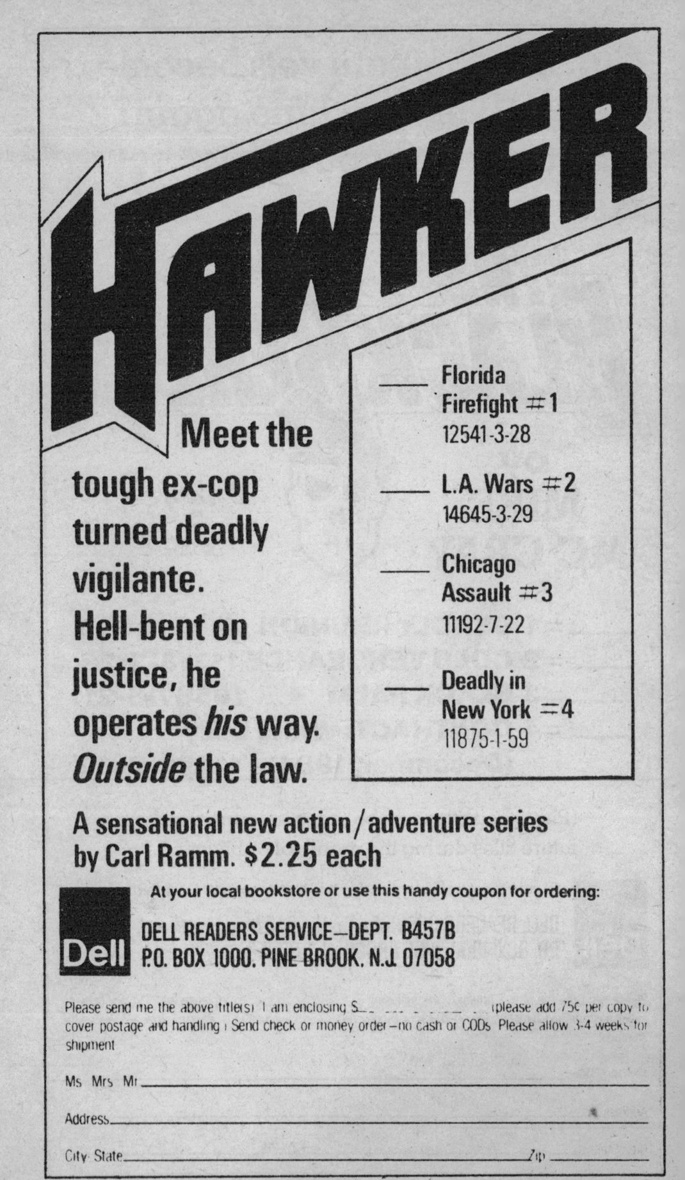
HAWKER
Meet the tough ex-cop turned deadly vigilante. Hell-bent on justice, he operates his way. Outside the law.
Florida Firefight #1 12541-3-28
L.A. Wars #2 14645-3-29
Chicago Assault #3 11192-7-22
Deadly in New York #4 11875-1-59
A sensational new action/adventure series by Carl Ramm. $2.25 each
At your local bookstore or use this handy coupon for ordering:
Dell
DELL READERS SERVICE—DEPT. B457B
P.O. BOX 1000, PINE BROOK, N.J. 07058
Please send me the above title(s). I am enclosing $ (please add 75¢ per copy to cover postage and handling). Send check or money order—no cash or CODs. Please allow 3-4 weeks for shipment.
Ms./Mrs./Mr.
Address
City/State
Zip